To :

Enjoy!
Raen Smith

House of
STEEL

RAEN SMITH

ps. Thanks for making a
wonderful daughter!

TO BRANDON

For your tireless support and love

PROLOGUE

Proverbs 15:3 - The eyes of the Lord are in every place, beholding the evil and the good.

Life has a way of coming undone. It could be one single moment or a series of moments that set the undoing in motion. Our neat, tiny stitch of life slowly unravels, perpetuating into a reckless spiral toward death. At first, we are unaware and unflinching, watching as days, weeks and years are deducted from our already borrowed time. One day, we are awakened to the light, to the moment that makes us question who we truly are - to the significance of our own lives in this constant world of forward moving life. We question humanity and the greater purpose. We question who is truly watching us, keeping vigil of the dangers. The line between good and evil becomes infected, blurs. Or maybe, just maybe, there is no line at all.

1

DAY 1: Thursday, December 18 –2:00 a.m.

Be vigilant. The words coiled in her mind, leaving stinging marks in her skull. V crouched deeper and rested against the house as she watched the woman stagger toward the man beneath the streetlamp. He had been waiting on the front porch since 1:00 a.m. He arrived only minutes after V had made her final lap around the house. After several empty bangs on the front door, his hard body had settled onto the porch steps, waiting for the last hour. V, tucked behind the twigs of a bush, and the man, huddled on the steps with his hands shoved in his jacket, were both waiting for Delaney Jones.

The man now stood in the middle of the sidewalk, the letters LU splashed across his knit hat. His smooth, vibrant skin was taut against his face. He was young, maybe in his early twenties. As V studied his muscular body, she predicted he was an athlete; a wrestler or a football player. He was definitely a student. She adjusted her own body, feeling the burn in her quads as she bent further against the wall. No one had seen her, and they never would. At 4′11″, she was astute at this line of work.

Her eyes narrowed beneath the black ski mask as she watched Delaney address the man waiting for her. Delaney's body swayed, her movements telling of too many drinks. V felt the sprawling crucifix tattooed across her shoulders flex as her arms hunched upward. The ink seared into her back as she watched the man bend down and swallow Delaney's lips. Despite the burning desire to look away, her eyes penetrated the couple as they stood embraced, kissing underneath the light. It was wrong. All wrong.

V's mind raced to her employer. The dedication. The time. He had scrutinized Delaney's every move for months. V's eyes scanned the quiet street just a few blocks from campus. The brisk air was silent, unmoving, as large snowflakes hung momentously in the air as though the embrace had been encapsulated in a snow globe. She breathed in, trying to escape the tingling sensations that ran through her back when she caught sight of the familiar black sedan across the street. V slipped her hand inside the pocket of her leather jacket and lifted the night vision scope. 135-HP3. The number on the license plate pricked her eyes. She hesitated, knowing that she didn't need to see the man behind the black Buick to know it was the Neanderthal with his Icelandic blue eyes and platinum white hair, but she moved the scope higher anyway, capturing the outline of his square jaw. His eyes glowed back neon yellow, deep into her scope. The penetrating gaze looked passed the couple embracing on the street, digging layers into her skin.

It had been twelve years since she had seen Gunnar last. She had been fifteen then. Pure. Unsuspecting. Submissive. Everything she wasn't at the ripe age of twenty-seven. Gunnar had morphed her with his smoking .22 hand gun and tonight, he had walked back into her life. She had been waiting for this, a diligent student preparing for this moment. Gunnar only meant one thing. Her employer was closing in on Delaney. He was ready to make his move. Delaney Jones was now the target.

Adrenaline coursed through her veins as she scanned back to Delaney and the student now making their way up to the house. V had sensed the time was coming, but she hadn't known it would be this soon. Her employer wouldn't let Delaney get away with this calloused lack of judgment. The disgusting fall from grace. Whatever pedestal Delaney had been on, she had fallen. Hard.

2

DAY 1: Thursday, December 18 – 2:00 a.m.

Delaney Jones stepped outside the door of Atlas Pub just before bar close. Three more inches of snow had accumulated on the ground during her five-hour stay at the bar, making a cool foot of blanketed frost. A Wisconsin winter. Twenty-eight years of this shit was getting old. She stumbled into the night as her breath was cut short, inhaling the icy air. With only five blocks to walk, she had convinced her university colleagues and the sober bartender that she would be more than capable to walk the short distance home. It was Appleton, the shining community voted as one of the best small towns in the United States to raise children. The approval ribbon gleamed across the town, prompting feverish chatter and boasting from its residents. Delaney had reminded them of this before she had leaned across the sheen of the dark mahogany wood to flash the bartender - a man with a thick neck, chiseled jawline and muscles bursting from his inexplicably small shirt - a strap of black lace underneath her low-cut sweater. It had worked. It always did.

As she moved through the snow, the fresh air invigorated her. It was the first time in fourteen years that she had walked alone in the blackness of the night. Wrapped in the down jacket her father Michael Jones had given her during her first year of college, wool hat, and sub-zero boots, she moved in and out of the glow of the streetlamps, feeling the crunch of the fresh snow beneath her boot. She finally felt safe. A sense of euphoric liberation buzzed through her legs as she trudged forward passed the last few bars lining the main street that coursed through the tight community's revitalized downtown.

Atlas Pub. Anduzzi's. The Bar. There were thirty-eight bars in Appleton for its population of seventy thousand. That was including the residents under twenty-one. A handful of Leighton students toppled out of the door in front of her, apologizing through laughter as they stumbled to follow the street back to campus. *God, they look young.*

Delaney turned, passing St. Mary's towering and ominous steeple on the second block, knowing that she would never walk the concrete steps to the entrance. Michael Jones had noted the church on their first visit to Delaney's house only weeks after moving in six months ago. She had venomously refuted the notion of attendance through her customary, polite smile. Her mother, Ann Jones, had nodded in agreement.

The brittle frigidness of deep winter sunk into Delaney's bones by the fourth block as she rounded the corner to her street. In front of her house, stood a man, dressed in a black wool jacket and hat beneath the soft haze of the streetlamp; a light dusting of snow fell off the lamp and onto him with each gust of wind. Her heart thudded underneath her layers as she slid her hand into her pocket, wrapping her fingers around the long cylinder of pepper spray.

The silhouette lifted his gloved hand with a short salute; Delaney's grip released around the cylinder as the air released from her lungs. The playful gesture he had executed after every class had always sent a thrill pumping through her despite the mental anguish that screamed at her body to stop. Delaney moved forward, her hands clasped together in front of her chest to huddle any ounce of warmth she had close to her body, inching herself to him.

"Ms. Jones."

"Theron."

"The semester is over, you're not my professor anymore," he said. His eyebrows raised beneath his LU hat before he smiled. Her legs weakened beneath her.

"And?"

"And here I am. I've seen you watching me."

"You're still a student."

"Not *your* student." He put his hands in the air, the large flakes melting into his knit gloves.

"True." Her lips curled. It was a technicality. The words of Leighton's President Givens stung in the back of her head. *Once a student, always a student.* The mantra taunted her.

"Let me take you out." He reached to touch her clutched hands still wound tightly to her chest. She let him cover her hands with his, feeling her body flood with eagerness spawning from the heat of his gloves.

The alcohol disoriented her, taking the edge off the plaguing feeling of regret. She closed her eyes as her body swayed beneath her, feeling the cool wetness of a single snowflake that landed on her flushed cheek. As her eyes fluttered open, she could see his face leaning into her. His lips brushed against her cheek where the snowflake had landed, replacing the coolness with warmth. He paused before moving his lips onto hers. Her body became instantly gratified by his lips and as she pulled him closer to her, the chill previously around her body vanished. They stood kissing underneath the soft glow long enough for dozens of flakes to speckle her wool hat when his hand reached for her face. She pulled a few inches away to look at him.

"It's cold out here, why don't you come in?" she whispered. The words had come out before she could stop them. There was no going back.

She grabbed his hand, led him to the front porch and through the front door into the warmth of her house. As Theron shut the door behind them, he moved to kiss her again, frantically peeling off her layers. Delaney mimicked the movements, feeling his hard body underneath his clothes. They staggered down the hallway, their lips moving hard and fast against each other, until they both stood naked in her bedroom. Her eyes settled on the pink mask and laptop lying on her desk before Theron interrupted her as he pulled her close into his body.

Don't do this. She ignored her own words.

***

Huddled against the warmth of his body, Delaney's eyes sprung open at the sound of a knock echoing from the front door. She shot up to see the mid-morning sun shining through a crack in the half-closed curtains. Her eyes followed the stream of white light radiating from the window to the rough stubble lying on the pillow next to her. His wrinkle-free skin was stretched firm over his face as his nostrils flared with oxygen. *Damn.* She nudged him with her elbow, stirring him to release a low grumble from his throat. Delaney shoved harder, driving the elbow deep into his ribs. Theron's eyes flashed open, his pupils dilating before they focused on her waiting face. This wasn't the way it was supposed to happen. Not with her student.

"You have to go," Delaney whispered as she swung her legs from beneath the covers. "Mark is here." Her eyes caught the grey heap of clothes lying on the chair. She tossed a tattered sweatshirt over her head and hopped on one leg, pulling the sweatpants up. A second knock.

"Who the hell is Mark?" Theron prodded as he leaned one elbow on the pillow, exposing the bulge of his bicep.

Delaney spun back, feeling her stomach tighten at the sight of his packed chest poking out from the blanket. "My brother," she replied as she turned toward the hall to scoop up his jeans, thrusting them behind her back. She moved forward to grab the Leighton football sweatshirt and ran back to the bedroom. Delaney wavered in the doorway, letting the blue fabric fall between her toes on the beaten, wooden floor before she cast her eyes down. Theron stood naked alongside her bed, posing like the Statue of David in all his glory. He had cast his face at the slightest angle, exposing the thickness of his neck. His eyes gazed outward in a pure mockery of serious contemplation. The military dog tags around his neck swayed, clinking together before they stopped to rest on his defined chest. His dead father's tags, he had told her last night. She kicked her leg forward, lifting the sweatshirt into the air. Theron reached his arm out, snagging the cotton in his ready hands.

"Jesus, Theron. Get dressed," she scolded before disappearing into the hallway again. She gathered the rest of his belongings in her arms and turned to shove them into his hands, now open and waiting a few feet behind her. A third knock.

"There's a back door in the kitchen," she ordered.

"No kiss goodbye?" He smirked before he put his head into his sweatshirt and pulled it down to cover his chest. Delaney exhaled, briefly considering the gesture of thankful regret she felt obliged to give.

"Don't forget your pants." She pointed to his bare, vigorous legs before pushing him toward the kitchen. She set her head back to the front door and moved to the sound of a fourth knock that had transformed into a full out fist bang against the door. The muffled yell of her brother's voice followed. She reached for the handle, stealing a passing look at her reflection in the mirror to see a disheveled woman with bloodshot eyes and ratty hair staring back. She licked her fingers, scrubbing the black streak of mascara underneath her eyes to a dull gray and matting her hair down to a snarly tease. *From meth addict to recovering stripper. Perfect.* Her hand pulled open the front door to her brother dressed in a dark gray suit with a canary tie adorned by blue dots hanging around his neck.

"Sorry for rolling you out of bed so early, professor. You realize it's almost eleven, right? Late night with the students?" Mark joked. His tall, trim body leaned against the doorframe before he moved his arms to embrace his younger sister. His high and tight, dirty blonde crew cut contrasted against her dark, snarly mess of hair. *You have no idea, Mark.*

"Delaney," he said, pulling her body away from him, holding her an arm's length away. "How long did you stay out last night?"

"It's good to see you, too. Come in," she replied as she opened her arms to lead the way into the house, now empty of Theron's clothes. Mark walked in and took a sharp left toward the kitchen.

"Hey," Delaney cut in, trying to step ahead of him.

"I'm starving. Let's eat quick before I head back to the office." He stopped, turning back to let Delaney slide passed him. She led him into the kitchen, pausing to look out the window to see the back of the twenty-one-year-old student's head moving down the sidewalk a few houses down. Theron pulled his jacket on as he began to jog, creating a white fog that swirled around his head. *That was close.*

Delaney yanked the refrigerator open, squinting at the fluorescent light that blinded her bloodshot eyes. A box of leftover take-out Chinese and a near empty gallon of milk stocked the only shelf. She felt Mark watching her from the table, studying her unkempt hair and loose clothes that hung from her thin frame as she heated up his leftovers.

"Leftover sesame chicken sound good?" she asked, even though he didn't have a choice. She snapped the refrigerator door shut before he could see inside the abysmal nothingness of the shelves.

"Sure. What the hell happened to you last night? When I left the bar, you were fine." His eyes penetrated her, just short of accusing. She slid the paper container of sesame chicken across the small table that was tucked tightly against the wall. The same table Theron had just passed seconds before he escaped out the back door a few feet away. As she moved closer to sit down, she felt a sudden lurch in her stomach.

"I'll be right back," she said, turning on her heels. "The forks are in the box next to the fridge," she yelled from the hallway behind her shoulder.

Delaney broke out into a run, covering her hand over her mouth as she made her way to the bathroom adjoining her bedroom. She snatched her loose waves behind her head and bent down to vomit into the toilet water waiting below. Her body retched, emptying her stomach over and over. She wiped her mouth with the back of her hand and flushed the toilet while the smell of alcohol permeated from every cell of her body.

Shuffling her feet across the cold hexagons that patterned the bathroom floor, she gathered her hair and tied it back with an elastic band. As she pulled the toothbrush in and out of her mouth, she studied the outermost corners of her eyes where the lines of crow's feet were setting in deeper on the delicate skin. She rubbed them, looking back at the reflection of the woman staring at her. At 5'9", Delaney had inherited her mother's lean body, rich, wavy hair - which they both had always kept long- and full, peach-colored lips.

Delaney had been "kissed by an angel," according to one of her photography professors, who one day had held Delaney's face in his hands while emphatically describing the beauty of the Sistine Chapel. She had heard, several years after she'd taken his class, that Dr. Bohide had been fired based on several accusations of sexual harassment. It hadn't surprised her. He had triggered her instinctual sexual predator sense; that same sense that most sane and mentally capable women employ on a daily basis. She hadn't doubted the accusations from students for one moment.

As she thought of Dr. Bohide, her stomach lurched again while her mind replayed the night with Theron. She had just jeopardized her career, the last eight years of school and her accomplishments in the art world. The potential to land in the gutter right next to Dr. Bohide nauseated her consciousness. She had slept with a student. Her student. Not to mention that Theron, despite the fact that he most likely hadn't known - or at least she hoped he hadn't - was the first man she had ever slept with. *Willingly.*

Her bare feet fumbled back across the worn, wooden floor of the bedroom as she felt the ache in between her legs. The alcohol had dulled her senses early this morning, but she felt Theron's after-effects now. She hadn't meant to sleep with him, but her growing desire to have sex on her own terms had culminated through his semester-long pursuit. She had longed to know what it would feel like to return to the place she had been raped after she had been freed from his restraints. To be born again as a woman. Delaney would be standing in the church again in just one day when she returned home for her brother Ben's wedding. The physical intensity between them, along with the liquid courage, had made her relent to her student.

Theron had locked his brown, unsettling eyes on her that first day of Drawing II from the back row. He had lounged back in his chair, smiling with a dimple under his right eye, and jotted notes as his eyes moved with her across the room. His hard body had filled most of the small, wooden school chair. Her first classes in the fall semester, as a newly Christened and not yet revered faculty member, were held in the oldest building that hadn't been renovated. She would later find out that he was a football player for the university, something she despised; however, it gave reason to his need to regard his body with such seriousness. She had appreciated the devotion last night.

Despite the fact that Delaney often had men admiring her, not one of them had made her feel the way Theron had on that first day. No one had ever made her feel so alive. So *desired*. She had felt her cheeks flush as the intrigue grew, wondering what it would feel like to brush her lips against his. Yet she had left that class period vowing to never let a student destroy what she had accomplished. She had needed to remind herself of her promise throughout the semester as Theron closed in on her. Less than eight hours ago, she had recklessly and undoubtedly shattered that promise.

As Delaney passed the vintage desk she had salvaged from a curb back in graduate school, she shut the open laptop and opened the top drawer to sweep the pink domino mask into the drawer with one single stroke of her hand. She walked back into the kitchen to see Mark still sitting at the table, finishing the leftovers.

"So, how was the meeting?" she asked as she slipped into the chair next to him. She needed to avoid any further questioning from Mark. Despite her best efforts, she had always been unable to keep anything from him. Almost anything. He was her conscious, her sounding board.

"Good, I guess. We presented the progress of Parker Tower to President Givens and the board. They seem satisfied. You really don't have silverware unpacked yet?" he asked, stabbing the last piece of chicken with the plastic fork. The utensil bent with his thrust.

"I told you, I've been busy. So, three weeks into the new job, and you're presenting on the multi-million dollar building?"

"They don't pay me the big bucks for nothing." He looked up from the food, winking as he held the fork in the air.

"You've earned that right to revel, so I'll let it slide," she said as she watched him shovel the food into his mouth, just as she had years before. *Some things never change.*

Mark was brilliant, but he had spent the last six years at an engineering firm down in Milwaukee making less than half the pay and paying twice as much for the same house he could get in Appleton. Parker Enterprises had pursued him, offering him a generous salary and benefits package, enticing him to move two hours north. He was now an executive for Holston Parker, the owner of the prestigious and well-known company that specialized in commercial construction. A business-savvy Parker had developed his own company, a self-made mogul that began with the construction of his first building, a small manufacturing facility for lumber, right in Appleton. From there, it grew exponentially, expanding from commercial construction to real estate. Parker Enterprises had made Holston Parker one of the wealthiest men in the state under the age of sixty, and Mark had gotten the golden opportunity at the young age of thirty-two to work under him, moving into the corporate apartments three weeks ago. Over the last ten years, Parker had notoriously hired young men in their thirties, weeding them out quickly to find the ones that had what he was looking for. Mark knew this and decided to take his chance.

"Well, I've got to get back to the office. Thanks for the quick lunch," Mark said as he got up from the table. He threw his fork into the sink. "Looks like you might need this again. It was the last one." Delaney ignored him, looking down at her phone that had alerted her to a new message.

She slid her phone out of the pocket of her sweatshirt and opened it to see a message from Theron. *Thanks for last night, Ms. Jones.* Her skin tingled as she shoved the phone back into her pocket to see Mark staring at her.

"Are you sure you don't want to ride back home with me tonight?" he asked.

"No, I'll come down tomorrow for the rehearsal. Ben doesn't need me," she replied, embracing her brother quickly before he pushed her back to walk out the door.

"I don't want anyone to smell the alcohol," he joked as he ruffled the top of her brown waves like a child. Her mind flashed to the first time he had showed this doting brother affection. It was exactly fourteen days after Mark had stepped onto her uncle's driveway in his dusty cowboy boots with her younger brother, Ben. They were her new, adopted brothers, Michael Jones had insisted. Mark had tousled her hair outside in the yard among the brittle leaves of the fall afternoon. She was six. He was ten. That's all it took. Mark and Ben were her brothers.

"Take a shower, will ya?" he yelled before he hopped into the truck, giving one last wave before backing down the driveway. She watched as the snow crunched beneath his tires as he left.

Delaney shut the door behind her, pausing to survey the living room scattered with boxes. The only furniture in the space was the worn leather couch she had toted around for the past five years as a hand-me-down from Aunt Emma and Uncle Walt. She couldn't even consider the small coffee table and mounted TV as furniture. The house was hers, though, and she vowed she would start cleaning the space later, just after she emptied her body of the lingering alcohol that coursed through her veins.

She fell into the couch, letting her body sink into the leather, as she examined the charred brick on the fireplace. *A service call.* That's all she needed, according to the realtor, to get the fireplace up and running. She put her feet up on the coffee table and reached for her phone, opening her previous messages.

Under Olson, she typed a response. *Plans tonight? – Ms. Jones.*

She slid the phone back into her pocket, her stomach turning at the slightest touch. A groan escaped her lips before she shifted her legs and pushed her body off the couch and into the kitchen. She opened the cupboard, revealing bare shelves except for a near empty bottle of red wine and one green tea bag. Although she had moved in six months ago, she barely spent any time here. Her office at the university occupied her entire semester and existence at the moment, something she had longed for while finishing her doctoral degree - a career to continue her devotion to her creative expression.

Cheers. Delaney uncorked the wine, swigging the last drops straight from the bottle. She had never consumed alcohol straight from a bottle before. In fact, last night had marked only the second time in her life that she had actually gotten drunk. Somehow, swigging from a bottle felt warranted to her. The wine settled reluctantly in her stomach as she heated a mug of water in the microwave. The steam of the hot water welled into her face as she moved in front of the window, envisioning Theron's head moving down the sidewalk. She tried to reason with herself, despite the uneasiness of treading dangerous, uncharted territory. She let her chest collapse in, exhaling a deep breath, before moving down the hallway into her bedroom.

Delaney lifted the mug toward her lips, hesitating at the sound of a car door shutting outside. She peered out the double window facing Drew Street before closing the curtains on the white flakes scattering to the ground. As she placed her mug down on the desk, she reopened the laptop to a pink box that contained the familiar, one line.

"Are you there, D?"

I always am. Her lips turned upward as she slid open the drawer to retrieve her mask. She felt the pink satin fabric slip between her fingers before she slid open the metal drawer of the green file cabinet to move a stack of file folders. A pile of lace in varying colors revealed itself. She picked a matching black top and bottom, setting them on top of the desk before dancing her fingers across the keys.

"In five minutes. 12:15." She paused before entering the next line, "CST."

Delaney walked over to the full-length mirror, encased in gun-colored metal as she lifted the sweatshirt over her head. She released the elastic tie in her hair, allowing the brown waves to fall to the middle of her bare back. Her disheveled hair wouldn't matter now, not after she was done getting dressed. She slipped the sweatpants down, kicking them gently to the side. Standing naked in front of the mirror, she studied her body for the transformation. Her supple breasts looked the same, alert and full. Her smooth, milky skin still shined an unblemished sheen. The bones of her narrow hips jutted from her pelvis, just as they always had. Her body had effectively remained unchanged. But she felt different. Her body was hers.

She stood straight as she placed the mask over her eyes, tying a knot over the back of her hair. Her eyelids fluttered free as she stared at the reflection. A beautiful, naked woman in a pink mask. She stepped into the lace and fastened the bra, lifting her large breasts even higher than they naturally were. Unlike the rest of the women in the My Campus Hotties community who took their clothes off for men, Delaney's only client had a special request that she had conceded to, happily. She stepped into a long, floor length black dress that clung to her body over her lace underwear. Even though she hadn't needed to put the matching lace set on, it had given her a satisfaction knowing what she had underneath. What he was missing.

As she finished plumping her hair, she reached for a paintbrush and scooped out a canvas underneath her bed. She looked one last time at the reflection of a woman in a black gown and pink mask before moving to her laptop. She began to type.

3

V's knee-high laced boots sunk into the snow as she moved in silence to the back of the house. Her eyes wandered to the neighboring single-story home. She wondered what she might look like to the inhabitants if they saw her. *A small white flash? A child?* V thrust the thought out of her head. She wouldn't be caught. Not now. She felt the knit of the white ski mask rub against her face. Her pristine gloves, jacket, pants, and boots were all white. She was pure.

The sound of a car door shutting echoed from the front. The rumble of an engine followed. She peeked around the corner, watching the truck back out of the driveway and onto the road ahead. Mark Jones was gone. She turned back to the house, watching Delaney move inside through the kitchen, swigging from the leftover wine bottle on the counter. V ducked underneath the window as Delaney turned her head, looking out the same window. V held the air in her lungs until the burn was too much to bear. She exhaled, letting the cool stream of white fog blow in front of her. The student was gone. She had watched him leave, fleet out of the kitchen door half-dressed, into the brisk morning turned afternoon air. V followed the brown head of hair into the bedroom around the side of the house, watching as Delaney turned to her laptop.

Another bang shattered the stillness of the day. Delaney's brown waves reacted to the noise in the front, drawing her to her bedroom window. V tucked her head down, this time breathing inside her elbow to mask the vapors. She tucked her body close to the siding as she heard the curtains close; the same siding she had rested against for more than an hour last night.

V slipped through the backyard and onto the back street. She lifted the ski mask from her head to reveal cropped, dark brown hair and porcelain skin. She would return to the office so they wouldn't miss her. But, she would come back. The cameras would have to wait.

4

DAY 2: December 19 – 9:00 a.m.

Delaney stepped onto the small porch outside her front door and into the fresh morning air, locking the door behind her. With her bag slung over her shoulder, she moved sideways down the steps that had been covered with the previous night's snowfall. Only an inch of snow had dusted the cold concrete, and as Delaney stepped, she felt the usual layer of ice underneath the snow. The winter. God, did she hate the cold. She spotted a bag of salt and a shovel leaned up against the side of the house on the porch. Mark was too good to her.

As she bent down to lift up the garage door, she noticed the door was cracked open on the bottom, revealing a scattering of snow just inside the garage door. She planted herself and yanked the door up, rattling the thirty-year-old aluminum as it rested on its track near the top of the garage. Her eyes scanned the garage, but nothing had been moved. Her white Civic remained in its place as she had left it – in the dead center of the one-stall garage. *No one-stall garage. No non-motorized garage door.* Her father and Mark had pointed out the house's deficiencies *after* she had signed the contract and moved in. They were right, though; they usually were.

She opened the door and threw her bag onto the passenger side seat, noticing how small her bag really was. She didn't need much for the weekend and the dress was already at the house. *Waiting. Just like everyone else.* Her youngest brother, Ben, was getting married tomorrow and despite the fact that she had to spend the late afternoon hours in the one place she feared the most, she was genuinely happy for Ben and Meghan. She would smile through the sympathetic looks she would get from everyone else who didn't know that she never planned on getting married. That consisted of most everyone, except for her mother, Ann Jones.

Her chest tightened as she thought of the relentless woman that she had left. When Delaney had hesitated to move to Appleton because she had wanted to spend more time with her mother, Ann Jones had insisted, even yelled at her daughter to leave. Her wig, dangerously close to tipping off her head, had waved back and forth in disgust when Delaney mentioned staying in Milwaukee. Delaney had been shocked at her disapproval; the enveloping wing she had kept over her daughter was retreating back, but Delaney hadn't known that her cancer-ridden mother had already realized her protection was waning. Ann's expiration date, as she called it, was nearing.

Four months ago, Delaney had purchased the 1920's bungalow after the real estate broker, who unofficially coined himself the realtor to the "ivory tower of Leighton," finally convinced her that the house on Drew Street was the idyllic home for her. The fourteen hundred square foot home, after all, was just five blocks from campus and it *had* been better than the first six houses he had shown her. It was also the smarter choice when compared to renting, according to Michael Jones.

When the realtor had opened the front door to the bungalow, the resemblance to her family's house back in Milwaukee - the house she'd grown up in starting at the age of six - had been unsettling. She had moved from one room to the next, surveying the architectural details. She had run her fingers across the craftsman trim, repainted several times from previous owners, in the living room just as she had as a child. She had even closed her eyes while standing in the middle of the kitchen, envisioning her mother standing in front of the sink washing the dishes in scalding water - water that was always too hot for anyone else to touch. Delaney released a sigh before she backed out onto the driveway, got out to close the garage door and pulled onto the quiet street to head two hours south.

The desolate campus radiated a beautiful eeriness; an undisturbed dusting of white covered the sidewalks and streetlamps surrounding the buildings. It was winter break after all, and most of the student population had headed home to spend the weeks with their families. She wound her car down by the river and passed the new academic building, Parker Tower. The exposed steel beams erected sixty feet up loomed over the remaining buildings that constituted the one hundred fifty-year-old campus. Parker Enterprises was constructing the massive building funded through private donations, including a cool $6 million from none other than philanthropist extraordinaire himself, Holston Parker.

The relatively quaint and historic riverside campus in Wisconsin remained a reputable liberal arts college with a student population of only about fifteen hundred. The campus notoriously attracted prestigious academics graduating from elite institutions, including Harvard and Brown. So, when Delaney had received the call from the chair of the Fine Arts

Department the previous spring asking her to visit campus for a tour and to discuss the recent vacancy, she had dropped her weekend plans and headed north without hesitation. Within weeks, she had signed her contract with the university to become the new Assistant Professor in the department. A job. Her first real job. A job that encouraged her to continue to paint. It had been the next logical step to take. She would be crazy not to accept the offer. It was, after all, an honor. The word hummed in her head, yet the current state of the campus stood in stark contrast to the lush green landscape and rolling river on her first visit.

Delaney had spent the entire past semester buried in her office and textbooks, trying to learn the ropes of teaching at Leighton. The tenured faculty members with more than thirty years of experience were polite and encouraging, but they remained skeptical of her young age and accomplishments. She tried with fervor all semester to meet their standards, staying well past midnight most nights in the studio to produce pieces for a display at Appleton's Trout Museum of Art. Showcased at the end of December, it met lukewarm reviews across the art community, only igniting her further. She would prove her place in the tier.

It wasn't an entirely unfamiliar place for Delaney to be, and it didn't bother her that she would spend more of her spring semester dedicated to her work. After all, she had endured eight years of post-graduate education moving to this point. She was all in.

While her college classmates were busy drinking and having one-night stands, she had spent her evenings with Winsor and Newton; the oil paints that, in most cases, always listened. She would then nap for a few hours in her studio amid black teas on the same couch now stationed in her living room. Despite the social media craze that had hit during her last years, she had also avoided the mindless, time-sucking idling of her generation, with the small exception of her sessions on her My Campus Hotties account that was leading to a small stockpile of cash. Her preferred methods of in-person meetings were "archaic" according to a studio mate. It had been better that way, Delaney told herself, fostering her relationship with her art instead. She had flown below the grid for so long, but had finally resorted to a smartphone when she moved to Appleton to maintain contact with her family, particularly to keep tabs on Ann.

Her Civic continued to hum against the road, moving along the river and her usual morning running path. Her legs itched as she eyed the trails. She had skipped her five mile run the past two days and knew she would miss it again tomorrow, but she would be back on Sunday to beat on the trail. She longed to stretch her legs and to inhale the clean air into her lungs. Running always had a way of clearing her mind, the physical counterpart of painting. Delaney watched as the academic buildings turned to two-story, Victorian houses packed together, only about ten feet separating one from the other. Bikes and shabby couches spotted the porches, half-covered with the snow that had accumulated over night.

Theron. She looked at her phone lying in the console. There were no messages. It had taken all of yesterday to determine that she couldn't make the mistake of seeing Theron again. She was grateful that he had pushed her past the hurdle of her quasi-virginity, if she could call it that, at the age of twenty-eight. She would always remember that, but she had made a huge error in judgment. She knew almost nothing about him except that he was a football player with a ridiculous eye for perspective drawing and that his father died in combat overseas, the military tags never straying from his neck. They could never have a relationship; the ties needed to be cut. It had to be quick and painless. It had to be everything unlike the night that had left her a wounded, scarred teenager.

Delaney had, unsuccessfully, attempted to rid herself of the traces of that night. Yet, even the smells lingered. She could still remember the scent of the votive candles burning only inches from her face. The odor of her singed hair nauseated her on days when she took too long to blow dry her hair. And, she couldn't stomach to be close to people with colds for fear she might get a whiff of the menthol on their breath.

It had been rainy that night back in April when she was just fourteen. She had stayed late at the after-school art group held weekly in the basement at St. Luke's, the Catholic Church just six blocks from her house. Mr. Rowan, the thirty-something, exceedingly religious group leader with a pitted face and the spotty hair of a sixty-year-old, had insisted that she finish her most recent painting of Saint Agnes. He had brought Delaney a picture of the saint just a few weeks before, declaring that the statuesque woman was the most beautiful and worthy of them all. Delaney had adored the small lamb that the woman saint had coddled in her arms so she had happily obliged to paint the portrait. The rest of the small group of ten students had gone home around five, meeting their families for dinner, but Mr. Rowan had contended he would give her a ride and explain her tardiness to her parents.

As she had finished rounding the slightest glint on the lamb's eye, she had sensed the presence of Mr. Rowan leaning in behind her. She had stepped forward, closer to the painting, before she had felt the weight of his hand on her hip. Delaney had jerked forward as he shushed her and wrapped his entire arm around her waist, grabbing to pull her into him. She had let out a gasp before he had covered her mouth with a piece of duct tape. He had shook his head in disapproval as his eyes hardened deep inside his blemished face. Those eyes. She could still see those eyes.

Delaney had squirmed beneath his arms as he pinned her down, her small frame not matching his robust physical strength. He had reached for a votive candle that had been burning in a rack near them, setting the small glass jar next to her hair that fanned across the concrete floor. She had screamed again to no avail, the tape stifling any sound her throat willed her to produce. She had kicked her legs, trying to wiggle her way free when he had tilted the flame to the end of her hair. Delaney had smelled her hair burning before he had snuffed it out with his hand. Her hair. What would Ann Jones say about her hair?

"Kick again, and I won't put the fire out." His words had broken the fight. The smell of menthol had permeated her nostrils as the cough drop clanked against his teeth. He had unbuckled his pants, pulling them down before Delaney had realized what was about to happen. She had caught a glimpse of the tattoo inked on his neck, 1 John 1:9, before she had closed her eyes. Her body had recoiled as she felt his calloused hands fondle her developed chest. She had squeezed her eyes tighter. *Let me go home. Let me go home.* He had poked and prodded her before she felt the searing pain below her waist as he raped her. The tears had poured down her shut eyes, wetting her hair next to her temples. She had waited until he stopped moving back and forth to open her eyes.

"Now that wasn't so bad, was it?" he asked as he had stood up, buckling his pants. She had lain on the cool slab, immoveable as her body bled while he merely handed her a paper towel, indicating that she should clean herself up. Her mind had screamed to her to run. Her body disobeyed.

"And my precious, Delaney," he had continued in a low and steady voice as he kneeled next to her, "If you even make a whisper about this, your family and friends will discover that you are just a little whore. That you begged for sex in church. You wouldn't want that, would you?" He had run his fingers along her face before he had stood up before the rack of votive candles. He had lit another candle and bowed his head in prayer.

Delaney's body had trembled as she surrendered to his orders. She had climbed out of his car after a silent six blocks and bit her lip raw as she walked the painful steps to the front porch. Ann Jones had met her on the porch, returning the wave to a smiling Mr. Rowan before he had driven off. Later that night, with eyes steadied on her reflection in her bedroom mirror, Delaney had chopped six inches from her flowing locks much to her mother's dismay. Ann Jones simply shrugged it off to the rebellious teenage years. She was her first and only daughter after all.

In the following weeks, Delaney had made every excuse to miss Mr. Rowan's art classes that she had once reveled in. She'd treaded cautiously every moment for three weeks, only going to school and back home again with the guardianship of her brothers, until the Tuesday morning she had seen his pitted face on the news. The smells churned deep inside her. He had been captured and charged with sexual assault and narcotics possession. As she had gazed at the profile of her father watching the segment, she knew she could never find the words to tell him or anyone what had happened. She had gotten her period two days later.

Delaney had attempted to suppress the deep wounds, abandoning painting and any sexual encounters with men for five years. Church, on the other hand, was abandoned indefinitely.

5

The gray sedan backed out of the long, winding driveway and onto the road. V watched as her employer left his seven thousand square foot mansion. She had never caught a look inside the stuccoed fortress. It was disgustingly beautiful, she was sure. V would have enough time - and space - to finish her preparation. She gave one final gaze to the house before she swung her own gray sedan in reverse. She had never been good enough for him, and she had stopped trying, without him knowing, a long time ago.

V laid her foot on the accelerator, watching the three-story house disappear in the rearview mirror. The past few years had been particularly agonizing, waiting and preparing for the right moment to seek her revenge. Her knuckles, the physical proof of that time, were raw and swollen between the joints as they gripped the wheel. The boxing instructor had vehemently denied V's demands to fight without gloves the first three weeks. But she was unyielding, punching the bags until her knuckles spit blood. He liked her tenacity, so he let her stay, never letting his eye off her during her biweekly visits. She was smart about the time in the ring, ensuring that her employer never knew about them. The yoga studio next door was her alibi in order for her subsequently lean and toned body not to draw questions. She was a quick study. Agile - powerful force in a tiny package as long as she controlled the rage. With over a thousand sessions, she felt ready, but her employer had made it difficult with the thugs that periodically visited the house in the middle of the night. He was the master of illusions; a monster that reared its ugly head only occasionally. So she waited.

She sped back to her apartment to finish the research she had started. It wouldn't be long before Gunnar made a move, but she needed to be one step ahead of him. Always. She hadn't been the first time they'd met. V needed to know more about Theron Olson, and she needed to finish packing her bag that was already stashed with cash and her .9 millimeter.

6

Delaney gripped the wheel tighter, her long fingers white, as a pickup truck flew passed her, kicking a flurry of powder onto her windshield. *I knew there was a reason why the streets were quiet when I left – a blizzard.* Her small car had served her well at college for the past ten years in the cramped space of downtown Madison, but the flat, empty terrain of the freeway made a wind tunnel of blowing snow and torrential gusts. The winds tugged and whipped the tiny car as snow piled onto the road. She leaned forward to look closer at the road. When she had accepted the job at Leighton, her father had tried to convince Delaney to buy a SUV for the "trips back home." She had smiled at him, knowing her father had wanted her to stay in Milwaukee, but urged him she would be fine in her Civic. She had purchased the car on her own; she was going to hang on to it as long as she could. *Michael Jones was right again.* Yet another time that her father's annoying habit of being right had presented itself.

Delaney surveyed the road ahead of her. The visibility had diminished to mere feet as the snow pummeled her windshield.

Glancing at the clock, she debated taking the next exit ramp to wait out the storm. *Plenty of time before the rehearsal dinner at six.* She had wanted to spend the afternoon with her mother, though. Delaney shifted her hand to the volume on her radio, stifling the low hum of the music. It needed to be silent. As her eyes moved back to the road, bright red illuminated in front of her before brake lights appeared only a few feet ahead. Her foot slammed the brake, locking her back tires into a fishtail. She jerked the steering wheel in the opposite direction of the spin dutifully, but the wheels refused to grip the slick surface. Within seconds, the car slid onto the other side of the freeway, crossed passed an empty lane of oncoming traffic, and slammed down into the ditch below, skidding twenty feet further down the road. The car slammed to a stop as Delaney's head thrust forward, along with her open bag on the seat next to her. She sat frozen in her seat, both her hands now trembling from the grip on the wheel. After a moment, she slammed her hands against the wheel and screamed into the silence.

The windshield, covered with white chunks, stood in better condition than her front end that was now buried in a foot of snow. Delaney looked up the freeway to her right, no cars passing in sight and the car that had been in front of her was long gone. *How had it come up so fast on me? Everyone else knew the storm was coming.*

Since she could remember, Michael and Ann Jones had watched the weather segment on TMJ4's local news broadcast every morning before heading to work - her mother as a secretary at the *Journal Sentinel*, Milwaukee's largest circulating newspaper, and her father at Miller in the brewery. As a teenager, Delaney had asked her father once about their obsession detailing the weather mid-breakfast before her short walk to school. He had stared at the TV, as if the weatherman would answer her question, before turning to her and responding that, "Old habits die hard, Delaney. Real hard." He had then walked over to the garbage, scraping his half-eaten pancakes with his fork into the garbage, and placed his dishes into the sink without another word. She had locked eyes with Ben, who shrugged his shoulders in his adolescent indifference, and watched as her father walked out the door.

It was seven years later when Delaney finally understood what her father had meant that day. It was when she was dating a guy named Titus, who she'd fervidly denied several dates just because of his name. Titus had grown up on a farm, and his fascination with keeping tabs on the weather had eventually led to Delaney to the discovery of her father's deeply embedded roots. Titus had commented that the upcoming rain would prevent his father from taking off the crop. His father's life, and subsequently his family's life, had always been dictated by the weather. "Farmers live and die by the hand of God and the Heavens," he had said. Michael Jones had been a farmer prior to living in Milwaukee; his old habit of watching the weather still lingered despite his new, urban life. Delaney ended up leaving Titus a few weeks later. Titus couldn't get passed that she wouldn't set foot in a church, and she couldn't get passed his name.

Delaney picked up her phone to see a small envelope icon on the top of her screen. *Too busy heeding the storm to hear my phone.* She groaned as she dialed into her voicemail to hear her father's voice warn her about the snowstorm, urging her to skip the rehearsal dinner and head to Milwaukee the following morning. *Perfect timing for spotty reception.* She threw the phone on the passenger seat next to her.

The snow accumulated on the windshield, piling up until she could barely see out of it. She grabbed the mittens from her console, another Michael Jones's reminder, and rubbed her hands together as she calculated what to do next. She would wait to call her parents until she was at least out of the ditch because the last thing she needed was Michael Jones plowing up here in his pickup truck. She still had plenty of time before the dinner.

Delaney scooped her phone back up from the passenger seat and searched for 'tow services' in her web browser; her iPhone populated a list of five locations within a forty mile radius. She started from the top, dialing Lomira Towing. A young girl answered and told her that it would be one hour until they could get to her. All of the trucks were already out. Delaney had politely declined through clenched teeth and moved on to the next business on the list, Joe's Towing. No answer. Just as she finished dialing the number for the third location, her phone beeped twice. She looked at the red flashing battery icon on the top of her phone. *Low battery.* She waited for someone to answer at Phil's Towing. *Maybe Joe and Phil are brothers.* She grumbled at the less than innovative names that plagued the towing services in the middle of nowhere.

"Yeah," a voice answered on the other end.

"Is this Phil's Towing?" The phone beeped again.

"Yeah."

"Great, can you send a tow truck? I'm in the ditch on Highway forty-one heading south. Not sure where exactly, one hour north of Milwaukee?"

"More details, little lady," he said.

"I don't have any, but my phone is almost dead and it's freezing," she urged. *Come on.*

"Well, probably about two hours out. That is if I can find you," he replied.

"A white Honda Civic headed south on the east side of the"—beep, beep, beep—"road," Delaney finished, looking down at the blank screen on her phone. She slammed her phone on the steering wheel then looked at out the passenger side window at the freeway above. She knew that even if a car happened to drive past, the odds were slim that someone would notice her white car buried in the ditch below amid the flurry of white. She resolved that she had two choices, although neither options were favorable in the conditions of blinding snow and sub-zero temperatures. Without any notion of how long the blizzard would last, she opened the door in dire hope of flagging someone down.

She exhaled as she pulled out her hat from the console, adjusting it over her head full of waves to fit snug over her ears, and then reached to pick up her overnight bag from the passenger side floor. Just as she moved to place her mittens on her hands, she glimpsed a pair of headlights flashing on and off up on the side of the road to her right. Through the white-filled haze, she spotted the glare of red blinking lights on the tail of the truck; the driver had turned on his hazards.

A tow truck.

Her eyes followed a man in a full snowsuit and ski mask, carrying a shovel as he made his way down the embankment toward her car buried in the snow. *Jesus, a ski mask? I'm bait.* A headline from her Uncle Walt, editor of the *Journal Sentinel*, sprawled through her head, *Missing Woman, 28, Abandoned Car Amid Worst Blizzard of the Decade.*

She looked around her car for a sharp object but found nothing to alleviate her paranoia. He made his way around the car to her driver side where he stood, almost knee-deep in snow, motioning her to roll down her window. She hesitated instead, and reached for the key in the ignition. The distrust evident in her eyes, he took off his ski mask, unveiling a middle aged man with gentle eyes and a goatee. A friendly wave with his gloved hand followed. She smiled back, rolling down the window to a whistling wind of arctic breeze and flakes.

"Looks like you are in a bit of trouble, miss," he said, pointing his finger toward her car. His goatee moved back and forth with his mouth. The hair reminded her of her bristle brush. "I'm Joe."

"Sorry about that, Joe. You just scared me a bit with your full suit and ski mask. I'm Delaney, by the way," she replied as she reached out her hand to shake his because that's what you did in the Midwest. Even in the midst of a snow storm, you were polite.

"Nice to meet you, Delaney. Not, of course, under these circumstances, but I'm glad I saw you down here. I won't be able to get your car out now; the snow is too thick and it's too dangerous, but I can give you a ride if you'd like. Back to my shop," he said, pointing to his truck up on the side of the road. *Back to the shop. Do I have a choice?*

"That would be great. Thank you so much for your offer. I can have someone pick me up there if you have a phone I can use."

"Yeah. Now, let's get out of here. It's colder than a penguin's pecker out here," he said as he looked down at the snow piled high on her driver's side door. "It looks like I'm going to have to dig you out a bit. Your door ain't going to open." He pulled his black ski mask back down, protecting his face against the harsh wind, and began heaving the snow away from the door over his shoulder with quick movements. *Of course, he's done this before. He's a tow truck driver.*

Delaney closed the window and gathered her phone with her overnight bag before waiting for Joe to stop shoveling. He paused and motioned his hands before yelling "Give it a try!" She pushed the door with her shoulder, shoving all her body weight into the plastic next to the window. The door opened four inches.

"Close it!" Joe yelled, signaling again with his hand. He began digging deeper to free yet more of the snow built up on the door. She watched as more snow flung over his shoulder ten feet behind him. His hunched body worked mechanically much more efficient than she anticipated from a relatively bigger man in - what she guessed - his early fifties. "Try 'er again!"

She lowered her shoulder again, pushing the door open wide enough that she could fit through. The door scraped against the snow as she squeezed herself out of the safety of the Civic and into the white fury of hell that pelted her whole body. The cold wetness seeped into her thin leather boots as she sunk a few inches down. She put her head down and covered the side of her face with her hand as she tried to move forward, the wind whipping her body like a ragdoll. Joe climbed back up the ditch, motioning for her to follow in his path of footsteps as he reached to grab her forearm to help her up the slope. The grip was firm, hoisting her onto the side of the road next to the truck. She climbed into the passenger seat of the truck after she noted the "Joe's Towing" sprawled on the door.

The four-by-four plowed south down the freeway toward Joe's shop, just ten miles away from Delaney's stranded Civic. She looked over, examining Joe's blue snowsuit, letting her eyes follow the red stripe up to his face. With his ski mask pulled up, resting on top of his head, and gloves set aside next to his seat, Delaney caught a better look at Joe's face that was clearly aged with years of hard labor. His hands were rough and thick with calluses, dirt gathered deep under his nails. He noticed her staring at his hands gripped loose on the steering wheel.

"I bury a lot of bodies," he rumbled with a crack in his lips. Before Delaney could reply, he continued in a serious tone, "I'm joking, dear. I suppose not the best time to joke given the situation."

"The ground's too hard to bury any bodies now anyway. You better wait until the spring then you can get a little deeper," she replied, looking straight ahead.

"Well, then, Miss Delaney, I guess I know who to call if I'm ever in a predicament of that nature." He paused, looking over at his passenger, her brown hair falling over her shoulders beneath her hat. "You never can pinpoint those lady-killers, can you?" he finished.

"Well, I'm surely not one of those, unless I'm provoked, of course." She looked at Joe's face as his smile spread wider.

"You remind me of my daughter; you're a feisty one. What possessed you to drive a Civic in this snowstorm, by the way? You know that's a terrible idea," he said. *You sound like Michael Jones. A father of a daughter.*

"My brother's getting married tomorrow in Milwaukee and I was headed down to spend time with my family. I didn't bother to check the weather like most normal people in Wisconsin, and I just happened to lose reception when my father called, urging me to wait the storm out. So here I am," she said, lifting her hands off her lap, gesturing toward the truck. "Thank you, by the way. How old is your daughter?"

"Elizabeth was sixteen when she died twelve years ago. She

HOUSE OF STEEL

would be twenty-eight, about your age, I'm guessing," he said, looking back at his passenger.

"I'm sorry, Joe. Yeah, I'm twenty-eight," she replied, her face flushed with the sinking feeling in her stomach.

"Car accident. By herself. They said she was driving too fast," he said before clearing his throat. "You're lucky I was driving past to pull someone else stuck on the side of the road. I caught ya' out of the corner of my eye. You couldn't have been in the ditch long; the tracks were still pretty fresh. Does anyone know that you were in the ditch?"

"Well..." she paused, looking out the passenger window at the white haze. "I did leave a message with my brother right before my phone shut off," she lied.

"Good. Once we get to the shop, you can call your brother to come and get you later today. He should wait until this blows over," he replied, leaning forward over the steering wheel to look out the windshield, as if he were able to calculate the blizzard's longevity and severity. *Another connoisseur of the weather.* Nothing except white.

"We're just about there," he added, shifting his truck into third gear to get through a massive drift. She hadn't seen a snowplow for the last forty-five minutes.

"I usually plow this road myself. It takes too long for the county workers to get out here," Joe said as he turned into a driveway Delaney hadn't even seen. *A driveway that leads to nowhere.* As her fingers gripped her bag tighter, the vague outline of a building began forming. He pulled the truck to a stop. The dark gray metal buckled and wavered against the gusts of wind and snow.

"And here we are. Not much to the shop, other than a phone, some cars, a vending machine and heat."

39

"That's all I need. Are you headed back out?" she asked.

"You got it. I'll be running in and out all day. Snow is my gold," he replied, tapping the steering wheel of the tow truck. "Make yourself at home, dear."

"Thanks, Joe, good luck out there," she said as she heaved the door open against the force of the wind. She ran in front of the truck's headlights, giving Joe one last wave before grabbing the handle of the black door stenciled with "Joe's Towing and Body Shop." The door reluctantly swung open into a dimly-lit, small waiting area that had a few chairs and the vending machine. She shut the door behind her, kicking the snow out of the way in order for the door to click shut and turned into the room, waiting for her eyes to adjust to the darkness before going further into it.

The waiting area opened to a pair of adjoined small offices to the right. She slid into a vinyl swivel chair with its high back and massively structured arms behind a metal desk amid the stacks of grease stained papers in the first office. The vinyl, with tiny tears where white fuzz poked through, squeaked against her jeans. She moved her body forward, but the chair didn't come with her. Her eyes traveled down to the bottom of the chair – three wheels. In the place of the fourth wheel was a wooden block. *What are you doing with that gold, Joe? Get a new chair. As well as a new phone.*

She picked up the chair by its arms to reach the phone. The coils of the cord uncurled only the slightest bit as she raised the receiver to her ear to silence. Her breath quickened as her body shot up, frozen in place with the phone still at her ear. *Dead phone.*

Delaney set the receiver back down, looking at the lights flickering in the waiting room. As she held her breath, she tilted her head, listening to the quiet hum echoing against the walls. Images of her Uncle Walt's cottage in northern Wisconsin amid flashes of lightning and torrents of rain flashed through her mind. She felt her lids close. The lights were on a generator. *No power. No phones. Man in a ski mask. Warehouse in the middle of nowhere. Whiteout.*

She crept toward the door, still clutching her bag, as she looked around for a sharp object. *Settle down, Delaney. The phone's old. It may not be working anyway.* She envisioned a masked man with black leather gloves, cutting the wires, scissors still in his hand as he smiled. Shaking her head at the thought, she exhaled and moved into the other office, her back running against the wall for safe measure. The room was fractionally larger. Most likely Joe's office with the same old office furniture. She picked up the cordless phone, sparking an idle hope that the phone purchased within the last decade would produce the familiar hum. She pressed the call button and was rewarded with a dial tone.

"Hello?"

"Mark." The sound of his voice rushed a swell of relief through Delaney's body.

"Tell me you're not driving," Mark answered her call.

"I'm not," she replied.

"Good."

"Well, it's not exactly good. I'm not driving because my car's in the ditch."

"God, Delaney," Mark said. She waited. "Are you okay?"

"Yes, I'm okay, asshole, but I need you to pick me up. I'm at a body shop in the middle of nowhere. A guy named Joe picked me up with his tow truck and brought me to his shop," Delaney replied.

"Yeah, I'll come get you. What's the address?" Mark asked.

Delaney picked up an invoice on the desk, scanning the content for an address. "927 Parker Drive. Lomira. Wherever the hell that is," she said.

"I'll be there in two hours. Don't go anywhere," he joked.

"Funny. By the way, my phone is dead so call this number back if you need me. And please spare me, don't tell Dad."

"Delaney?"

"Yeah?"

"You there alone?"

"Yeah."

"Be safe." Mark hung up before she could say thanks.

Delaney sighed, setting the phone back down on the charger. Her stomach rolled as she looked up at the plastic clock hanging on the wall. *12:13 p.m.* She fished a crinkled dollar bill out of her wallet and headed out to the vending machine in the waiting area to locate the last bag of M&Ms in the near-empty machine. She watched as the candy landed with a clank on the bottom. As her hand fumbled around the bottom of the tray, a soft ball of fur brushed against her fingertips. She recoiled, letting out a scream.

"MEOW." The animal's screech pierced the waiting room as a small head with glassy eyes appeared from the tray. The cat hopped out of the vending machine, stretching its legs while keeping an eye on her intruder.

"Jesus," Delaney said to the calico cat as it left small smudges of grease on the floor. Delaney nudged the cat with her leg as it rubbed against her jeans. A dangling silver ID tag gleamed from its neck.

"Parker, huh?" Delany said. She replayed her motions, opening the black door of the vending machine, but peered in to scope out the bottom tray before she placed her hand back in to retrieve the M&Ms. As she tore open the top of the bag, she noticed a door of blackened glass that, she assumed, led to the warehouse. She put her hand on the cool metal handle and pushed down. *Locked.*

"What's back there?" She spoke to fill the hum, attempting to calm her nerves. Yet, the voice she had directed at the cat fell flat in the stale air. She turned around to an empty spot on the dingy linoleum; the cat was gone. The slight buzz of the lights and vending machine filled the otherwise silent space.

Adrenaline pumped through her veins as she stepped back to Joe's office and the only window in the cramped warehouse space. The flurry of white outside had cast a bright reflection into the room, making it the least offensive place for Delaney to wait. The dismal view outside settled into her stomach. It would be awhile. Her eyes scanned the rest of the walls. Crowning achievements of certificates, licenses and accolades filled them. She peered closer at three particular certificates grouped together, scrutinizing the stamped signature that inscribed all of them. *Holston Parker.*

As she moved on to other framed pieces, the office walls of Leighton University flashed through her mind; the departments filled with pretentious faculty and their achievements. She had always thought framing achievements was a bit ostentatious. Even as a child, she wondered why doctors or dentists framed their walls with their schooling and praises. Her mother had once told her that it was a "diversion from their inadequacies in life." Delaney had agreed.

Next to the framed accomplishments hung smaller, colored frames with pictures of a young girl. She looked closer at a picture of the girl in her teens sporting a polka dot two-piece, standing on a white, sandy beach with an expansive lake behind her. *Lake Michigan?* Her hair was slicked back, wet from the water as she stood, posing at the camera with a wave and smile. She had the same gentle eyes as Joe. His daughter, Elizabeth. A boy, slightly older, stood with his arms crossed behind her. *Brother? Boyfriend?*

Another girl, about the same age, except with long, dark hair, sat on a bench a few feet away. Her legs were tucked into her chest, her arms hugging them with ferocity. Unlike the girl posing, she stared straight into her knees as if she was purposely avoiding the picture. Her dark hair hung dry, half-hiding the rest of her face. Delaney placed her hand on the wall as she moved closer to look at the girl with the dark hair, the wood paneling flexed with the pressure of her hand.

Delaney caught another picture that showed the same girls sitting on a swing that hung from a large oak tree in front of a sweeping cabin. This time, the dark-haired girl's eyes penetrated the camera, staring at Delaney with translucent blueness. She shifted her eyes to the forty-something man dressed in khakis and a poplin shirt. He stood leaning against the oak tree with a hat half-tipped on his head, not looking at the girls, but gazing off to the side; his pronounced jawline stood outlined in the picture. The angles protruded sharp in his hard face as if he objected to the girls' happiness. The picture was, most likely, an unknown capture of time to the man.

She shifted over a foot to glance at the other pictures surrounding the young girls. Pictures of Joe and Elizabeth at various ages filled the frames, some hand-decorated by, Delaney presumed, the daughter herself. Her blonde curls, a contrast to her father's dark hair, decorated his daughter's vibrant face. She was beautiful, yet feisty as Joe called her; a picture of her standing on top of a shed roof, blonde curls falling effortlessly around her devilish grin, exemplified this. Delaney smiled back at her standing tall on the roof with the blue sky surrounding her. *I wish I could have met you.*

Listless, Delaney began examining the items on Joe's desk. An old desk clock. A greased gear – something she only knew thanks to her mechanically inclined father. She had spent hours of her childhood watching him tinker with an old Chevy that he never was able to run, at least not for a consistent period of time. Also on the desk was a fist-sized stone used as a paperweight to hold down a stack of invoices. She lifted the stone last, running her fingers along the cracked grooves, turning it over in her hands to feel the roughness against her skin. Feeling a poke against her skin, she turned it over to see a small key adhered with transparent tape to the bottom.

Really, Joe? She peeled the tape off the stone with her fingertip, freeing the small brass key from the hard surface. Letting it rest in her hand, she closed her fingers to feel the ridges roughly stab her skin. She opened her hand back up, watching as the white imprint of the key disappeared from her skin, resolving to the flesh color of the rest of her hand. *I shouldn't.* Her eyes wandered to the drawer that had a small, circular keyhole half-hidden behind the handle.

The soft rumble of an engine startled her as she drew her eyes to the window. It had been twenty minutes, if that, since she had called Mark. She slid the key back under the stone before she squinted through the white haze to see the outline of a vehicle pull right along the side of the shop. Her head cocked as she stumbled to her feet. It wasn't a tow truck.

7

DAY 2: December 19 – 12:30 p.m.

V swiped her employee badge along the scanner, waiting for the red light to turn green before she pulled the glass door engraved with Parker Enterprises open. The scanner had obliged, just as it had almost every day for the past ten years. As she slipped through the door, she wondered what it would feel like to stop going through it. Would the pain vanish? After last night, she had realized that today was the last day she would go through that door as the Director of Security at Parker Enterprises.

The sprawling corporate structure stood four stories high with 150,000 square feet for just over four hundred employees. It was dim, with no cars in the parking lot, no Kelly at the front desk to greet everyone and no employees wandering the campus. It was Saturday. All the employees were at home huddled in the warmth of their houses as the snowstorm dumped blankets of white onto the ground. She slipped down the hall with the empty backpack slung over her shoulder. She knew the surveillance cameras in the halls would pick her up, but it didn't matter because her team wouldn't question it. It was rare that she missed a day in the building. It was as if the walls expected her every day with the exception of Sunday. Her white boots treaded light against the carpet, the fibers of the nylon only absorbing a trace of saturation. She pushed the elevator button, watching as the silver doors opened slowly to bring her to the fourth floor.

The elevator dinged as it propelled her upward, one step closer to cutting herself off from Parker Enterprises. The doors opened to a brightly lit executive floor, the outside elements reflecting into the floor to ceiling glass. It was an intricate building, designed with Holston's touch of modern meets luxury. Although she had despised what the building stood for, the empire that he had built, she had always marveled at the beauty of it. She couldn't deny him that. She turned to the right, walking past Mark Jones's office – the brother of Delaney Jones. He had only been here a few weeks. She hadn't realized who he was during the interview process, but the five minute Google search she did just a few days ago tagged him to Delaney. Holston Parker was interested in their family. The intrigue grew.

V stopped at the heavy double doors to her left. The doors, made of African Blackwood, glistened in their rich, saturated oils, telling of the daily polishing. The silver handles of the door called her, beckoning her to come in. She punched the code into the keypad on the wall, waiting for the familiar click before she pulled the door open into the vast office surrounded in glass. He secured his office, or at least he thought. V had put in a master key for all the Parker Enterprise's buildings, though; one that only she knew. Getting in and out of Holston Parker's buildings and offices was effortless. Uncomplicated. Everything she wanted her life to be.

The office's masculine space consumed her as she crept toward the desk in the middle of the room. The large, wooden desk spanned over ten feet. It's high, black executive chair hung still and empty in the air. She ran her fingers along the desk, feeling the polished surface of the same rich wood that the doors were made of. The desk had been handcrafted in South Africa by a talented tribesman; it had taken him a year to make his creation. Holston had always reveled in that fact. Her eyes fell to the sheen of the empty surface. There were no pictures of the ones he loved. No portraits of a happy family. In Holston Parker's heart, there was nothing other than blackness.

Although she knew there was nothing here for her, V needed one last look at the office without him. She had rifled through his office months ago, searching for clues that would help her find the incriminating evidence she needed. V had seen it with her own eyes, but it hadn't been enough. She had thirsted for more. One last thread that explained it all to her. She wouldn't find it here, though. He was carefully meticulous in his methods.

She slipped her hand into her pocket near her knee and flicked open her knife. Despite that she longed to drag the knife along the surface of the desk, she knew she couldn't. She couldn't risk being tracked. Instead, V tucked her head underneath the desk and, with the blade sturdy in her hand, she brought the pointed edge to the wood. Slow, she dragged the knife down and back up again, carving a deep V. While she planned that he would never see it, the pleasure of defiling his precious commodity still coursed through her veins.

V stood up and took one last look at the room before exiting out of the double doors. It would be the last time she saw that office and the desk with the rich grains and polished top. She moved down the hallway, taking the last right into her office with nine foot windows spanning two walls. It was nothing like

Holston's, but she didn't want it to be. The office was white, almost sterile in its appearance with its blank walls and glass desk. The desk was clean and light. As she slipped into the chair, she set the backpack on top of the desk and pulled open the drawer nearest to her. She dug to the bottom where a small, silver case lay buried beneath a stack of papers. She slid open the case, looking at the cameras the size of quarters set inside the foam. They would be perfect. She reclosed the case, locking it shut before she slid it into her bag, already packed with her white clothes and ski mask. She would change in the car.

8

Delaney shuffled through her bag, frantic to find the pepper spray she never left home without. Layers of fabric slipped through her fingers, but there was no long cylinder. She was sure she had packed it. Delaney closed her eyes, feeling the small groan erupt from her throat. Her open bag had flung onto the mat below during the impact of the accident. The pepper spray was in her car.

Delaney's eyes followed the tall man as he emerged from his sedan, letting the wind and snow pummel his body as he strode toward the door. She looked down at the desk and scanned the surface for anything to defend herself with – a letter opener. Even a pen for Christ's sake. Anything. She contemplated grabbing the old clock, but exhaled instead before she moved through the doorway and into the waiting room. A barrage of cold air whipped her skin. The man ducked through the door, clinching against the howling wind outside. His electric eyes traveled up her body first and finally came to rest on her face.

"Hi," she said.

"Humph," he grunted in response as he studied her standing before him. He hadn't anticipated that anyone would be at Joe's shop, and definitely not Delaney Jones.

"Uh, Joe picked me up after my car went in the ditch." She paused, waiting for him to respond. To say anything intelligible.

"Oh," he replied, his eyes still inching up and down her body. Her skin crawled with black spiders, their legs dotting her entire body. Her face drained as her defense mechanisms thrust into overdrive. She wrapped her arms around her body, hugging it close as she examined the man's face.

At 6'6", he towered over her, his thick neck producing a huge Adam's apple that moved up and down with each grunt. His bright eyes were set in a muscular and well-defined face. A large scar snaked down on the right side of his temple, its thickness protruding from his skin. Her eyes caught the movement of his hands as he unclenched his rough fists, resting them on his side. She noticed the start of a tattoo near the cusp of his jacket, reaching far up onto his arm. Other than his black leather jacket and boots, he had no other gear to protect him from the cold. No hat. No gloves. His white hair matted down from the snow, hidden in the platinum hue of his strands.

I–," she started again, feeling her body crumble beneath his presence. *Breathe, Delaney.*

"I'm Gunnar," he grunted before his lips turned up into a coy smile. The wrinkles around his eyes and forehead multiplied into a pit of snakes slithering through his face. In his mid-forties, he had yet to learn the social standards acceptable to Americans or really any human. He turned to sit down in a chair next to the vending machine, his body overflowing in the small, plastic seat. Delaney exhaled, feeling a slight release of tension.

"I'm Delaney," she responded. The hum of the generator

filled the stifling room as he continued to watch her from his chair. Her cheeks flushed a deep crimson as his face contorted; the satisfaction of her discomfort evident in his reflection.

"Are you waiting for Joe?" she asked.

"Not really," he replied.

"The weather's pretty horrible out there. Did you get stranded?" she asked, the words flooded from her mouth. *Not really?*

"No, he's just fixing my other car. I need something out of it," he replied, his face stoic and unmoving as he watched her. Delaney's ears tried to discern his thick, heavy accent. It was definitely European. He studied her as if he was calculating something, if there was anything in his brain that allowed him to process information. "I didn't know you were here," he added.

"I'm sorry. Do I know you?" she asked, flinching at his words. Her gut wretched inside as her mind calculated the improbable possibility.

"No," he grunted again as his eyes lit up to the movement of her body. "I didn't know that *anyone* was here."

"I'm just waiting for my brother to pick me up. He'll be here any minute," she lied. It would be at least an hour before Mark got there, if not longer.

"Oh?" he said, his voice piquing interest as he laced his thick fingers together in his lap. He hadn't planned on staying, but since she was here, he felt compelled to stay. To watch.

The wind whistled against the thin walls of the shop. Delaney turned her ears at the sound of a muffled banging noise. Her eyebrows creased at the sound, but she didn't really want to know what it was. "Is that Joe?" she asked, walking to his office to look out the window. She knew the answer, but played it anyway.

"No," he answered from the other room without looking. He stood up and walked to the back door with the blackened glass. He slid a key into the lock and disappeared through the door; the sound of a click was followed by a dim haze glowing through the window. She craned her neck forward despite the nagging voice that told her to stop. Run. She lurched forward anyway, glancing through the door to see a small overhead lamp near a workbench that illuminated outlines of painted aluminum. The rest of the shop was dark. Another muffled bang carried through the wind, sending another shot of fear through her body. *The phone.*

Delaney sprinted into Joe's office, taking a glance at the car parked outside, before picking up the phone. The dial tone echoed in her ear as her index finger shook uncontrollably over the '9'. There was no possible way that the police would get here in time to stop Gunnar, but at least they would know. Someone would know to look for her if something did happen. Her head throbbed as she pressed the '9,' but she hesitated too long to press the next numbers. Her eyes shut to the sound of the warehouse door opening. She set the phone down and rushed into the doorway of the office just in time to see Gunnar lock the door behind him. With the shop on the other side completely black, he turned around to see Delaney leaning against the frame of the door.

"You know it's not safe for you to be here by yourself," his voice rasped in the same low, monotone grunt.

Delaney forced the hardness down her throat, swallowing before she opened her mouth to reply. But her voice eluded her, the words refusing to leave her lips. She cleared her throat. "My brother will be here any minute. Did you get what you needed?" Her voice barely filled the air.

"Yes." He hit the chest of his jacket as he moved through the waiting room, closer to Delaney. Her feet fumbled underneath her as she staggered back against the wall - a prime victim, defenseless against his pursuing body.

She gripped her bag, ready to swing at his head when the heavy smell of cigar permeated just inches from her nostrils. The nauseating smells of singed hair and menthol came swirling in. It was going to happen again. She would be raped here, but this time, Gunnar would finish the job. He would stab her to death and cut her into a million little pieces. She held her breath as he paused with inaudible thought to give her one last stare. The same contorted look appeared on his face before he walked past her. Delaney's chest burned as she held the oxygen tight in her body, her lungs calling to exhale. As she released, the black leather stopped. The boots rotated to face her.

Despite the fact that Gunnar wanted nothing else than to stay and watch her squirm under his careful eye, he had a discrepancy in the form of the man he had tied up in the trunk. The hunting knife that he had just picked up would help alleviate that issue. He had always saved the knife for his most enduring victims. He would take pleasure in ending the life of the man in the trunk. As he envisioned the knife sinking into the man's chest, he stared into Delaney's blue eyes, wondering how she might feel about watching him. He reconsidered his plan.

"I need your help before I go," he said.

"Oh?" Delaney replied. Her hand instinctively reached up to her empty pocket. She knew it wasn't there. The pepper spray was in her car, but she longed for the comfort of the long cylinder so she shoved her hand into her pocket, trying to look unaffected.

"I just need a quick push to get out of the snow. Joe didn't plow much in front of the shop. I've got a car," he finished, trying to coax her to come out on her own. He knew his employer wouldn't approve of hurting her to get her to come outside. Not yet anyway.

"Sure." Delaney despised the word as it spilled from her mouth. She wouldn't be a victim, not again. If she could get him outside first, she could quickly shut the door of the warehouse and lock it. She knew it wasn't an infallible plan, but she had nothing else.

"Good," Gunnar grunted, turning back to open the door. The gusts swirled again into the waiting room as his boots stood transfixed, holding the door for Delaney. She wanted nothing more than to knock him down with a blow to his groin, but there was no way she could get off the kick. She walked through the door, ducking her head as the snow pelted her.

"Delaney, do you happen to know this man?" he grunted behind her as the trunk to his car opened. She stopped, her body mesmerized as she looked down at the bound man in the trunk. He screamed, but there was no sound. The duct tape over his mouth left a muted nothingness that disappeared with the wind. His arms and legs were tied beneath him with plastic restraints. Delaney turned away as terror surged through her body. She wouldn't let Gunnar take her like this. She tried to sprint away from the car. Two steps. His hands grabbed her arms, yanking her back to the trunk.

"Look, Delaney," Gunnar said as he dragged her back to the car. Her feet kicked in the air as he held her head toward the trunk, forcing her to look. The agony in the man's face tortured her. Delaney's eyes traveled down to his neck where she read the tattoo inked into his neck, *1 John 1:9*. Her body went limp. *Mr. Rowan. Richard Rowan. St. Luke's Church.* He had aged; his hair was now gray and the fullness sucked from his deeply scarred and pitted face. A face she would never forget. A face that had haunted her for fourteen years.

"He was released from prison a few weeks ago," Gunnar began. Delaney could feel his hot, stale breath on her neck. "I didn't get a chance to kill him before the police got him. Right after he raped you." The fear in Mr. Rowan's eyes pierced Delaney as she felt Gunnar release her. They pleaded for help – disgusting plea for mercy. Her feet sunk several inches into the snow as Gunnar moved closer to the trunk. He perched his legs and reached inside his jacket to retrieve a knife. He raised it high above his head, pausing before he grunted his well-rehearsed chant. The man began violently twisting along the plastic that lined the trunk beneath him while Delaney silently begged for it to stop.

"Your sins will never be forgiven." Gunnar thrust the knife down, sinking it deep into his chest. Delaney's scream vanished as she watched Mr. Rowan's body go lifeless in the trunk. Blood pooled beneath his body and onto the plastic sheet. Her legs failed her, buried deep in the snow. Her feet somehow chained to the ground, she stood next to the experienced killer, her body pulsating as it threatened to verge into convulsions. He pulled a white cloth from his jacket and inched it across the blade, wiping his knife clean. He turned it over in his hand, examining the point, before he tucked it into a sheath near his chest. Leaning forward, he swept his hand over Mr. Rowan's empty eyes, closing his lids. Gunnar rolled the ends of the plastic toward his body before shutting the trunk.

"He got what he deserved. You should feel redeemed, but you should be more careful next time. With that student, I mean. Errors in judgment lead to devastation. Consider yourself," he waited as his throat released a grotesque noise, "notified. I don't want to see you again."

Delaney sputtered, unable to formulate anything comprehensible. Instead, she stepped back, watching him get into his black Buick. The sedan's wheels spun as snow flew into the air. The red taillights vanished into the white as she stood, empty, listening to the wind thrashing against the warehouse.

9

V swung open the back door that led into the kitchen and slipped through, closing the door tight behind her. All the residents of Appleton, with the exception of her, were holed up in their houses, waiting out the storm. To her, this just meant more time. V rubbed her white boots on the rug stamped with "Welcome" eradicating what wetness she could. Contemplating unlacing them, she reconsidered, just in case. She stepped forward, hearing the slightest squeak against the wood as she moved through the kitchen. Delaney's living room was just a few feet ahead.

Swinging the white backpack around, V placed it on the floor and unzipped it, revealing the small silver case. She flicked open the clasps of the case, lifting the lid up to expose the two circular lenses. Sliding off her white gloves, she picked the first one up with her index finger and thumb, carefully cradling it in her fingers before scanning the room. There was barely anything in it. A couch. Coffee table. Mounted TV. Boxes of unpacked belongings. Her eyes turned toward the charred fireplace adorned with an old, wooden mantel. A built-in bookshelf to the left of the brick had books along the first row. She would be able to set it on a book without Delaney noticing. It wasn't perfect, but it would work. She slid her hand into her pocket to retrieve her phone, sliding through the interface with ease. An image of her body appeared on the screen. A small wave of her hand mirrored on the display. V's eyes scanned back to the blackened fireplace. By the looks of it, Delaney hadn't touched the fireplace since she moved in. She would have to do something about that. It was the perfect spot to dispose of unwanted items, whatever that was.

Running her finger along the edge of the thick spine of a book, V placed the first camera on the top of it. *The World According to Garp.* She had never read it; she wasn't much of a literary study anymore, not since she was a teenager. The inconspicuous camera blended into the dark space. Satisfied, she picked up the silver case and moved down into the hallway to Delaney's bedroom. She stepped onto the cracked floor, skimming the room for the drop before narrowing in on the desk tucked against the wall. It had a direct view to her bed. She crept forward, placing the silver case onto the surface.

Her eyes scanned the contents of the desk. She picked up a frame with a picture of smiling people sitting close together as if they actually enjoyed each other's presence. Their happy faces looking back at her, one by one. Taunting her. The girl had taken after her mother - blue eyes and long, wavy hair. Yet, the two boys didn't look like the parents. Both had light hair, contrasting to the dark strands of the parents. They had rounder faces and their deep eyes were wider, set further into their skulls. The two boys weren't theirs. They couldn't be. She set the frame back down, slipping out the second camera from the case. Placing a piece of tape on the back of the camera, she adhered it to the frame before bending down to see the angle it would capture. Flawless.

V turned her attention to the bright green filing cabinet next to the desk. She pulled it open, exposing a handful of files that she shuffled through. There had to be more. As she dug further, she felt a fistful of lace and silk. She sighed, digging the bras and underwear out of the drawer and into her bag. 1:28 p.m. There was more than enough time. She turned back to the living room to begin the process of cleaning the fireplace.

10

Delaney squinted as she looked out the passenger window into the blinding glare of the sun's reflection. She turned to look at Mark's profile in the driver's seat. His eyes were covered in sunglasses, the lenses staring ahead at the road. She had waited two hours for Mark to pick her up, huddled in a fetal position on the carpet of Joe's office for the first hour, willing Gunnar's face out of her head. But she couldn't remove his face, his eyes. They plagued her just as Mr. Rowan had. Her body had finally released, allowing her to crawl to the vending machine to almost empty its contents. She had stared at the grease soaked cat while eating far too many bags of junk food that exceeded their "fresh by" dates. She blamed the uneasiness in her stomach to the stale pretzels and chocolate melted and solidified several times over. That made sense to her.

She had been unable to dial 911, although she had tried several times. Her finger convulsed over the last digit, but she had nothing to say. No details to give about Gunnar. The license plate was a blur. His accent, imperceptible. His knowledge about Mr. Rowan, unfathomable.

Only two people had known about that night and now, one was dead and the other, herself, was a silent doll. The police wouldn't find Gunnar. The man was obviously a trained killer, plunging the knife in the precise location to minimize the blood loss in the most efficient stroke. Gunnar had also made it exceedingly clear that he would have no problem finding her because he already had. Her body toyed with the twisted sense of relief that the only living, breathing connection to that night had been immortalized in the trunk of that car.

The Ford truck blazed through what snow remained on the road after the blizzard had ceased. The snow crunched beneath the wheels and spurted out the sides with ease. The snowplows had emerged from their sheds, clad with their salt and large blades, moving the snow off the freeway and piling it high in the ditches below. The salt and warm sun worked to melt the remaining snow that covered the roads.

"Please tell me that was enough to convince you that the Civic has to go," Mark said with his eyes still focused on the road ahead. Delaney smiled. Her lips felt stiff, almost cruel in their gesture. She didn't expect anything different from Mark. Michael Jones would say the same.

"Joe's getting it out of the ditch. It still could be in good shape," she said. She couldn't wrap her mind around how she could possibly tell Mark what she had witnessed. "By the way, Joe has some ties with your new employer, Holston Parker."

"Good shape, huh?" He laughed before looking down at her in the passenger seat. "And Parker Enterprises is everywhere. Wisconsin. The Midwest. Even the East Coast now. You realize his net worth is over a billion dollars, right?"

"Yeah, I realize he shits money, but don't you think it's strange that he is connected to a redneck auto shop in the sticks?

Why would Parker be connected to such a small shop?" she asked, turning to look outside the window at the flat landscape, its redundancy lulling her eyes.

"Did you go through his stuff, Delaney?" he prompted, accusing her from beneath his sunglasses.

"No," she replied, thinking about the key underneath the stone. "His signature is everywhere. A stack of invoices are sitting on the desk with the header of Parker Enterprises, as if the shop is owned by Parker. The shop itself was located on Parker Drive, as you obviously saw. Even the cat is named Parker." Her voice rose as she finished the details, unable to even process the words coming from her mouth. She didn't care about Holston Parker.

"So, obviously Parker Enterprises owns Joe's shop. Maybe he's a longtime friend and helped him get started. I'll check it out. He owns a conglomerate, Delaney. That's what makes him a billionaire. He's not working on the floor at the brewery. He's out investing and growing businesses," he replied, looking back at Delaney who was leaning forward in her seat, pushing her hand against the dash.

"Low blow to dad," she shot back. "I see how it is. New job. New status."

She was edgy, but the topic of their father's profession was always a sensitive one. She had spent most of her adolescence defending her father's job to the wealthy students of Xavier Academy - the private school just blocks from their house - whose pedigrees often included a long line of doctors, lawyers, and independent business owners. When Mark had turned fifteen and been accepted to the prestigious school, with no financial assistance, Ann and Michael had poured most all of their middle-class earnings and savings into his education because, as their father had once said, "None of you damned kids will be blue collar, not if I can help it." They had hoped tuition would stretch to the remaining two children, but they never had to stretch or make a decision about whether Delaney or Ben would attend the academy. One month prior to Delaney's first day of school, they had received a stamped letterhead from Xavier Academy's Admission Board and Foundation stating that, "They were pleased to extend a full scholarship through a private donation to such a remarkable young girl full of promises for a strong future." The family had rejoiced in the fact that they could now send all three of their children to the academy.

"I just mean it as a frame of reference, Delaney. Holston Parker is not you or me or ninety-nine point nine percent of the rest of society, for that matter." He moved his hand off the steering wheel for emphasis. The hum of the road hung in the air.

"By the way, you could have warned me about the massive snow storm that was looming." She was blaming him without reason, but she couldn't stop herself.

"It came on pretty fast, and I didn't know that I was your personal meteorologist. Didn't Dad call you?"

"Of course, he did and of course, my phone didn't have reception so I didn't get his message until *after* I was in the ditch," she said, looking down at her phone that was plugged into Mark's charger. Her mind rushed to Theron's last message on the morning he left her. She hadn't heard from him in over twenty-four hours. Gunnar had known about Theron and the night they had spent together.

"Well, you better call Mom and Dad. I figured I would let you –" Mark started before he paused, looking at her.

"Right after I send a message to a friend." She stopped, returning his gaze. "Okay, I'll call her." She moved the screen away from Theron's message and onto her contacts screen, scrolling through to find her mother's smiling face, flush with color and rich brown hair. *A healthy Ann Jones.*

"A friend?"

"Yeah, June, from my department. Co-worker. Friend," she lied, but not about June being her friend. She actually considered June a friend so she might be able to pass through Mark's scrutiny.

"You have a friend?"

"Yeah. I actually have two, believe it or not."

"Yeah, you were never that good at making friends, were you?" Mark teased as he sat straight, both hands on the wheel. Mark had always been a real sucker for following the rules. There was no way she could tell him about Gunnar. Not after she didn't call the police.

"Not really," Delaney said while looking out the passenger side window. "You know I prefer it that way." James Anderson's face surfaced in her thoughts as she stared at the white landscape suffocating the fields to her right. James was one of her only friends growing up. They had met during a lunch break in the first week of high school, not in the cafeteria of the school where the rest of the four hundred some students sat, but in the back of the school library, next to the stuffed shelves of classic literature. She had just pulled John Irving's *The World According to Garp* and was idly paging through it, crouched near the bottom shelf. She hadn't heard him come up from behind her; instead, she had spotted a shadowed movement in the wall of windows ahead of her. Her body had quickly turned and jolted up as he had leaned forward to look

65

over her shoulder at the book.

"He dies at the end," he had said, looking straight into her blue eyes. "So now you know."

"Thanks for sparing me the pleasure of the book," she had replied, looking back at the boy with his shaggy, brown hair that hung low near his brown eyes. The ends, bleached with the remnants of the summer sun, curled with a youthful touch. His smooth, olive skin lay stark against his bright white, uniformed shirt. Her heart had fluttered in adolescent excitement despite her complete annoyance with his sabotaging statement.

"Anytime, Delaney. You know, the library is a bore," he had said, turning to go with two books tucked securely beneath his arm. He had disappeared in the shelves before she could reply. They would meet again the next day, in the library, in a different row of books. This time, Delaney had come up on James, blurting that Lenny would accidentally kill the puppies. He dropped Steinbeck's *Of Mice and Men* back on the shelf. They had spent every lunch hour together for the next four years in the library at Xavier Academy.

Delaney snapped back to the truck at the sound of her brother's voice. "My sister, the lone wolf," Mark said, staring back at the road ahead.

"All right, get off it. I'm going to call Mom and Dad. I'm sure they're wondering where the hell we are," she said as she looked down at a smiling, older version of herself on her phone. She clicked call.

"How long until Dad tells me to get rid of the Civic?" she asked Mark while waiting for her mom to pick up the house phone. The answering machine clicked on, Ann Jones prompting her to leave a message.

"No answer at home. Is she with Ben?" she asked, clicking

back through the contacts to find her parents' cell phone number. They had finally gotten a cell phone, albeit a shared one, a few years ago after much cajoling from their three children. She called the number only to hear her mom's voicemail again.

"Nothing?" Mark asked, looking back at Delaney. His eyebrows disappeared beneath the darkness of his shades.

"That's strange. They always answer that phone. I remember once when Mom answered my call during a wedding. She had whispered into the phone, telling me to call her back because she was in church."

"Typical," Mark replied.

Delaney fell silent, still trying to wash the image of Gunnar out of her mind. She opened her mouth, desperate to formulate what she had witnessed. But instead, her lips clamped shut, her throat suffocating the noise deep inside. The memory of Gunnar would settle with Mr. Rowan, forever wrapped in a tiny, sealed package. There were just some things in life that were never meant to be said or remembered. Surely, Mark would understand.

11

As she secured the door with the key, V rotated her head into the pelting snow and torrential wind. She wasn't ready to go back to her apartment for the evening to deluge herself into more research; her rented space was not exactly what she considered a home. She hadn't had a home since she was fifteen, though, and quite possibly, she thought, as she crept around Delaney's backyard and onto the sidewalk, had never had one at all.

V's childhood, of what she remembered, was lonely and still. Her days often filled with being passed from one neighbor to the next while her father was away, working tirelessly to provide a "better life" for them both. As an adult, she still didn't know what that meant. Her dead mother was never spoken of, her father never bringing home a replacement to dote on the pixie-like child. Her parents, for all she knew, had abandoned her to fend for herself.

She grew quiet, watchful through school as girls and boys played and teased each other. A self-inflicted wallflower, she often wondered if she would blow away in the wind. One day she had tried, jumping ten feet from a playground's steel support in a summer dress onto the pebbles below, but she had only cut her knees instead, soaking small dots of blood through the cotton. Her father had burned the dress when the neighbor woman he paid to do their laundry hadn't successfully removed the stains. V had tried to blow away again the next day.

Her only friend as a small child was a boy a year older than herself who had come to live with her and her father for a short time when she was five – Ethan, with a broken leg and blue welts all over his scrawny body. They huddled together for that year, Ethan teaching her how to play and fight back against older kids, if trouble ever stirred. But for the wallflower, trouble hadn't arrived until she was fifteen, and Ethan was long gone. She had returned to him some time after the summer of two deaths – the black summer she now referred to it as – for help and guidance; he had dutifully obliged.

It had been years of silent preparation and studying, anticipating the right moment for her revenge. She had enrolled in basic nursing courses at the technical college near her apartment, using the alias of deceased Jane Frieburg from Missouri. Identity theft and tampering with the school's recordkeeping system had turned out to be an alarmingly simple, yet gratifying, task for her. And the blood and needles, well, that had never bothered her. The human body was an intricate system of organs and tissues, fragile in its entirety.

The target training at the same facility was what she found pleasure in the most, though. The handle of the gun sent a feeling of life coursing through her veins; she became one with her own body. Her precise shots were dead-on from the beginning once she had found her .9 millimeter. "A light, deadly pack from a tiny punch," the instructor had told her. It had all been so natural.

12

DAY 2: December 19 – 4:15 p.m.

As Delaney and Mark made their way back to the house on 7th Street that they had called home for more than twenty-two years, she couldn't help but feel the memory of their first meeting flood back to her. Ben and Mark had set foot on her uncle's driveway with her father; the man she had not seen from age three to six. Her Uncle Walt, Ann's brother, had taken Delaney and Ann into their home in Milwaukee when they had left their former home in Amberg.

Ann and Michael were indisputably in love with each other despite what the rest of the small, rural town in northern Wisconsin had thought. In fact, during those excruciatingly long three years apart, a day had not passed without her parents telling each other anything different. Each night, before Delaney and Ann had crawled into the twin bed they had shared in the upstairs spare bedroom of Uncle Walt's house, Michael had told his two girls it wouldn't be long before he would be with them again. He had stayed true to his promise when he arrived three years later on the driveway.

He had arrived driving the pickup truck Delaney remembered from the picture her mother had taped to the dashboard on the day they had left. By then, the picture had been worn around the edges with a large crease down the middle. For one thousand ninety five days, without fail, Delaney had stuffed the picture of her father into the tiny pocket of her jeans, right next to the torn piece of paper that counted the number of days of his absence. For this reason, she had refused to wear anything except clothing adorned with pockets. As an adult, she still kept true to this ritual.

The trees of early October had littered the grass and cracked driveway with fallen leaves. The warmth of the day had succumbed to the coolness of the autumn night and the darkness had closed in on the once-blue sky, now partially lit by the glow of streetlamps. Delaney had sat at the family dining table situated in front of the home's large bay window facing the street. Her cousin Levi, then eleven, had sat across from her when she caught the flicker of a light out of the corner of her eye. She had peered outside to see the street flooded with slowing headlights. The shine of the rusted pickup truck turned into the bay window and straight into Delaney's clear blue eyes.

One large silhouette had come into sight behind the steering wheel along with two small outlines next to each other. Delaney had pushed the chair back, sliding the legs along the wooden floor with a scratching noise. Inhaling a deep breath, she had moved to peer against the glass of the window as the man behind the wheel turned off the lights. Michael Jones had walked back into Delaney's life on the driveway of the two-story brick colonial just as he promised every day. Delaney knew then that her dad was the most honest man she would ever meet.

The six-year-old Delaney had pushed past her cousin and yelled to her mom as she sprinted into the cool night. She had hesitated on the front porch as she waited for her father to move toward her, tears welling in his deep brown eyes. As soon as he was close enough, Delaney jumped into his outstretched arms and buried her head into the nook of his neck to breathe in his smell of hay masked with Ivory soap and Old Spice. "Delaney, girl," he had said, "I can barely lift you. *You've grown*."

"Dad, I think *you've grown,* too. Look at the picture," she had replied. He had more lines around his face than she had remembered and more hair than what her picture had captured. She had slid her hand into her pocket and retrieved the tattered picture.

"You still carry this? I'm so happy to see you. Where's Mom?" he had asked as the passenger door of the truck opened.

"Who's that?" Delaney had asked as she looked around her father toward the truck. Two boys had stood close to the pickup truck, next to each other, waiting to move forward. Each had worn tucked in flannels and cowboy boots; the taller boy had placed his hand on the younger boy's shoulder.

"Come on, guys, meet your sister, Delaney," Michael Jones had said. The taller boy had stepped forward first. His dirty blonde hair had looked as though straw had been plucked from a nearby field and adhered to his head strand by strand. The lean body had moved forward with a fluid motion to stand next to Delaney, who had scrambled down to stand on the driveway to get a closer view of her father's passengers. Delaney's head had reached his chin.

"I'm Mark, and this is Ben," the taller boy had said. The shorter boy had stood behind his brother, peeking around the lean framework at the mention of his name. Unlike his brother, Ben had a thicker and stockier framework as if he was a perpetual hay bailer in-training. His waves of thick, blonde hair curled behind his ears and poked recklessly at his collar.

Delaney had stood face to face with Ben.

"Michael" Ann Jones had cried as she came pouring onto the driveway, embracing her husband for the first time in three years. Tears had wet Michael's face as they held each other. Slowly, Ann had pulled away to set her eyes on the two young boys standing next to Delaney. "Michael?" she had asked.

"Ann, meet Mark and Ben," Michael had replied before adding, "our sons."

"Our sons?" Ann Jones had stood immovable next to her husband of ten years, chained in place like one of the cattle back at the farm. She had finally released a smile, stumbling toward the ten-year-old Mark and five-year-old Ben, bending down to give them a closer examination. She had rubbed her dress flat and moved the hair from her eyes, smiling at Ben as he slid further behind his older brother to kick a stone with the tip of his cowboy boot. The tip had been so worn that his toe was dangerously close to peeking out the other side.

"Well, Ben, we'll have to do something about those old boots, won't we? It's nice to meet you," she had said. She grazed the tip of his boot with her index finger and gave his pants a playful tug. She had held out her hand for Ben to shake. The boy had moved around his brother and reached out to Ann, feeling the warmth in her hand as it closed over his own. He had looked into Ann's blue eyes, wrinkled around the corners and had smiled.

Ann had stood up and looked closer at Mark's face, deeply bronzed from the warmth of the summer sun. "And you, Mark, it looks like you could use a haircut. Good thing you came when you did, otherwise, you wouldn't be able to see anything with that straw hanging in your eyes," Ann had said as she brushed the hair that hung low on his forehead. Embarrassed, Mark had shook his head and pushed back his hair with his hand. She had given his shoulder a small squeeze.

Uncle Walt had led the dinner prayer, as he always did, and had thanked God for the gift of a second chance. Delaney, who instead of bowing her head, watched as her father and uncle exchanged a silent understanding. She hadn't known, as they did, that a second chance like this was only for the lucky few.

Mark and Ben had told their stories of how Michael introduced them to farm life, teaching them the daily chores, but never allowing them to milk the sixty head. Ben had moved his hands up and down, making a sucking noise to emulate the milkers for Delaney, which resulted in a swift elbow from Mark who was seated next to him. Michael had glossed over the quiet years spent in the trailer before the arrival of Mark and Ben. "Business as usual," he had said, spending time hammering and fixing up the barn and looking for a potential buyer.

It was only when the kids had retreated upstairs that Michael recounted how he had first met Mark and Ben back in an adjacent town's hardware store. "Old Hank" behind the counter had told Michael about his grandsons, Mark and Ben, who were working in the back of the store. Old Hank had been taking care of Mark and Ben for the past four years since their dad, Hank's only son, had passed away from liver cancer. In Hank's words, it was the "slut of a mother's" fault that his only son was driven to drink and subsequently developed liver cancer.

According to Hank, his son's future coffin had been sealed the day she took off with another man in a Mustang and turned over both Mark and Ben to the care of her ex-husband, who was jobless and heart-broken. The last they had heard was that she was in California, living on a beach and working in a tattoo parlor. Old Hank had taken in his son and two grandsons, then two and six.

Without the help of his wife, who had "graced him by leaving this earth" five years earlier in a fatal heart attack, Old Hank's feeble attempts to occupy Mark and Ben while their father drank himself to death were futile. The boys had spent endless hours in the hardware store sorting nails, hex nuts, and washers, as well as, sweeping floors and cleaning the store's front window. During the summers, the two young boys would set up their lawn chairs, drinking Ting on the sidewalk, watching one or two cars pull into the hardware store each day. They rarely saw their father, except at night, when Old Hank brought the boys back to the house to sleep.

Their father's funeral was held exactly four years later on the anniversary of their mother's escape with the man in the Mustang. According to Old Hank, the rains had poured all morning until the exact moment in which his coffin was lowered into the ground as if God turned off the sprinklers. The forgiving April sun shone the remainder of the day. It was only one month later that Old Hank had his first heart attack that left him weak, yet still "ticking." Without any other family, Old Hank had been looking for someone that could take them in to keep them busy and out of trouble without all those fees from the crooked attorneys. "Because God knows, they've had enough trouble," he had said. Michael had left that day with his hinges to fix his shed door and two young boys in his pickup truck. Ann had signed the papers to adopt Mark and Ben, making Delaney the middle and sole biological child of the family of five.

***

Mark pulled his truck in front of the craftsman ranch, braking to a stop before pulling onto the side of the street. Eight inches of snow had collected into a heavy, undisturbed blanket on the driveway. The truck idled as they both first looked at the driveway and then each other. He pulled the truck into park and pulled out his cell phone. In twenty-five years, their father had never left the driveway unplowed. Often he had his own driveway plowed and the two neighbors' driveways on either side cleared before anyone else along the street even attempted to begin the snow removal process. Delaney's phone rang, prompting her to look down to see her mother's face looking back at her.

"Mom, where are you?"

"Delaney, it's Dad. We're at Froedtert," he replied. He cleared his throat, attempting to cover the strain in his voice.

"Froedtert?" Her small voice sliced through the air as she looked at Mark who had already shifted the truck into drive and pushed down on the pedal heading to the hospital.

"Mom was real out of it this morning after her chemo treatment yesterday so I brought her in. She was admitted this morning. You might want to leave Appleton now that the storm is done."

"I'm here with Mark. We're not far. Do you need anything from home or anywhere else? Do you need me to call Ben?" Her voice cracked. The wedding was tomorrow.

"We're good. I'll call Ben. You didn't get my message about the storm, did you?" he asked.

"I did. We'll see you in a bit," she replied, looking at the windows of the buildings passing by. The gas station. Walgreens. The hospital's landscape came into view. Mark followed the signs leading to in-patient care, although he hadn't needed the signs. They both had been there before, only a few short months ago.

Walking into the hospital suffocated her, the smells of sterilization laden with human ailing and bodily fluids only worsened with the fact that Ann Jones was here. An oncology nurse had once told her that it would get easier, the wounds would sting less with each visit. *She was wrong.* The pain of losing her mother to a slow, unyielding death was excruciating for her, for everyone. She looked at Mark walking along side of her. He would stifle his agony, bury it deep to stay strong for the family, just like their father.

"Delaney Jones?" A voice called across the lobby. Delaney and Mark stopped; their wet shoes both slipped on the entry floor as they turned their heads to the sound. A man in a brown jacket and bright red scarf moved toward them, maneuvering between chairs and waiting people. Delaney leaned forward, taking a closer look at his olive skin and brown eyes. His height, the build. Her stomach dropped.

"It's James," she said under her breath, her stomach twisting with each of his steps.

"James Anderson?" Mark asked. "When's the last time you saw him?"

James smiled and waved that same half-wave he had displayed the first day they had met in the library at Xavier Academy. Delaney, frozen in the entrance of the hospital, would recognize that wave anywhere. The sound of the automatic doors opening behind them startled her. She moved forward into the lobby, glancing at Mark as James approached. *James Anderson. Not now.*

"Delaney Jones."

"James Anderson." Her heart pounded as she thought of

the last time she had seen James. It was spring break of her sophomore year of college. She had booked a ticket that day costing her four hundred eleven dollars and an empty bank account. Six years of built up tension had brought her to the unreasonableness, or at least that's what she had told herself. She had decided that she couldn't let James go.

She had hopped in a cab for the first time and showed up on the doorstep of his fraternity house unannounced on a Sunday night in the warm California spring, telling the cab driver to wait - just in case. A girl with long, platinum hair and deep bronzed skin clad in her underwear and tank top had opened the door. Her chest had bulged out of her top, waiting to spill over with the slightest movement. She had hung on the door, flashing her white smile at Delaney when James had come stumbling behind her asking how much they owed. A pizza guy. James had mistaken her for the delivery man. As he tugged the girl's underwear, he had moved his eyes up to Delaney's. The color had drained from his face. Delaney had turned on her heels and climbed back into the cab, telling him to drive. The cab driver had sputtered something her mind didn't register before she had yelled. James had followed her, calling her name as he ran onto the lawn of his fraternity house in his underwear, but she had never looked back, not once to see him running after her as she traveled down the street headed back to Wisconsin. She had to call Mark to buy her another ticket back; he had conceded without an earful, much to her surprise.

"What are you doing here?" he asked, not moving his eyes off Delaney. She stared back, studying a different James than she had left standing in his underwear seven years ago. His hair was cut short and his face had filled out. His brown eyes were still youthful, but displayed a sense of experience and age. A more masculine and distinguished man had replaced the boyish charm James once radiated. She felt her face flush as she tried to suppress the anger and embarrassment she had felt for so many years well inside her. James Anderson was still gorgeous, still got under her skin. She thought of her appearance; soaked leather boots, knit hat covering her mess of waves and a puffy, tear stained face. She hated herself for letting him affect her like this.

"It's good to see you, man. It's been awhile. What the hell are you doing here?" Mark jumped in to save the silent Delaney, holding his hand out to give James a handshake.

"I'm here in Milwaukee scoping out offices. My firm wants me to relocate here, open a division in the southern Wisconsin market. I got a call about two hours ago from my assistant back in California that a potential client, apparently a significant one, wanted to meet me here. I was about to leave since he never showed up," he replied. "Then I saw you, Delaney Jones." He repeated her name like he had seen a damn unicorn.

"Moving back to … Wisconsin," she said, lingering on the last word. *His assistant back at his firm.* He had finished law school, just like he said he would. Delaney had written him off, deleting all emails and voicemails he had left her after the incident in California. But she had just watched a man get stabbed, threatened by the killer, and now James Anderson was standing before her. December 19th needed to end and fast.

"Why don't I leave you two, looks like you might have some catching up to do," Mark started, moving toward the elevators. "Just come up when you're done, Delaney."

"No, it's okay. Mark, just wait," she said, never taking her eyes from James. The hairs on her arms rose at the thought of staying with James, enduring the awkward conversation when she wasn't ready. "We're headed to see our mom and our dad is waiting for us. I should go. "

"I'm sorry to hear that. Is she okay?" James asked.

"Cancer," she replied flat, feeling the emptiness of the disease that was consuming her mother.

"Oh." His face fell, closing his eyes to the stinging revelation. Ann had been a second mother to James during high school, replacing the absent mother from his childhood. "Delaney – "

"I know," she replied, knowing that the dying mother card wasn't one she wanted to play, "You're sorry. We're all sorry."

"I can let you go, but will you call me?" he asked, his eyes pained by the question.

"Uh, sure," she replied as her feet moved to catch up with Mark at the elevator.

"You have my number?" James called to her, still standing in the entrance.

"Yeah." She waved to him as the elevator doors opened, waiting to whisk her away. Mark hit the number three, a movement engrained in his brain - a number they hadn't needed to ask for. Delaney cast her eyes up just before the doors closed, locking eyes with James still standing, watching her. "Like branding on cattle, burned in my memory."

"Not that I need to know your business, Delaney, but shit happens. You were good friends and those are hard to come by. Just remember that."

13

The statue, raised twenty feet in the air, floated in the deep shadows of the church in between two large, stained glass windows. His face dripping with blood, half-hidden as he looked down, exhibited a calmness V had admired since she was a child. His hands and feet, bloodied with nails driven through them, hung from the cross. His side spewed out even more red liquid. He had endured. God would give her the strength she needed to follow through. To end what her employer had started.

V had trudged the four blocks to St. Mary's, the church she had attended weekly since she was a girl. The intricate architecture and gold embellishments ran from the floor to the culminating steeple of the church. Her eyes followed them up to the large dome where the lavish angels guarded the alter down below. The angels with their large, gold-tipped wings had always made her feel safe. Protected. She sat in the first pew, watching as the votive candles flickered against their glass holders, casting shadows that danced along the wall. She could hear the sweet, low chants of Father Hasken's voice. Her arm hairs rose beneath the layers of white as chills ran through her body. She inhaled, smelling the rich aromas of incense lingering in the air. V closed her eyes to see the vision of Father swinging the gold chains of the thurible. The white smoke drafted from it slowly as the earthy smell permeated her nostrils. The metal clinked as he swung it over the casket back and forth, back and forth, in the sign of the cross. The body inside the casket needed to be raised to God to be judged. Her employer's acts couldn't be forgiven.

The vision burned in her mind as she reopened her eyes to the dark, empty church. She doubted that anyone else would be attending the 5:00 mass, but she knew Father Hasken would be here, with or without his parishioners. He would perform the ritual regardless, but she would leave before he started; she knew she wouldn't be able to face him. Not after what she was about to do.

It had started three months ago, when she had followed Holston. She had tracked him two hours north, near his cottage, to a small town called Amberg. What she had seen there was unfathomable, even for him. She had crept up to the run-down barn that he had entered alone, just minutes before, peeking in through the cracked glass of a shattered window. Inside the barn had stood a group of ten girls in their early adolescence to mid-twenties. Barely clothed, they had huddled together whispering and crying in muffled sounds like wounded animals. An older woman, her long blonde mess of hair scattered to the middle of her back, stood on the edge of the pack. The woman had turned, looking toward the window V peered through, before turning her attention back to the huddle of girls. Holston had walked around them, examining them, before turning to speak with a man who had walked forward from the shadows of the dark barn. They had exchanged words she couldn't make out before Holston had reached into his jacket, revealing a thick, white envelope. The man with the burly red beard and overalls had taken the envelope in his hand, checking the contents, before shaking her employer's hand and then laughing, slapping the butt of one of the girls before disappearing once again into the darkness. Another gray sedan had pulled up moments later as her employer led the girls out of the building. She had sunk into the ground, realizing that he had just bought the girls. Holston Parker was a human trafficker.

14

The elevator halted at the third floor with a ding, opening to the in-patient care unit of the academic medical hospital. As Delaney finished writing both of their names in registration, the tall frame of Michael Jones walked through the double doors dressed in his signature plaid, button-down shirt. He outstretched his arms at the sight of his children. She looked up at her father's eyes that smiled through the dark, heavy bags under his usually bright, translucent eyes now dulled with lack of sleep. His once dark brown hair was replaced with hundreds of gray hairs that speckled his strands. The gray hair was spreading, threatening to take over the once rich, thick hair she had remembered. Age was creeping up on Michael Jones.

"What happened to you, Delaney? It looks like you saw a ghost," Michael asked as he embraced her and moved to give Mark a quick man pat on his back. The time hadn't come that would warrant a full embrace for the two grown men. Ann's encroaching death seemed surreal.

"Relatively speaking," Mark started.

"We saw James Anderson in the lobby," Delaney finished, placing her hand on her father's arm before shooting Mark a

84

sideways glance, warning him. "But that's unimportant. How is she?"

"They are taking good care of her. Her body is real weak from the treatment, and she's not eating. But they are pushing fluids, and she's resting now." He put his hand over his temple, rubbing the wrinkles that had begun to settle into his forehead. Aging was a bitch.

"Let's sit down and let her rest for a bit," Mark replied, pointing over to a group of chairs in the corner, set against windows overlooking the city.

"No, we better head back to the room. Mom knows that you were coming. She would kill me if I let you sit in the waiting room," Michael said. "Ben's on his way with Meghan. They should be here within the half hour. And, for the record, the wedding is on, and Mom plans on being there." He pointed to each of them before turning to lead them back through the double doors and into the hallway. The path was dotted throughout by nurses at various work stations, moving in and out of rooms as if orchestrated, calling to each other for updates and help.

"It's busy today," Mark said as he paused his step to avoid a nurse running across the hallway into the room on his right. Mark's idle chatter annoyed Delaney as she noted a crimson streak down the front of the nurse's scrubs. The blood pooling beneath Mr. Rowan's body had been so quiet, moving in synchronous beats out from his body. He had left this world in a gruesome peacefulness.

"Yeah, Mom's down this hallway. It's a bit quieter over here. I think she'll be able to go home tomorrow. She's doing much better than she was early this morning. Whether or not she makes the wedding is debatable but not according to her,"

Michael whispered the last sentence as he moved swiftly through the hall, taking the next left to room 547.

Sunshine flooded in from the two large windows that covered the wall straight across from the door. Several inches of snow were visible on the ledge against the window, glistening in the afternoon sun. Ann Jones lie with her back to the door, facing the vibrant blue winter sky scattered with fluffs of white clouds. Her thin body stretched the length of the bed, leading to her bald head that lay on the pillow. A long, wavy brown wig sprawled out next to her on a table. She refused to go anywhere without her wig.

"Mark and Delaney are here," Michael said, his voice quiet as he walked into the room. She turned her head excruciatingly slow at the sound of the voice to see her two oldest children walking into the room. A small smile leaked from the edges of her lips as she tried to maneuver the rest of her body toward her guests. The painful movement bore into Delaney's gut as she watched the emaciated woman turn toward her. This woman was completely unfamiliar to her. She couldn't be Delaney's mother.

"Oh, no you don't, lady. Let me help you." Michael jumped forward, helping his wife of thirty two years move to her other side. Delaney watched as the woman's frail arm emerged from underneath the covers and wrapped around her father's strong neck. Her skin hung loosely from her arm in a pale grayish tone bordering on translucency. Delaney felt another pang in her stomach, forcing a smile, as the woman finally finished turning toward them. Her eyes had hallowed out with lack of sleep and food. Their brightness had vanished and been replaced with a dull glaze. The woman had transformed in just a few short weeks. *Death had crawled into Ann Jones's bed.*

"Oh Delaney, wipe that smile off your face. I know I look terrible. Where's my wig?" She moved her hand around on the table next to her, fumbling until she felt the strands of synthetic hair along her fingers. She picked up the wig to put it on.

"Jesus, Mom. Don't worry about it. You look great. I always wanted Mr. Clean for a mom anyway," Mark said, grabbing the wig from her hands. Ann broke into a gurgle that eventually subsided, her body swallowing any force of laughter. Michael ignored the wretched sound and produced a laugh deep from his gut. Mark followed suit. Delaney exhaled, but her body refused to yield any sound.

"You're lucky you're my favorite oldest son, otherwise, I might have to get out of this bed and kick your ass," she replied pointing her finger accusingly at Mark. Ann had always joked that Mark was her favorite oldest son; Delaney her favorite only daughter; and Ben her favorite youngest son. Ann Jones didn't have her body, but her mind had yet to fail her.

"How do you feel?" Delaney asked, regretting the words before she even finished.

"With my fingers," Ann replied, wiggling her bony fingers just inches above the blanket.

"I should have known better," Delaney replied as she felt the rest of the tension release. *Ann Jones is still with it.*

"By the way, guess who they ran into in the lobby?" Michael asked, moving to sit on the end of the bed by her feet. He placed one hand on her foot buried deep in the blanket. Delaney groaned inwardly as she glared at Mark. She felt like she was being thrust back into high school, her family plotting to improve her social life.

"Who?" Ann rasped, moving her head off the pillow with a slight jerk before she surrendered, laying it back down.

"Relax, Mom. It was just James Anderson," Delaney replied, looking at her father. *If this is how they react to almost hitting James, how can I tell them about what I saw? About Mr. Rowan?* The repeated images in her mind of the knife sinking into his chest made her shudder. Sleeping with Theron had sent her world into a frenzy. She had been pushed into oncoming traffic, dodging one horrific scene only to stumble blindly into the next.

"He's back in Wisconsin? Good thing I was here." Ann's eyes glimmered for a moment while she waited for her daughter's response. She had always wanted James to rescue her loveless Delaney. Both her parents had always adored James. He was a frequenter at the Jones' house since his father often worked late at the office. By the end of their senior year at Xavier, Ann Jones had joked that she inherited another mouth to feed, but they hadn't seen James since he moved out to California, and Delaney had failed to mention why they had stopped talking several years ago, avoiding the topic all together.

"I guess he's moving back, but that's irrelevant. Let's talk about the wedding before Ben gets here," she said, dodging the James discussion.

"What's there to talk about? I will be there. Dr. Hansen mentioned I should be discharged - if the night goes well - by tomorrow morning," she reported. The exertion of energy was too much for her as her breathing shallowed. She looked down at Michael who had lifted his hand from her foot to remove his glasses. He once again began to methodically rub his temple, massaging it. Delaney had always heard about the mental and physical toll caregivers shouldered, though she had never seen it living, breathing before her eyes like she did now.

"You think you'll have enough energy for the wedding, Mom? I think Ben might prefer that you stay home and take care of yourself," Mark said, leaning against the chair Delaney sat in for support. Convincing his mother to stay home from Ben's wedding, he knew, would be insurmountable. Ann Jones was the most incorrigible woman he had ever known and in most scenarios, this quality benefitted her and everyone surrounding her. They had all believed her sheer determinedness was why she was alive today; in fact, she was three years past Dr. Hansen's projected "expiration date."

"Absolutely not. No more discussion on the wedding, and I swear to you, Mark," she whispered as she curled her finger, beckoning him to come closer to her, "I will cut you right out of the will." Mark, who had leaned in closer to her, gently pushed her finger aside before he cracked a smile and moved back by the chair. Ann let out a small, raspy laugh before beginning to cough. Michael reached for the glass of water on the tray next to her, placing it to dry her lips. She swallowed hard. The water line hadn't moved.

"I tried, for the record," Mark said, lifting his hands up in the air, drawing attention away from the painful vision of her swallowing essentially air. "Ben's going to try to convince you, too. Just so you're prepared."

"You Jones boys don't scare me," Ann said as she adjusted her legs in her bed and looked back down at Michael who had once again placed his hand on her foot. "I will be there."

Delaney glanced out the window of the fifth floor room to avoid eye contact with her mother. Her eyes scanned the ledge, stopping at a light brown teddy bear that had a pink bow tied around its neck. Her mind flashed to the tattered teddy bear she remembered from her childhood. The muffled voices of her family filled the background as she tuned out the conversation, focusing her eyes on the bear. She stood up, feeling her legs buckle underneath her, as she walked over to the ledge to feel the satin bow slip between her fingers. The bow was wound tight around its neck as if it were strangling the teddy bear. *The satin. The pink.* She hadn't recognized the resemblance before, but this teddy bear had the same hued pink, satin fabric of her mask. Her mind shot back to her bag in Mark's truck, the mask buried deep inside. She felt a rush of warmth run through her body.

"Who sent that?" Michael asked as Delaney stood holding the teddy bear in her hands.

"I don't know. It was just here," Ann replied, dismissing the teddy bear and turning back to talk with Mark. Delaney set the bear back on the ledge as her chest tightened. She needed air.

"I'll be right back," she muttered as she stumbled out into the hallway of the hospital, allowing the heavy door of Room 547 to shut behind her with a click. She inhaled the sterile air of the hospital and leaned against the wall next to the door, closing her eyes as the sketch of her mother's waves blowing in the wind appeared. Her rich, long strands blew across her back as she sat in the driver's seat of the old car. Delaney had remembered clutching the teddy bear next to her in the passenger seat.

***

According to her mother, Delaney had been born, unwillingly, in the unpopulated town of Amberg on a dairy farm. She grew up knowing nothing of farming and its particular demands, not by her own choice, but by the hands of the uncompromising Ann. On Delaney's third birthday, her mother had packed her only daughter's handful of clothes, with tags still intact, into a worn, leather child's suitcase and put Delaney, clutching her sole toy - a light-brown stuffed bear with a pink bow tied around its neck - into the passenger seat of the family's '79 Impala. With a small handbag of her own, filled with one change of clothes, Ann had taped a freshly-printed picture of Delaney's dad on the dash. He had stood, half-leaning against the rusted Ford, in a cowboy hat and red flannel tucked neatly into his jeans. The nearby wheat field and an old wheelbarrow had completed the landscape of the portrait.

With one last glimpse of the faded red barn and single silo glowing in the sunset, Ann had driven down the dirt path, through the small town of Amberg, passed the old grain store turned coffee shop she had once adored, and onto the concrete of I-43 headed south. Her dark brown waves had gathered loosely on her neck as it fluttered in the fresh breeze of the open driver's side window. She had stared straight ahead, not once looking in the rearview mirror. She would never set eyes on the sixty-year-old farm she was raised on again or the town of Amberg or her few close friends from childhood. She had smiled down on Delaney in the passenger seat, reassuring her young daughter with a slight pat on her knee.

Four hours later, Ann and Delaney Jones had arrived at the two-story colonial house in the Milwaukee suburb of Waukesha to their waiting relatives: Uncle Walt, Emma, and Levi. The soft glow of the TV inside showed movement in the house as they had pulled into the driveway. Soon all three stood on the porch, watching as Ann turned off the key and stopped the hum of the engine. They had been waiting, after all, for two days. Delaney had learned much later that it had taken her mother that long to leave Amberg.

Uncle Walt had cradled a sleeping Delaney into his arms

while Emma ushered Ann into the house to unpack - although Emma hadn't realized how little *packing* Ann had done - and showed her the birthday cake decorated with a single purple flower waiting for Delaney on the dining room table. All four had huddled around her in an enclosed cocoon and sang quietly to the three-year-old, half sleeping in the chair, lulling her to sleep. The hues of the three spiraled, pink candles had flickered against the darkness of the room.

Delaney's small head, with the same thick waves as her mother, only shorter, had rested on the massive table as they finished the last notes of the song. She had lifted her head as the singing stopped and looked up at her mother who had a single tear sliding down her face. It had been the first time Delaney had seen her mother cry. She hadn't known it would be the only time she would see her mother cry.

***

The memory washed over Delaney as her feet moved beneath her, carrying her to the end of the hallway. She stopped, her eyes a foot away from a Van Gogh print of a wheat field. Black crows scattered against a blue, looming sky in a large, ornamental gold frame. The print intricately detailed the strands of wheat sweeping through the vast field. The golden yellow contrasted beside the dark blue sky. The placement of the print, among the sick and dying at a hospital, seemed a distasteful choice as she looked closer at the crows circling through the field. A tear rolled down her face. Ann Jones had never looked so vulnerable.

Delaney wiped the tear with the back of her sleeve and turned her back to the print on the wall. She slid down the wall and pulled her knees into her chest, cradling them as she breathed in deep, closing her eyes to Thanksgiving four years ago on 7th Street.

The Jones family, along with Uncle Walt and Emma - Levi was living in New York at the time - had congregated, as usual, to enjoy their annual turkey feast created meticulously by Ann Jones. The aromas of fall filled the air; the warm smell of pumpkin pie and turkey had occupied the Jones' kitchen and adjoining dining room. They had all gorged themselves, just finishing their choice of two desserts that Ann had crafted the night before when she said in passing as she cleared up dishes, "I have cancer. I thought I would let you all know. Stage Three." Ann had said it so matter-of-fact, as if she had been commenting on the weather. She hadn't missed a step, continuing to move dishes further into her arm, stacking them as she gathered more. Ben had dropped his glass on the wooden floor, shattering it on contact. The rest of her family still seated at the table stared at her, not moving or saying a word. The doctors had given her three hundred sixty-five days, give or take a few.

Ann Jones had spent the last four years, trying various experimental treatments and aggressive chemotherapy. She had been close to remission, a treatment almost eradicating the cancer cells, only to experience another severe spread of the cancer. Her health moved in waves, on sliding scales from better to worse and back again. But never had Delaney seen her mother so weak and vulnerable. Her eyes, for the first time, had lost the vibrancy and sheer determinedness that had brought her mom this far. Ann Jones had begun to let go.

Delaney opened her eyes to the sound of a door shutting down the hallway. Her eyes adjusted and focused in on the door and the man across from Room 547. His fleeting eyes made contact with hers for a moment as if he was surprised to see her sitting down at the end of the hall. He darted his eyes away and turned to walk down the hall away from her. His body, with perfect posture, stood tall as he took long, strong strides. His dark hair with speckles of silver glistened in the light of the hallway as he moved effortlessly in a black leather jacket. As he turned the corner, he placed a gray fedora on his head and in a moment, he vanished from the hallway as if he had never been there in the first place. Delaney stood up, stretching and rubbing her eyes as she took a snapshot of the man's face in her mind; his dark eyes penetrated the sketch.

Her legs moved her to the door of Room 547. She lifted up her hand to open the door, but set it back down at her side before turning to the room behind her. Room 546. The door had cracked open to display just a small glimpse into the room. Her eyes moved up and down the vacant hall. She listened to the silent space before turning to move toward the door behind her. Her head peeked into the room as she pushed the door to get another inch of sight. There were no visitors standing in the room. She poked her head another inch closer. The bed was empty.

***

Delaney shut the door behind her, locking it, and turned into the bedroom her parents had left untouched for ten years. Mark had dropped her off at her parents' house, leaving her to stay by herself while he spent the night with Ben. The rehearsal was cancelled, Ben claiming that "no one needed to practice standing anyway." Michael and Ann were still at the hospital, despite her mother's plea to be discharged, and Delaney had welcomed the chance to be alone, a chance to breathe. Gunnar had threatened her, but this strange sense of relief was comforting her. Mr. Rowan was gone. A dark, psychopathic angel had taken her rapist.

She felt the stitching along the purple patterned quilt her mother had sewn for her back in high school. Each square was so small and intricate. Delaney realized, for the first time, how long her mother must have spent sewing the quilt; the same time that was so limited now. She sat down on the edge, plucking at a stitch that was unraveling before noticing the teddy bear sitting on the pillow. Tattered and worn, the almost thirty-year-old teddy bear still had the same pink satin bow tied around its neck. She hadn't seen it in years, assuming it had been long gone from her childhood. Picking it up, she felt the pink bow, gritty from years of dragging it along as a child. A strange feeling consumed her as she thought of the teddy bear back at the hospital.

8:22 p.m. She had eight minutes. She wouldn't miss another call with *him. It would be therapeutic,* she reasoned. She needed to release the anxiety threatening to overtake her body. Her hands slid open the zipper of her black bag and into the contents, searching for the pink mask buried underneath the clothes for the weekend. She pulled the laptop from the bag, turning it on before gathering her mask, brush, and rolled up canvas. Her fingers wrapped around three different shades of black and gray paint. He only ever wanted black. As she waited for the laptop to start, she closed the curtains and pulled the sweater over her head revealing the red lace bra. She pulled down her jeans and peeled off her socks, standing in only her bra and underwear in the middle of the room. Sliding them off, she stepped into the one-piece, black dress. It hugged to her body as she pulled the straps over her shoulders and drew the bottom down to hang just below her upper thighs.

Glancing into the small mirror leaning against the dresser, she hadn't imagined what it would be like to be back in her bedroom like this. The rush flowed through her veins. She couldn't help herself as her fingers placed the mask over her eyes, tying it tight behind her head among the brown waves. She felt transformed. *A woman.* Delaney Jones needed to escape her reality.

Her fingers flashed across the keyboard, hitting each key with ease as she logged into her account. The welcome screen popped up reading, "Welcome Back, D. Your show is in three minutes. Your guest is waiting." She noted the two thousand dollars deposited into her account, but the money didn't matter to Delaney like it did for the rest of the girls in the online stripping community. She wanted nothing else than to never *need* the money. The stockpile was for Ann.

Her studio mate, Kandy with a K with DD cups, had recommended she try it. After all, it was what had gotten her through graduate school without any loans. Delaney had even caught a glimpse late one night before finals, walking in on Kandy with a K's session. "Easy and harmless," she had said through a smile. Delaney had used a makeshift mask from a bandana that covered the lower portion of her mouth - Clint Eastwood western style - for her first session. Awkward, sure, but not entirely bad. It had exhilarated her, something her non-existent sexual life had been clearly lacking. The next night, she had picked out a pink mask from The Red Flamingo, the adult store just blocks from her apartment. She had walked past the store every day for four years, never entering. It had taken her a week and four sessions with strangers to realize how ridiculous it was to strip for men she would never meet. With her final dissertation nearing, she had forgotten to take the picture of herself clad in the pink mask, holding a paintbrush between her teeth, off her profile page. And when House_of_Steel had messaged her, asking for a private show with one condition - that she paint for him fully clothed and send the paintings to a PO Box - she had conceded and kept the mask. Ann Jones's health was failing.

The man behind House_of_Steel had intrigued her, drew her in. He convinced her to keep coming back, fully clothed, with canvases ready, making her feel a deep sense that she was needed. They had met weekly online for the past three months, but in the last two weeks, he had requested two visits each week. He had deposited over thirty thousand dollars into her account, and she had dutifully mailed out each canvas to the PO Box listed in New York. She opened the tube of paint and buried herself into the silence of the room, her mind quieting before she clicked on the "Enter room" button. The icon of House_of_Steel flashed on the screen before his deep voice pierced the silence, his video blocked. He had always refused to display his video.

"Hey, D."

A woman in a black dress and a pink mask appeared sitting on the edge of a bed, a brush poised in her hand.

"A new backdrop. The teddy bear makes for an interesting mix," he said, his voice serious. She turned around to see the teddy bear's glassy eyes staring back at her. A crawl trickled through her skin.

"What would you like tonight?" she asked as she turned around, dismissing the toy. She knew the answer, but she asked anyway, as she always had for the past few months. She needed this.

"A barn."

Her hand began to make long, sweeping strokes along the canvas, building the panels of the wood that created the walls of the structure. The sound of the bristles against the duck cloth repeated. It was the only sound that filled the silence for sixty minutes.

15

The final winter light began to fade on the horizon, disappearing beyond the river's edge. V's eyes traveled down the river to the old factories and paper mills that lined the shores on the opposite side. More than one hundred fifty years ago, the town of Appleton had started as a milling town, booming with activity from logging camps that sent the logs floating down the Fox River to Appleton to make paper. Most of the mills were vacant now, though; some had been renovated into apartments and restaurants near Leighton University. This Appleton was different than what she grew up in. Parker Enterprises was building the city one brick at a time and one murder at a time. Her eyes shifted to more than five blocks away where the steel beams of Parker Tower stretched into the sky. The building was covered with the layers of snow from yesterday's onslaught of accumulation. Her employer's crews would be back on Monday to start clearing the snow to continue the construction. It was silent, much like the rest of campus - except for the man inside the house she was watching.

Her eyes settled back onto her target, Theron Olson. She had found his name on the university's website, his name and face plastered on the Leighton Football roster page. She had recognized him immediately. It wasn't his large build, stocky shoulders or brown hair - ten of the pictures had fit that profile - but the dimple on his right cheek that she had spotted when he escaped out the back door of Delaney's house was a dead ringer. He had only one dimple, beneath his right eye. Once she knew his name, it was easy to find his fraternity house. Leighton students could only live off campus if they were in a fraternity or sorority, or if they could provide a reasonable explanation for their inability to live in the dorms. Almost all the football players were in Beta Theta Pi. He lived with several of his teammates in the two-story, colonial fraternity house along the shores of the river that she stood outside of, tucked behind a garbage can. She was better on foot.

Theron walked past the window again, back to the kitchen. He was one of three roommates that were in the house, most likely the only ones living there through the break. He was shirtless, despite the freezing temperatures outside, his hard muscles flexing with each of his movements. He was handsome, but it was wrong. Scandalous. However, it didn't warrant what she assumed Gunnar would do. Her employer knew about Delaney's indiscretion, but V hadn't discovered why Delaney Jones was so important to him. Not yet anyway.

Out of the corner of her eye, V saw a familiar black sedan creep down the road, passing by the fraternity house. She squinted, distinguishing the outline of a tall frame with white hair behind the wheel. Adrenaline rushed through her body as she realized he was here already, watching Theron, waiting. Gunnar was the only person, next to her employer, that she had an unrelenting need to unleash her revenge upon. The hourglass had run out of sand.

16

The white flakes swirled in a gust of wind and landed delicately on the window in front of Delaney. She stood on the other side in a deep blue, floor-length dress cradled by the warmth of the register blowing near her feet and the faux fur wrap Meghan had convinced both Delaney and her maid of honor to wear. Delaney hadn't wanted to be a bridesmaid for Meghan, not because she didn't care for Meghan, but because she had no will to be in the church. She had initially declined when Meghan asked her, but Ben had convinced her otherwise, as always. For her brothers, Delaney would do anything even if that meant returning to the only place she had vowed never to return to.

When Delaney had walked through the door of St. Luke's, she had expected an earth shattering revolt from her body. She had anticipated smelling the singes of the hair. The menthol of his breath. She had inhaled deep, letting her chest well high beneath her blue dress, but she hadn't smelled any of the scents from that night. Instead, the odor was of stale heat blowing from the registers along the walls of the church. She had expected to feel the excruciating pain that he had inflicted upon her radiate into her pelvis. It was nothing like that. She had felt a sense of power that she was returning despite him. Gunnar's words rung in her ears. Richard Rowan had gotten what he deserved and she had prevailed. He had taken her virginity, her innocence, but he hadn't destroyed her. Delaney had eyed the stairs that led to the basement, but she had decided against it. Not today. Not when they were celebrating Ben. She would come back.

Delaney wrapped the white fur tighter against her bare arms, hugging the warmth against her body, as she stared out the window at the cemetery of the church. Most of the headstones were buried deep under the inches of snow that had fallen the day before. Only the tall headstones, mainly large crosses, protruded from the blanket of frost. A large cross near the middle of the cemetery stood stark against the rest. The dark black granite contrasted against the ivory snow with circling footprints around it. Someone had brushed off the headstone this morning. She squinted, reading the letters that ran from the top of the cross to the bottom.

LIVE.

She refocused her eyes, blinking to remoisten them from the heat below her. *LIVE.* The letters were clear, but Catholics had always confused her. She hoped, for the deceased below that headstone, that there was a Heaven, and she hoped, for the sake of Richard Rowan, that there was a Hell. She knew that he would be there, despite the fact that he had somehow believed God would forgive his sins. It had only taken her a day after the rape to look up the 1 John 1:9 verse he had tattooed on his neck: "If we confess our sins, he is faithful and just and will forgive us our sins and purify us from all unrighteousness." Richard Rowan had believed that after raping her, and many others she assumed, that he would be redeemed. There was no forgiving the act of requesting a young girl to paint Saint Agnes, the patron saint of rape victims and chastity, before destroying her. The cruel premeditation had been a dagger embedded and then twisted deep into her heart.

Delaney turned around to see her mother sitting in a wheelchair next to Meghan. When Michael Jones had opened the chair in the vestibule of the church, Ann had sworn like a pirate in the house of God. Michael's hopes of a docile reaction from his wife in a place of worship were dissolved as he shushed her like a four-year-old misbehaving in church. She had conceded finally with threats by Ben who had promised her that he would refuse to marry Meghan if she would, in fact, refuse to sit in the chair occasionally throughout the day. She sat waiting in the chair before any of the guests could see her.

The black gown hung from her body, the extra material flowing on all sides of her. Ann had purchased the dress not more than three months ago. Earlier in the day, Meghan had helped her pinch the sides of the dress underneath her arms tighter, holding them together with a few pins. It had improved the fit, but the dress still swallowed her in a sea of black satin. Meghan had brought along a shawl for Ann, which - at least to some extent - hid the fact that her frail body was drowning in the dress. All of the fluids the nursing staff had pumped into her body had bloated her face, which in Delaney's opinion, was masking the hollowness she had seen the day before. The brown wig hung from her head in cascading waves of chocolate just as Delaney had remembered of her mother twenty years ago as a child. At least, she had something.

"Are you ready?" Meghan asked Ann as she turned to face her soon-to-be mother-in-law. Meghan fingered the lace of her fitted, vintage dress. Her short, blonde hair was pulled loosely back and gathered at the nape of her neck with a small flower.

Her green eyes poked through the netting of her 1920's style veil that covered only a small portion of her face. She was stunning.

"Are *you* ready?" Ann asked Meghan as she set her hand in Meghan's, placing a small, blue sapphire ring in it.

"Oh, Ann, I can't take this," she said, tears welling in her eyes. Delaney stepped forward to look at the ring her mother had worn around her neck for as long as she could remember. The small, silver band was intricately twisted to encase a singular, oval shaped sapphire protruding from the middle. It had been Delaney's grandmother's ring that Ann had inherited on the day she had married Michael. Too small to fit her fingers, but unwilling to enlarge the ring, Ann had worn it around her neck since that day. Delaney couldn't recall a time that she *hadn't* seen the ring dangling from her neck. Until now.

"You will take it," Ann ordered, handing Meghan a tissue and covering her hand over the ring. "Now brush that tear away so you don't ruin your makeup. I might stage you up otherwise."

Meghan's face flushed as she looked at Delaney who was now standing on the other side of Meghan. She nodded her head and smiled. Delaney knew, just as her mother knew, that she would never get married. She covered Meghan's other hand with her own.

"Are you ladies ready? The show is about start," Michael Jones said as he opened the door to the waiting area where they sat.

"You better believe it," Ann said as she stood from the chair with the help of Delaney. "And yes, I will be walking down the aisle."

***

Delaney's eyes landed on the nail driven through the bloodied feet of the statue. She followed the legs up to see the remaining body of Jesus nailed to the cross. The looming statue stood prominent with a backlight, the shadow shone dark on the wall behind it. Candles lit throughout the alter area flickered and burned bright against the dimness of the church. She watched them dance, admiring their beauty and freeness. She had been raised a Roman Catholic, mostly by the influence of her father, attending mass every week in the same church she stood in today until the age of fourteen. Michael would bring the three Jones children while Ann would only attend mass on occasion and only then to appease her husband. Delaney had spent her childhood listening to the chants, miming the directions, but her attention was always drawn to examining the artifacts and intricate architecture of the building. Even as a child, she was an artist with a curious eye. The church, she felt, had so much to hide within its massive walls and stone statues. Ann Jones had once told Delaney that she had given up on God when she was twenty-eight. Delaney had given up when she was fourteen.

The sound of clapping hands echoed against the arched ceilings, snapping Delaney's head back to Ben and Meghan kissing for the final time. They both turned to their guests as Ben thrust his fist in the air with a triumphant pump before walking down the aisle. That was Ben. The melody blasted through the organ pipes as she stepped forward to face Mark, wrapping her arm in his. Their steps aligned as she scanned the small crowd that had gathered for the sunset service.

Meghan's guests, mostly friends, had only filled the first

two pews. Her family had been virtually non-existent her entire life as a foster child. Delaney wondered what it would have been like to not have a family. To not feel the closeness of her brothers' love or her parents' watchful eyes. It seemed entirely likely to her that Meghan could truly miss something she never had. It was selfish, Delaney knew, that she would want her mother back the second she was taken from her. She looked over to the left to see her cousin Levi, Uncle Walt, and Emma carefully eyeing Ann in the bench ahead of them. The extent of their family existed in just that one pew, but it had been all she needed. A few other friends and neighbors scattered throughout a few rows.

She glanced at the back corner of the church where the two elderly men sat who had offered up the collection. Behind them, she saw a profile of a man dressed in dark clothes walking toward the exit. His movements were quick and fluid, his long strides moving him into the back of the church as he placed a gray fedora on his head. Delaney watched as the man from Room 546 slipped through the side door and into the air of the brisk night. She yanked Mark's arm, her legs itching beneath her to follow the man as the fear coursed through her veins.

"What the hell are you doing?" he whispered, matching her pace.

"I've got to check something out," she whispered as they neared the door the fedora had disappeared through. She needed to see him, to find out what he wanted from her.

"I'll be right back." She waved off Mark as he joined Meghan and Ben in the foyer of the church, awaiting their guests. The door creaked as she opened it wide enough for her to slide through onto the ice. The crisp air stung her throat and chest as she inhaled the black night's oxygen. Her breath formed in a steady stream of white fog in front of her as she exhaled. Her eyes darted down the sidewalk. Small patches of a soft glow from the church paved the way down the empty sidewalk. She looked in the snow piles to the right and left of her. No tracks. She turned back to grasp the handle of the door, pulling it to find it had locked behind her.

Fedora.

She shouldn't be out here alone. The frozen wind whipped on her bare back as she turned on her heels to face the vacant sidewalk. Delaney looked down at her slipping heels with disdain as she stepped carefully into the dark night to the other entrance, her hands out to balance herself. The light of the church through the glass front doors glared in her eyes as she turned the corner. Her body jerked and hesitated as an outline of a man partially blocked the light. A man in a brown jacket and red scarf stood waiting at the door, looking in. She knew his build. The stance. The scarf.

"Jesus, Delaney." James jumped at the sound of her heels cracking behind him.

"James, what the hell are you doing out here?"

"I heard that Ben was getting married. After I ran into you yesterday, I needed to see you again. I figured you wouldn't call, so here I am. I did a little Facebook stalking to find out about the wedding. Busted. What can I say?" he said, lifting his gloved hands up in the air. James Anderson had been standing there longer than he would have liked to admit. She hugged the fur wrap tighter to her body, looking into his brown eyes that were glistening above his pink cheeks flushed from the wind. The soft radiance of the church's lights highlighted the grin that Delaney had always loved.

"Really?"

"Yeah, really. You're off the grid. No Facebook, no emails. You changed your number, so I had to look elsewhere. Your family doesn't seem to hate me as much as you do. I had to take one last shot, it seemed right."

"I don't hate you," she said, sighing. "Are we really having this conversation? Me hating you?"

"No, let's not do that. What the hell are you doing outside, though? It's freezing out here."

"You don't want to know."

"Delaney, you know I'm sorry. I never got a chance to tell you that." His eyes locked onto hers. "And I would give you my jacket right now, but I know you would refuse."

"You're right about the jacket."

"I know I am." The smile disappeared as he looked down at his hands, fumbling with his gloves. "It's been too long, Delaney."

"James, I don't know what you want from me." Her voice cracked as she felt a pang in her stomach. Seven years of bottled up anger fizzled inside, nearing the edge of overflow. The years harbored a serious amount of angst for her and she hadn't, despite better judgment, played out what she would say to him if she ever ran into James Anderson again. Planning had never been one of her strong points.

"All I want is an hour with you. I want to know what you're doing. I want to know how your mom is doing, how your family is doing. I want to know if you're happy. I need to know you again," he said, moving closer to her. He placed his hand on the fur wrap, his touch burning into her arm. She couldn't do this, not now.

"I finished my Ph.D. at Madison, and I got a job at Leighton University in Appleton. My mom is sick, real sick. Cancer sick.

The rest of the family is good. Ben just got married, as you know," she said as she nodded toward the church before adding, "and I'm happy. Perfectly happy," she lied. "You?"

"You know what I mean," he replied.

"Why are you moving back to Milwaukee anyway? I thought you were never coming back to Wisconsin?" she accused.

"Does it matter to you?" he asked.

"I'm not going to answer that."

"Believe it or not, I finished my law degree, and what I told you yesterday was true. I'm here this weekend scoping out office space," he said before adding, "and houses."

"James," she started, unable to process the permanency of his move and the possibility of him crawling back into her life as her back began to numb.

"Just one hour," he interrupted as he reached his hands up to her shoulders, rubbing them to keep her warm.

Damn you, James. She felt the anger dull, calming with his touch. *Maybe the stability of an old friend wouldn't hurt.* "One hour?" she asked.

"Coffee. Tomorrow morning at Alterra. Ten work for you?"

No. "I will see you there. You should go. I've got to get back inside." She moved toward the door, causing his hand to drop to his side.

"Delaney?"

"Yeah?" She turned back to see his eyes still glistening in a now softened face. This was the James Anderson she remembered.

"Thank you. Have a good night." He turned to leave, disappearing into the darkness.

Just like that, James Anderson was back. She exhaled before

placing her hand on the handle of the door, looking behind her once more toward the sidewalk where the man in the fedora must have walked. Her body shuddered as she finally reentered the church. The warmth enveloped her as she sifted through the quaint crowd. Uncle Walt's robust belly bumped into her, signaling an embrace. She looked over his shoulder to see the door of the vestibule hanging open, a single chair in her line of sight. On it, her black bag sprawled open for all to see.

She broke out of her uncle's encroaching arms. "I'll be right back," she whispered as she passed by him and through the door. She scrambled to the bag, searching through it, knowing that what she was looking for wasn't there. She shouldn't have brought her bag here just like she shouldn't have slept with Theron. Her mask was gone and so was he.

17

V's tiny frame weaved in and out of the snow covered trees. She was closing in on Parker Tower. It was only thirty yards away. It stood tall against the rest of the landscape, as a pillar of the next generation to come to the campus. It would be a striking building against the river, just like the rest of Holston Parker's buildings. They were always striking.

Crouching down behind an evergreen, she heard the needles scratch against her jacket before she moved inches to her left. She listened for the sound of Gunnar's voice, watching for any movement in the dark, but she was too far away to see anything in the shadows of the morning. She removed her black glove, placing her hand on the .9 millimeter tucked just inside her black pants. She pulled it out, holding it tight to her leg with her finger ready on the trigger, as her eyes scanned the openings of the building. Plastic sheeting that covered some of the openings flapped in the breeze. She leaned to the right, looking through a hole where the sheeting had fallen off and saw movement inside on the first floor. V waited, counting to five. This was it. Gunnar was here, as she had suspected.

She surveyed the area in front of her. There were no more

trees. She leapt up and flew to the wall with her head ducked down. Squatting again, she leaned against the exposed cement wall. She waited, counting to five again, before raising her head into the opening. Theron sat on the concrete in the corner, forty feet away, with duct tape around his legs, arms, and mouth. A black bag covered his head. The letters LU splashed across his chest underneath a black wool jacket. She moved her head back down underneath the opening, breathing heavy as she dug her boots further into the snow. He was alive.

With one hand gripping the gun, V ran her other hand along the outside of her pants, feeling the pocket near her knee. Slipping her hand in, she wrapped her fingers around the handle of the blade, pulling it out and onto the side of her leg. She looked to the frozen river where a slight haze of yellow hovered. The sun was on the horizon. Soon the daylight would flood the area and the building for all to see. Her time was running out and so was Theron's. She pulled the ski mask sitting on top of her head down over her face.

One. Two. Three. Four. Five.

The black ski mask peeked around the corner of the cement wall. V didn't see Gunnar, although she knew he had to be here. Somewhere. Springing forward, she ran to Theron, sliding along the concrete to his legs to slit the duct tape with one slash. She heard footsteps crashing in behind her. The blade sliced, releasing Theron's hands from behind his back.

"BITCH!" Gunnar's voice yelled as he closed in.

"Follow me," she whispered in Theron's ear as she pulled him up, leading him off the concrete and toward the opening on the other side of the building. As they sprinted forward, Theron yanked the bag off his head, letting it fall to the concrete. V turned back to see a flash of Gunnar's white hair hurtling in on them, his grunts becoming louder and faster. She took aim, raising the gun into the air to fire two shots in his direction before she turned to run again alongside Theron. No shots were returned.

"This way," Theron yelled as they ran through the opening of the building into the exposed air outside. She turned to take aim again, her arm extended out with the barrel of the gun pointed inside the building, when her arm slammed against the concrete wall with the contact of Gunnar's boot. The crushing blow of his boot caused her hand to stretch open, releasing the gun as it skidded against the concrete.

"Don't make me do this," he grunted as he swung his arm at her. V caught the glint of silver from a machete as he raised it above his head before it came thrusting down toward her. Theron turned back, stepping in front of V with his arm out ready to attack. Gunnar's arm swung through just as Theron pulled his away, making contact with Theron's chest. The blade sliced through his dog tags and skin, leaving a deep slash across his front and onto his side.

"AH!" Theron yelled as he grabbed at his chest, blood seeping beneath his cut shirt. The tags dangled loose to the ground. V kicked Gunnar in the groin before landing two hits to the side of his knee, dropping him to the ground.

"GO!" she yelled to Theron, who stood in shock against the wall. The tags fell to the ground when he staggered forward into the darkness as they gained a lead on a thrashing Gunnar.

18

DAY 4: December 21 – 8:45 a.m.

The sound of the register rattling as the heat turned on awoke Delaney from a deep slumber. She pulled the quilt over her pounding head, letting the heat of the cocoon consume her a few minutes longer. The sound of footsteps down the hallway prompted her to pull the cover back down. She breathed in the cool air of her old bedroom and looked at the clock. *8:45 a.m.* The night played back through her mind; the mysterious man in the church burning in her sketches. She had miraculously made it through dinner, numbing herself with alcohol until she found herself for a good portion of the late evening sitting on the toilet in the woman's bathroom. She had sat with her phone in contemplation, close to firing a host of warning messages to Theron, but she hadn't completed the task; Gunnar's words seethed through her brain. She would be good like he asked her to; he had lifted the burden of Mr. Rowan from her. And Theron hadn't done anything. Gunnar wouldn't possibly go near him. She rolled out of the old twin bed and opened the door into the hallway to sweet smells of cinnamon rolls and eggs.

"Good morning, sunshine," Michael greeted as she shuffled into the kitchen. He stood at the stove, spatula in one hand and the handle of the frying pan in the other.

"That's new," she replied surveying her father. She could have counted on her hand how many times she had seen her father cooking in the kitchen. It's not that her father hadn't helped around the house - he was a genuine Mr. Fix-it man, his days from the farm reflecting in his suburban transformation - but the kitchen was not his specialty. It was merely one more sign that Ann had relinquished her throne.

"Nice to see you up and moving this morning," Mark said as he glanced over the top of the *Journal Sentinel* that he held lightly in his hands.

"Did you see this, Delaney?" Her father nodded toward the small TV mounted to the wall by the counter. He still insisted on the news every morning, just to catch the weather.

"Breaking news from Appleton. There's a crime scene on campus, or at least they think. They found a bunch of blood, and a student is missing."

"What?" she asked, moving into the kitchen.

"See the ticker on the bottom? A student walking her dog came across it along that new building that Mark is working on," Michael said.

"Blood?" Her head throbbed, trying to process the information.

"Yeah and the blood was fresh. They don't know if the person is still alive or not," Mark added. "I'm going to have to head back to the office today to see if there is anything I can do. I'm sure Holston is trying to stomp out any fires. This isn't the best publicity."

"Maybe you should be worried about the person," Delaney replied, watching the screen. She couldn't help but think of Gunnar's warning about *the student.*

"They haven't given any details on whether it is a male or female or if there is a suspect." He turned back to the eggs that had stuck to the pan when he unsuccessfully attempted to flip them, the yolks running wild toward the sides of the pan. "Are you sure you need to go back, Delaney? I think you should stay a few more days. I could use the help around here."

"It will be fine. I'm sure it was some random drunk student getting into trouble. I have some work to get done before the students come back next week," she lied. While she desperately hoped that it was some random drunk student, the sinking feeling that something had happened to Theron consumed her.

"Where did you sneak off to for so long last night after dinner?" Mark asked. Michael Jones walked over to shovel a pile of dry, crusty eggs onto the plate in front of her. It took all of her energy to hold in the lurch her gut was stirring. He stood over Delaney with the spatula and pan in his hands, waiting for an answer.

You don't want to know. "I'm an adult," she said, looking down at the plate. *That's not going to work.*

"And?" Mark prodded.

"I wasn't feeling well. Too much vodka. I was in the bathroom. There you have it," she said, looking up at Mark.

Mr. Rowan. The mask. The teddy bear. It had all been too much. She had wanted to run out of St. Luke's, screaming to the world about Gunnar and the mysterious man stalking her, but what could she say? No one would believe her. She didn't even believe it herself. "Let's get over the embarrassment and talk about Mom," she added, trying to deflect the attention.

"What about me?" The quiet voice came from the living room. They all turned to see Ann Jones lying in a reclining chair, reading a book. The thick, fleece blanket covered her from breasts to toes in a sea of patterned red. She set the thin paperback down - she couldn't hold a hardcover book anymore, its weight too heavy for her frail hands - at the sound of Delaney's voice, resting the book on her lap.

"Don't talk about me like I'm not here because I'm still here, whether you like it or not. Delaney, a few more days wouldn't kill you. Maybe a few more days to catch up with James," she stated as if it wasn't a suggestion but an order.

"You read too many books, Mom," she called back. "Speaking of books, I'm headed to the bookstore downtown for a quick check on some I've been looking at for class. I'll be back in about an hour or so. Then Mark's going to drive me up to Lomira to get my car."

"Where's your car?" Michael asked, turning to look at his daughter moving through the kitchen and then to Mark sitting at the table. Her father had been too occupied to even notice Delaney's car wasn't in the driveway. He was slipping.

"Joe's Towing. A guy named Joe pulled the Civic out of the ditch yesterday," she said, shutting the door to the bathroom to shower before Michael could respond.

***

Delaney pulled into the parking lot of Alterra in the bright morning sun, looking casually in the windows of the brick coffee house located along Lake Michigan. *10:11 a.m.* She was late. She scanned the customers sitting alongside the windows overlooking the white, churning lake. The blue seemed to stretch far into the air as if there were no end, the two elements blending into one. The shores lay heavy with ice chunks, rocking back and forth in the intimidating tide. Still sitting in Mark's truck as it idled, she spotted James, polished in a gray blazer, tucked back into the farthest corner of the coffee house. His eyes fixated on the lake outside as he brought a mug to his lips. Her day old jeans and sweat stained sweater, which was a stinging red, seemed irresponsible, almost laughable. She took a deep breath in and could almost smell the fresh aromas of coffee brewing. The warmth of the coffee mug around her hands.

She envisioned James's face, laughing as they talked. His brown eyes settling in on her, absorbed deep in hers, as he had always done back at the academy's library more than ten years ago. No one knew her like James did, and she had shut him out of her life for seven long years. She longed for his embrace, his familiar touch. His voice. His words. After the past two days, she needed to feel safe, to feel grounded. She had even briefly considered telling James about Gunnar. She allowed herself one last exhale before a ringing tone sounded in her bag.

"Hey June," she answered.

"Delaney, I'm glad I got you. How was the wedding?"

Delaney let June's voice soak into her mind, waiting for her calm nature to radiate to her. "Beautifully painful. I mean, I'm incredibly happy for them, but you know me and weddings. I'm just relieved that my mom could experience it." She choked on the last words.

"How is she doing?" June asked, her voice quiet.

"She's taken a turn for the worse. I can't explain it in words, June," she said as she watched James look at his watch. "But I don't want to talk about it now."

"I understand," June added before she continued, "The reason I called was because of the incident on campus. Have you heard?"

"You mean the blood? The missing student?" Delaney

asked.

"Yeah, that," June replied. "A student found the blood while she was walking her dog. The campus sent out an official statement because they found military dog tags," she paused before adding, "They believe they belong to Theron Olson."

The phone slipped out of Delaney's hand, dropping to the floor of the truck. The words stung as she looked at her empty hand still hanging in the air. *Theron.* She closed her eyes to see the tags hung around his neck, glinting in the morning sun. *His father's tags.* She scrambled to reach the phone, her hand searching frantically to locate it. Her fingers wrapped around the hard plastic before she brought it back to her ear.

"Are you there, Delaney?" June asked on the other line.

"Yeah, yeah. I'm here," she responded, her hand fluttering to her neck.

"He was a student in your class this semester, wasn't he? I had him two semesters ago in one of my intro classes. A football player," June said. Delaney cleared her throat and wiped her eyes. *Theron.*

"How do they know it's his blood?" Delaney asked, not wanting to know the answer.

"I don't know, but they were his tags for sure, though. His dad's name is engraved on them, and his roommates haven't seen him since yesterday. The police reported that there were signs of a struggle, whatever that means."

"Oh." Delaney's voice was barely audible, the silence stifling. "Did they find anything else?" Her voice sounded foreign, although she had produced the words.

"Not that I know."

"Are they searching for him?"

"Yeah, they are, but I haven't heard anything else. News is

traveling fast around here. Rumors are flying. Students and faculty are panicking. I've got Robert here at my house, not that he's going to do much of anything," she said. Delaney heard Robert yell in the background. At five-feet-seven and maybe one hundred forty pounds wet, June had a better chance at fighting off an offender herself than relying on Robert. She looked through the window to see James still sitting at the table, now looking at his phone, then his watch, and finally back to the entrance toward the parking lot. She ducked down, her head parallel with the steering wheel.

"I'm coming back this afternoon. Keep me posted if you hear anything else," Delaney said, tucked underneath the driver side window before she hung up the phone. *Three days. No calls. No texts. Now, no Theron. It had to be Gunnar.*

BEEP. Her phone lit up in her hand with a message from an unknown number. *Go back to Appleton. Tell no one. Further instructions will follow to save him. Trust me.* Delaney read the words, feeling the life drain from her body.

It was Sunday. Three days since she had seen him last. The air in the truck suffocated her, the heat making her sweat through her sweater and down jacket. The stars. She saw stars everywhere. Her breath was quick and shallow as she brought her head upright. The dash spun in relentless circles as she blinked her eyes in a flutter. Her hand fumbled for the keys and moved it forward to start the engine before she grasped for the window controls, unrolling the glass half way to feel the cool breeze swirl through the cab and into her lungs. The truck rumbled as she backed up and maneuvered out of the parking lot.

As she turned onto Lake Street, she took one last glimpse of James sitting at the window. His eyes locked onto hers while he pulled the mug down from his lips as if to say something, but instead, placed it on the table, watching her flee. With treacherous Lake Michigan to her left, she sped on with her foot heavy on the gas, looking in her rearview mirror to see Alterra and James disappear.

***

Delaney pulled into the driveway of her parents' home and parked the truck back in the original location she had found it in, at the right side of the garage. Visitors always parked on the right side. She had held her phone tightly in her hand the entire twenty minute trip home, her finger hovering, once again, over the "9" on her keypad. Yet, she couldn't finish the call, just as she hadn't finished it back at Joe's shop. She needed to come clean, but she didn't know how it would be possible. Was she too late? Who was the mystery text from?

She stepped on the hard surface of the driveway, feeling the cleared concrete beneath her feet. Her heavy legs had begun to move her forward as she watched the white smoke from the wood stove escape from the chimney and disappear into the blue sky. She inhaled the deep smells of burning wood and fire into her lungs and found herself standing on the porch next to the white pillars. She had not remembered walking there, but there she stood, with the black entry door a foot from her face. *The door. The house.* Everything seemed to float around her, surrounding her from every side. It would get smaller inside, she knew that. The drive had been smothering. She swallowed hard and reached for the knob.

The door opened into the living room where her mother still sat reclined, now covered with two blankets, with her eyes shut and her book's pages spread open creating a fan on her lap. Delaney gasped as she looked at the small, hallowed out woman lying motionless. Her transparent face still and hard contrasted against the plush, deep brown chair huddled near the wood stove.

"Don't worry, she's just sleeping." The whisper came from the opposite corner of the room. Mark stood, leaning against the wall, looking out the front window onto the street.

"Jesus, Mark," she scowled, walking in to take off her shoes and jacket.

"She's leaving this afternoon with Dad. Dr. Hansen just called about an hour ago. He put in an order for an experimental treatment down in Chicago. There's an oncologist there that performs a specialized surgery that targets the pancreas. She'll be his guinea pig. The second patient in the nation to receive the treatment. If this doesn't work, well..." He hesitated as the words caught in his throat, "Her turn is up."

"And she's agreed to go?" Delaney asked, feeling the heaviness in her chest. "She's leaving now?"

"She put up a bit of a fight, but Dad convinced her to give it one last shot. She's tired. She's real tired," he said, looking at Delaney. Deep, bluish-gray circles surrounded his eyes as they welled up; Delaney had never seen Mark cry. She wondered if she was about to for the first time. The Jones family didn't cry. "It's going to be a tough week. She may not even make it through the surgery, but if she does, well, it's the only shot she has. The only shot *we* have."

Delaney, now standing next to Mark, mimicked his stare out the window before turning to embrace him. He wrapped his arms around her as tears began to flow from her eyes, streaming down her face against his chest. Her body released, feeling the slight relief of panic trickle from her body.

"You two are going to make me cry," Michael Jones said, walking into the living room wearing his jacket and hat. "But don't forget who we are talking about. If there is anyone, I mean, *anyone*, in this world that could get through this, it would be your mother." He stopped at her chair, setting down the bags he had packed for them both and placed his hand on her arm. She startled at the touch as she opened her eyes to Michael.

"Are you ready? Is Delaney back?" she asked, looking down at the bags next to her.

"I'm here, Mom," Delaney said, wiping her eyes and face with her hands. She walked to the woman, who was placed, like a small child, bundled in the chair, and wrapped her hand around the cold, bony fingers that lie on top of the blanket.

"Oh, you two. Don't worry about me, just take care of yourselves. I'll be fine," she said, looking into Delaney's clear blue eyes that had reddened with tears. "But you promise me that you'll be careful when you get back to Appleton. Dad will call you when they schedule the surgery later this week."

"Later this week?" Delaney asked.

"They are going to help her get some strength back before they do the surgery. Increase the odds," Michael paused, clearing his throat.

"Oh, hell, I'll just say it," Ann interjected. "Of living through the surgery. I've got to be stable before going into surgery." She spoke as if she was reporting on someone else. "But don't worry about me. We'll call when we know when the surgery is. Just be careful, Delaney. It sounds like there is some funny business going on at your school."

"You know I will," she said, bending down to kiss her mother's bald head; she felt the cool, clammy skin of her head against her warm lips. "And I will see you before you go into surgery. Don't worry – I'll let Mark drive."

"And, Mark, you should move into Delaney's house instead of those stuffy corporate apartments until you get a house," Ann said, pointing to Delaney who had stepped behind Mark as he embraced his mother.

"Don't worry about it, Mom," he said, picking up one of the bags to bring to the car that was waiting in the garage.

"Are you ready?" Michael asked Ann.

"Not yet," she responded, "I've got some things to take care of before I go. But you kids can get going before your dad gets my sorry ass out of this chair."

Delaney forced a small smile and turned to Mark to see a small tear sliding down his face.

19

V had to move fast, the time was dripping away. She crept along the detached garage in her day gear, the usual full uniform of white, with a backpack slung on her shoulders. She paused reluctantly, waiting for the man next door to finish shoveling his driveway. His body leaned forward. Scoop. Lift. Throw. The speed was painful to watch knowing how little time Theron had. He finished his last throw, placing the shovel inside his garage before ducking his head back into the house. Finally.

The snow removal service had already made its round to the driveway ahead of her. She had placed the call last night. It felt like a necessary measure. Would Delaney notice?

She sprawled forward, lifting the handle of the garage door with two hands. The door lifted a foot, enabling her to slide her tiny body beneath the crack. She sprung to her feet inside the garage and kicked the door down with her foot, shutting it tight against the cracked pavement. The backpack hit the ground with a thud before she unzipped it to remove the contents. She gripped the pen, carefully constructing the words along the note, when her eyes caught the tacky red streaks along the side of her jacket. There was so much blood. She wasn't trained for a wound

125

so deep and extreme. She hadn't ever seen anything grotesque as the torn flesh, the white of his ribs poking through the opening. The blood had gotten everywhere.

V placed the items from her bag in the garage before she opened the door and slid back out the bottom, the same way she had come in. Her eyes flashed to the house - the bedroom. She couldn't help herself. She sprinted to the back door, tipping the small tree stump on its end to reveal a brass key. Delaney was in dire need of taking basic security precaution. It was too easy.

She slid the key into the hole and vanished through the open door. She walked into the bedroom, standing in the middle of the room as she closed her eyes to envision the long, broad strokes against the canvas. It wouldn't take long. Her pants made contact with the floor as she lay on her belly, searching with her arms. V felt the frame of the canvas and hard plastic bin. Pulling them out, she grabbed the pink watercolor and a brush. It would have to be quick. She couldn't leave Theron for much longer.

20

The Ford hummed along the concrete that stretched against the vastness of the fields as it veered to the right to exit off the freeway. Delaney and Mark had spent most of the hour drive in silence while looking out the windows of the truck, watching the city and industrial landscape turn to open farm fields and tall trees that stood like beacons emerging from the layers of snow.

"Do you think you can manage the drive back to campus without landing in a ditch?" Mark half-joked as he took a left onto Parker Drive. She knew he was only trying to look after her, but he couldn't manage to express his concern in a normal, caring way. Typical sibling banter that, at the moment, exhausted her.

"Yeah. What about you? You're looking pretty tired," she jeered back, trying to compensate for the sheer panic that continued to fester inside. *Who is the man in the fedora? Where the hell is Theron? Are they after me, too? Should I call the police? What would I say?*

"I got this covered. Just be careful when you get back. I don't want to hear about you getting kidnapped or murdered," he said, turning into the driveway of Joe's Towing.

You have no idea. Delaney's stomach churned at the thought of the blood of the student she had slept with, but she hadn't divulged the details to Mark. She hadn't quite figured out how or if she would be able to tell him, or anyone, that she had slept with Theron two nights before he was found missing, maybe dead. Her career and life ruined before it even started. Then there was Gunnar, where would she begin?

His cellphone. Her number would be in his phone from her text. She placed her head against the coolness of the passenger side window, exhaling, causing a small patch of foggy condensation to develop on the glass in front of her. Her Civic was parked outside along the warehouse. In the afternoon sun, the run-down warehouse glared against the cleanness of the white blanket surrounding it. Areas of red and orange rust seeped along the sides of the building, running down the dark gray aluminum like a dirty blood that drenched it. The Joe's Towing sign hung crooked over the door. She closed her eyes to shut out the muffled noise of Mr. Rowan's scream, only to see the knife sinking into his chest. She couldn't do this.

"Mark," she hung on his name, opening her eyes to turn to him.

"Yeah," he replied, pulling the truck to a stop.

Delaney paused, her heart ferocious in her chest. Her phone burned in her hand.

"I remember asking you once when we were kids what your birth parents were like. You told me that you tried to forget. Do you remember that?" she asked. "Have you still forgotten what it was like?"

"For the most part, yes, I've forgotten," he replied, hesitant. "Why?"

"How do you forget something? Move on from

something?" she asked.

"You just do. Push it out of your mind."

"Do you still see anything?"

"Only bits and pieces, but it faded with time. Everything fades with time," he replied. "Delaney, is this about Mom?"

"No."

"Do I need to be worried?"

"No," she replied again before leaning over to hug her brother. "It'll be fine. It always is." She climbed out of the truck with her bag slung over her shoulder and walked up to the warehouse door. It was fine when she didn't tell anyone about Mr. Rowan. She banged on the door with her fist, waiting a few moments before trying the handle. Delaney would forget, just like Mark did. The door was locked. She turned back to Mark, waiting in the truck, who was pointing at her Civic. She opened the door of the car and saw a white piece of paper with a pre-printed header "Joe's Towing - Parker Enterprises" placed on the driver seat.

Delaney, This one's on me. Car is in good shape, just a few dings. Be safe. - Joe. She folded the note, placing it in her pocket as she began to search for the keys, but they were indiscreetly placed in the ignition of the car. She shook her head at the dangling keychain, glistening in the sun and threw her bag on the passenger side floor. As she paused for a moment to wait for the engine to warm up and the heat to kick in, she ran her hand along the floor of the passenger side mat. Her pepper spray was gone. Delaney took one more glance at the door of Joe's Towing, thinking about the picture of his beautiful, now-dead daughter Elizabeth and her friend. And Gunnar. And the lifeless body in the trunk. She shuddered, putting the car in reverse to make her way out of the driveway and back to campus.

***

Delaney slowed to a stop at her house on Drew Street, hesitating as she noticed her black driveway had been cleared. Piles of snow lined her driveway on either side. She peered at the houses flanking her own; she hadn't exactly befriended any of her neighbors to warrant the favor. *June and Robert.*

With the Civic idling in front of the garage, she climbed out and jerked the handle of the garage door. She kicked the jammed door with her foot and bent down again, grasping the door with two hands to lift it up with all her body weight. She jerked it free, swinging it half-way open, and readjusted herself to lift it above her head while the resentment dripped from her burning arms.

The door hadn't stopped moving before she spotted a dark heap lying in the middle of the stall. She walked closer, examining the black, crumpled piece of clothing. Picking it up with her index finger and thumb, the tackiness transferred to her skin as she recognized the black buttons she remembered unfastening just a few nights before. Her knees made contact with the concrete as she fell, letting the fabric fall through her hands back down to the garage floor. Her mouth let out a scream before she covered it quickly with her blood-stained hand, muffling the noise.

Theron's jacket. She glanced down at her hand to see a faint hint of red glowing back at her. Her head reeled as she wiped her hand impulsively on her own jacket, transferring the blood from her fingers onto it. Her face. She ran the inside of her elbow across both cheeks, scrubbing the skin raw where her fingers had been. Her feet moved beneath her body until her knees finally straightened, willing her body to stand in a crouched position. With the jacket lying on the floor, she spun on her heels, expecting to see someone behind her, but the desolate street was silent. *No one.* She looked back at the jacket to see a folded, white note lying next to it that had fallen out from underneath. In sprawling handwriting, the message only filled a small portion of the page:

Tell no one. His life depends on it. Your family's lives depend on it. Burn the jacket. You have until 5:00 to save his life. Trust me. V.

Delaney snapped her eyes shut, counting to three, and reopened them to see the same message written on the piece of paper held in her shaking hands. The text message. *Who the hell is V? Gunnar?* The paper fluttered to the floor as the garage spun around her, sending a warm snake slithering through her body. The coils of warmth tightened their grip on her insides as sweat beads formed near her forehead.

She stumbled to the cool breeze outside of the garage, her shoes disappearing into the frost as she lurched into the snow. Her stomach emptied, leaving repulsive streaks of brown and green against the white. God, she hated puking. Tears streamed down her face as she lurched a final time, nothing left to give. She wiped her mouth with the backside of her hand and staggered back into the garage. The stinging red letters streaked against a canvas in her head, searing as they branded into her head underneath the loose waves.

Your family's lives depend on it. Trust me.

She couldn't take it anymore. She couldn't do this alone. The police needed to know. The fact that she had slept with a student didn't matter anymore. Her job didn't matter. It was his life. Her life. Her family. Her mind spun to her family as she thought about Mark, Ben, her parents, all in coffins. Even if they all survived, if she survived, she would be an accessory to murder if Theron was found dead. The panic swirled in her head as she reread the note. It was almost 2:00 p.m.; she had three hours. *This is a sick game.*

Delaney nudged the jacket and note to the side of the garage with her foot, unable to pick it up with her own hands. She climbed back into her Civic and pulled it over the spot where she had found the jacket. The engine stopped silent with the turn of her hand. The impossible stillness permeated through her body. Paralyzed, her body refused to move forward out of the car. She rested her forehead against the hardness of the steering wheel. *I have no choice.*

Her hand reached mechanically for the door handle, pushing it open wide enough to climb out and onto the concrete slab six feet away from the jacket. The words chanted through her mind. *Burn it.* Her eyes scanned the garage before they narrowed on a black Hefty bag set beside several logs of split wood. *Another addition to the garage.* She picked up the bag, hesitating before she plunged her hand inside to find gloves and a book of kitchen matches with a deep silver cover embossed with a V. She fingered the cover, feeling the raised V against her skin. *Gunnar?*

She slid the matches in her pocket and inched her shaking hands into the gloves to shove the jacket and note deep inside the bag. The gloves. She peeled off the gloves and deposited them alongside the jacket. With the logs and bag tucked in her arms, she crept toward her house in the afternoon sun. Her neighbors. She was an accessory to murder, tampering with police evidence. She ducked her head down and turned to the back door that she had never used up until the morning Theron fled from her house. She swung the door open with a gentle kick of her foot. It was unlocked.

Her chest burned as she maneuvered the items into the living room dropping them next to the wood burning fireplace. The black fireplace trimmed in gold accents hadn't been used in years. The realtor's face flashed in her mind as she recounted his words after the house inspection. *Nothing a little clean and service couldn't fix.* The surrounding brick that had been charred with black streaks had been cleaned, exposing original dark red brick. She bolted to the kitchen, yanking open drawers until the gleams of the stainless steel edges caught her eyes. Her fingers surrounded the handle of the largest knife - a butcher knife her mother had given her as a housewarming gift. She hadn't ever used it. Gunnar would have a knife and so would she. Her eyes darted around the room as her body stood rigid and vulnerable underneath her. Silence filled the space.

She held the knife tight to her body as she crept back to the living room and retrieved her supplies one by one. Her eyes fell on the pile she had collected. Tick. Tick. Tick. The sound of a clock ticked through her head. Theron. Mark. Ben. Ann. Michael. Time was vanishing. *I have no choice.*

Bending down, she stuffed the logs and bag inside the fireplace. The sharp smell of sulfur filled her nostrils before she tossed a match onto the pile. The flames cracked and spread, melting the plastic to expose the wool jacket inside. The flicker of the flames burned in her eyes before she finally closed them. She turned her back on the flames and headed to the garage, hiding the knife in her jacket, to bring in her bag from her car. It seemed like a normal thing to do.

Delaney threw her bag on the floor of the front entrance and pulled her phone from her pocket. She scanned through it looking through emails and texts. No emails from the university about the incident. Her legs shook, begging for reprieve until she found herself huddled on the floor. The metal of the knife clanged against the floor as she crawled, the knife still gripped in her hand, to the door. She turned to lean her back against the door as tears flooded down her face. The snake coiled in her body from earlier, released itself, slithering away, leaving her chilled and shuddering. Her mind flashed to the silhouette that slipped out the door of the church. Down the hallway of the hospital. His blackened eyes flickering.

Fedora. Is it you? Who are you?

She shivered as she wrapped her arms around herself, rocking herself back and forth. Between rocks, she reached down to grab her phone next to her legs, her fingers dialing the numbers without thinking. Her eyes closed to see him where she had left him - his body hugging close against the window overlooking the lake. Her finger hovered over the call button when a sudden banging vibrated on her back. The scream echoed in her head, but it refused to leave her lips.

Crawling to the side window of the entry door, she peered out to see a pair of men's brown loafers. Her eyes followed the loafers up to a familiar brown jacket and red scarf followed by olive skin and brown eyes. She scrambled to her feet, wiping her face and eyes with the back of her hand, and kicked her scattered mess from her overnight bag to the wall.

"What are you doing here?" Delaney asked as she opened the door. The silver of the stainless steel blade in her hand sparkled in the afternoon sun.

"Jesus, are you okay? Your jacket. Are you hurt?" James reached to her as he pointed to the blood on the side of her jacket.

"Oh, that." The words fumbled out of her mouth as she

placed the knife at her side, wiping the dried streaks on her jacket with the other hand. Her expressionless face paled as she buckled in the doorway. "I'm just starting dinner. Tomatoes."

"Oh," James replied with a confused expression. "With your jacket on?"

"Yeah, it's cold in the house."

"Oh."

"I'm fine," she said, pushing his outstretched hand away as she moved back into the house. She glanced at the flames in the fireplace that had lowered and settled into a slower, methodical burn.

"What are you doing here?" she accused.

"When you didn't show at Alterra, I drove over to your parent's house. Your dad mentioned that you had gone to the bookstore, but you came back empty-handed, which I know is impossible for you. So you lied to them about seeing me. They said you were headed back to Appleton. He gave me your address." He looked down at his feet, his eyes catching her scattered bag against the wall.

"Are you sure you're okay, Delaney?" he pressed, his eyes penetrated hers.

"I'm fine," she repeated, bending down to gather her things, shoving them inside the bag. Her fingers refused to loosen their grip on the knife. The sound of the zipper filled the empty air.

"Really? That knife is making me nervous."

She looked down at her hand where her knuckles were now white. Despite the burning feeling to trust no one, she had almost just called James. It had been instinctual to reach out to him, to spill every detail of the past few days. She set it down on the console just inside the foyer. Her hand throbbed. She turned around to see James staring back at her, his eyes studying her face.

"Whatever you've got going on, Delaney, if it's more than your mom, I will leave it," he said, inching closer to her. He brushed a wave of her tear-moistened hair away from her face and rested his hand on the nape of her neck. Her body stiffened before it melted beneath the warmth of his soothing, familiar hand.

"Maybe you should sit down," he suggested.

"I'm fine. Really." Her voice shook, entirely unconvincing.

"Delaney," he whispered, moving closer to her until his body pressed against hers. *Why is he doing this?* Her body fell limp in his arms as he consoled her. She buried her face in his chest, feeling the coolness from outside still lingering on his jacket. She knew it wasn't right, but her body craved the comfort. The closeness of someone familiar. She felt empty. Vulnerable. She inhaled, breathing in the same soothing smell of James she had known ten years earlier. He brushed her long, chocolate waves through his fingers and rested his lips against the top of her head.

They stood embraced in the foyer when a sudden crack from the fire jerked Delaney's head back. Her eyes moved to the red and orange flames flickering in the darkness of the living room. She closed her eyes, backing away from James's arms that had just enveloped her.

Theron.

"I'm sorry, Delaney." James shuffled his feet backward and cleared his throat. He leaned against the wall, his shoulders and upper back resting along the faded paint.

"I just can't do this right now," she whispered under her breath. The flickers of the flames danced up and down, casting shadows that bounced along the walls.

"I need to know that you're okay," he said, pushing himself off the wall to stand in front of her. "Coming from the guy that chased your car in his underwear down the middle of the street."

"What are you talking about?"

"California. I ran through the neighbor's yard, down the sidewalk, and onto the street, running after your car. All in my underwear," he said, smiling at the last words while lifting up his arms as if he were about to take a bow.

"You did?" The details of seven years ago seemed grossly irrelevant as her mind spun to the next three hours. She had three hours to do what? Where were the instructions?

"Of course, I did."

"I must have missed that," she said, barely hearing his words.

"Too bad. I'm sure it was a sight to see. Delaney, I didn't know you were coming. Mark told me a few weeks later why you came. I had no idea. I thought you had written me off."

The crackling of the fire filled the silence between them. *I can't do this right now.*

"Before I forget, your mom sent along something to give to you. It's in the car. I'll be right back," James said, breaking the stillness between the two as he moved out the front door. She opened her mouth to scream to James, but nothing came out.

Theron, Ben, Mark, Ann, Michael...

Delaney snatched up her bag and the knife, running to the back of the house. She scanned the bathroom and spare bedroom before poking her head into her own bedroom. Her feet stopped before entering the room. The yelp of a wounded dog came from her lips, followed by the thud of the bag. She held the knife out, flashing her eyes around the room before settling them back on the pink staring back at her. It had been propped up on her bed, in plain view, in watercolor. A pink mask sketched on the canvas. Drops of red paint dripped from the mask into a red pool onto her bed. Her brush lay next to the painting. *Gunnar? The man in the fedora?*

She lurched forward, pulling the canvas down to face her bed. Breathless, she stood in the middle of the room, knife held high. The sound of the front door opening and shutting snapped her out of position.

"Delaney?" James called from down the hall.

"I'll be there in a second. Just wait," she yelled back. Her hands moved feverishly, wrapping up the canvas in the blanket before shoving it underneath her bed. She slipped down the hallway and back to the foyer where James stood half-bent in the entryway, removing his shoes. Her hand slid the knife back on the table in silence. She looked back to see him presenting a box that fit neatly into the palm of his hand.

"This is from my mom?" she asked as she reached out to run her fingers along the dark box adorned with alternating lighter wood accents.

"She said you would know what it was."

"I've never seen it before," she replied, taking it in her hands to feel the smooth wood against her skin and the cool metal clasp that locked it shut. The small, golden clasp swung open. She lifted the lid up, resting it on the matching golden hinges in the back. Red velvet lining encased the inside, cradling a silver ring in the center. She picked up the ring as she felt a hardness in her chest, tracing the lettering along the inside of the ring with her index finger. *Forever.*

"It's my mother's wedding band," she said, placing it back

in the box. The silver shone against the deep red velvet surrounding it as she clasped the lid tight with a click. Her mother had never taken the ring off. Until now.

"Delaney, I'm sorry. I had no idea. I…" James sputtered as he reached out to Delaney, wrapping his arms around her again as she lay her head on his chest. The pounding reverberated through her mind. Her mother, lying like a small child in the chair. The man in the fedora creeping through the night. Theron's bloody jacket turned to ashes in her fireplace. His life in her hands. Her family's lives in her hands. She looked down at the red streaks still on her jacket. Releasing his grip, she peeled off the jacket and turned to him.

"Why don't you grab a seat in the living room while I wash this bit of tomato off?" She nodded toward the fire that had simmered to smoldering logs.

"Sure, I'll throw some more wood on the fire," he suggested, turning to walk into the living room.

She opened her mouth to protest, but instead formed a forced smile. "Go for it. I'll be right there."

Relax. The jacket's gone. She turned and moved to the kitchen, her legs aching with each step until they stopped at the sink. She let the hot water run until steam formed around the steady stream. She grabbed a towel and ran a portion of it under the scalding water, allowing her hands to burn for a moment under the flow. Ann Jones had perfected that temperature. She scrubbed with vigor, washing the streaks again and again, until her fingers throbbed. Rinsing the washcloth, she wiped her fingers raw. Exhausted, she wrung the cloth and leaned against the counter to look out the window where a vision of Theron's head bobbing down the sidewalk was sketched into the landscape outside. She leaned forward to yell, but before the words could leave her lips, he disappeared from the sidewalk and out of her head.

"Ouch," she yelled under her breath as she pulled back her hands from the edge of the sink. The scalding water splashed against the sink and onto her forearms, the specks burning into her skin. She hit the faucet to stop the rush of water before throwing the washcloth in the garbage on top of the empty box of Chinese food.

Mark. Her phone felt hard against her leg. He would know what to do. How to help Theron. How to get her out of this hell. But she couldn't. Her eyes scanned the room, double-checking the lock on the door in the kitchen. Not that it mattered.

"Do you need some help?" James's voice called from the other room.

"No, I'm good," she replied as she appeared into the hallway. Lounged on the couch, James pushed his sleeves to his elbows exposing his creamy toffee skin. Relaxed was the furthest state of mind for her. He pointed to the TV with the remote.

"Did you hear about this? There's a crime scene on your campus," he said, staring at the news reporter standing in front of Maloney Hall, the location of the Art Department and Delaney's office. The woman was bundled in winter gear, her gloves holding a piece of paper that crinkled in the wind. Two other reporters were in the shot behind her, reporting in the distance to other stations, as police officers came in and out of the screen to set up barricades.

"Yeah," she replied with her eyes locked on the screen. *The police.* The worn leather of the couch squeaked as her jeans slid down next to James. She glanced at the time listed on the bottom of the broadcast. 2:03 p.m. *Less than three hours. It's only been maybe ten minutes.*

"It sounds like there's going to be a press conference soon with the Police Chief and President of the school." He turned to look at Delaney, sitting next to him, her body erect and forward with her eyes glued to the screen. "Are you okay? Do you know anything about it?"

"Yeah, I'm fine. A student's missing. Male," she added, turning toward James's imploring eyes. She was placating him at the moment, but she knew it wouldn't be long before it changed. He knew *something* was wrong. It was obvious. She placed her hand in his, feeling the comfort of his firm grip. She couldn't tell him. She couldn't tell anyone. As much as she wanted to push James out the door, she couldn't, not now. But, Theron was alive, and he needed help. Her silent cry muffled in her head.

"Looks like the conference is coming up," she nodded at the screen, releasing his hand. The camera panned the room. The large boardroom had been a stop on the tour of Maloney Hall June had given her in her first week. Her stomach dropped as the camera flashed passed a man in a suit, a fedora in his hands, leaned up against the wall among the reporters. Silver speckles spotted his dark hair. He disappeared as the camera kept panning. *That was him.*

She snatched the remote from his hands as President Givens and a stocky, shorter man in a black police uniform walked together to the podium. The screen flashed "President Givens and Police Chief Sanchez" along the bottom of the screen.

"Sorry," she whispered to him, realizing it too late.

"Good evening and welcome. We're here to provide you with the details of the last twenty-four hours that have transpired at the University." Sanchez cleared his throat. "This morning, at approximately 7:45 a.m., a student of the university was walking her dog when she came upon an unsettling scene. She called law enforcement immediately to report her findings. We have determined the area to be a crime scene according to the blood spatter analysis. A student has also gone missing on campus. We have reason to believe, although we can't be certain, that the blood belongs to Theron Olson, a twenty-one-year-old student on campus. In collaboration with the university police, we are conducting a search for both Mr. Olson and a potential suspect. During this time, we ask that anyone come forward with details relating to Mr. Olson and his last whereabouts or with details regarding suspicious activity on campus. Thank you." Sanchez stopped, stepping aside to let the gray-haired President Givens move forward in his suit to the podium. His eyes were glazed with bluish circles set in his wrinkled face.

"We plead that all students, faculty and staff remain calm and safe during this time. Although most of the student population is away from campus for the break, we strongly encourage anyone else remaining on campus or close to campus to stay close to people you know. We are doing our best, with the help of law enforcement, to find Mr. Olson and the perpetrator. A command center will be established in the Union for any student who has information or for any student seeking help. Police officials and counselors will be available to anyone seeking help. Thank you." President Givens stepped aside as a picture of Theron flashed on the screen.

Delaney felt the thud of her heart hitting the floor. Theron's eyes penetrated her as his brown hair flopped in boyish curls around his forehead. His bright white smile curled up in the corners. *So innocent.* He appeared so much younger than what she remembered from her bedroom. He was a boy. His face permeated the screen as she lurched forward with her hand on her stomach. Bolting down the hallway, she found her way to the toilet, dry-heaving into the bowl. She swung the door shut with her foot, laying back down to rest her face against the coolness of the tile when a light knock rapped on the door.

"Delaney, are you okay? Do you know him?" James asked from the other side.

"Yeah, I'm fine, James. Maybe you need to go." She feared him leaving. She feared him staying.

"Oh, hell no, I'm not leaving now. Unless you want me to get axed," James joked.

Silence.

"Sorry, that slipped. Was he a student of yours?" his voice softened.

"Yeah." She sat back up, her head hanging between her knees. A vibration buzzed against her leg and she shot her hand into her pocket. The words filled the screen in a tight bubble from the unknown number.

Police will call soon to question. Stay calm. Tell them he asked you to be a reference for a job. Send James to Mark. Wear the clothes in the bag in your bedroom - V.

Her breath quickened as she flashed back to Sanchez and his hard face staring back at her from underneath his police uniform. The messenger knew her number, knew her home address, knew about the mask. He even knew about Mr. Rowan fourteen years ago. Her eyes focused on the V. The moniker - laughed in her face as her mind sprawled. She moved her body onto her knees, wincing at the pain before standing up to look at herself in the mirror. Bloodshot eyes set into a puffy, almost indiscernible face stared back at her. She looked like a deranged drug addict on a bender.

"Give me a second," she said through the door. She pulled

her hair up, wrapping it tight with a hair band. She turned the handle, sending icy water through the pipes and out of the faucet into her waiting hands. Daggers pierced into her skin as she splashed it upward, washing away the salt that had dried on her skin. She couldn't let this happen. She wouldn't let this happen. *I am a Jones.*

The sting permeated into the layers of skin and traveled through her body, awakening her senses as she finished and wiped her face. The mirrored reflection was slightly improved; a woman with her hair pulled tight, a pink tone radiating from her cheeks. She opened the top drawer to find a bottle of Visine, a tube of mascara, and a container of lip gloss. She moved quick, fixing herself to a minimal standard that would pass. Exhaling one last time, she opened the door.

"Delaney? Delaney, I'm so sorry," James pleaded.

"It's okay. He might be alive yet," she said, looking straight into his eyes. She had to do this. *He is alive. If I do this right, I will save Theron, Ben, Mark, Ann, Michael...* "I was thinking we should go to Mark's place. He just started a job up here a few weeks ago and lives in a corporate apartment just a couple minutes away. Maybe we can catch an early dinner?" she asked, the words clear and steady.

"Dinner, really? The Police Chief just said we should stay in as much as we can. Weren't you working on something in the kitchen, anyway?" James asked, putting his hand against the doorway.

"Not much, and I'm not really in the mood to finish. It's not like the homicidal maniac is going to take all three of us down." She smiled as she waited for his response. *Maybe he would.*

"Okay, let's do it. I'm not going to leave you by yourself tonight anyway so we might as well grab dinner," James conceded. He had vulnerability with Delaney, and she knew it.

"I'll be right back. I'm going to change real quick. Feel free to grab anything in the kitchen you can find." She turned, heading to the foyer to pick up her mother's box before moving down the hall into her bedroom. She closed the door behind her, scanning the room for a bag. No bag. She ran to the bathroom, her eyes running over the counter and floors. No bag. *Where the hell is it?*

She moved backward into the bedroom and stopped at the desk. The vibrant green color of the file cabinet splashed against the wooden desk. She placed the box down before sliding open the drawer. A black bag lay in the place of her lingerie. Her bras and underwear were all gone. Wrapping her fingers around the bag, she pulled it out, tearing it open to find a pair of pink high heels, a black corset and pink jacket. She closed her eyes thinking back to her mask. It was a reminder. He was mocking her. With reluctance, she slid on the shoes and switched out her sweatshirt, clasping the corset shut. Her breasts pushed upward, overflowing the top. She slid on the jacket, covering some of her breast exposure. The fit was snug against her body. *He knows my size.*

Turning back to the desk, she eyed the box's gold clasp shining in the light. She disappeared into the bathroom to retrieve a silver chain. Her fingers pushed the clasp open, revealing the ring. She picked it up and slid it onto the silver chain. Moving to the mirror, she watched her reflection as she raised the chain up to her neck, letting the metal fall to her chest. The ring strengthened her, comforted her as she inhaled, feeling the ring rise with her breath. *If Ann Jones can fight, I can, too.*

James cleared his throat as she walked out of the bedroom and down the hall to him. "Pink heels, really?" he asked with a smile.

"I'll take that as a compliment, all things considered," she replied, trying to play her role with a certain amount of normalcy. "I'll call Mark." She pulled the phone from her pocket. Before she could start the call, her phone began ringing. An unknown number.

"Hello?" she answered.

"Is this Delaney Jones?" a man's voice asked.

"Yes, it is." *The Police Chief.*

"This is Police Chief Sanchez with the Appleton Police Department."

"Yes?" She forced a reassuring look to James, as if all was clear. That she hadn't been an accessory to murder. That she hadn't slept with a student. That she wasn't about to be interrogated by the Police Chief. The text from her mystery visitor had been right.

"I'm calling on behalf of the task force designated to the case involving a student at Leighton University. I assume you've been informed of the news of Mr. Olson since you are a professor on campus?"

"Yes," she replied, desperate to control her voice.

"We would like you to come down to the command center at the Union for a few questions. Time is of the essence as we attempt to locate Mr. Olson. We can send a car immediately to your whereabouts." His last words hung through the phone. The last thing she needed was a host of police officers at her house.

"I will come myself, anything to help. I don't want my neighbors to question me. I'm sure you understand seeing as this is a small town. I'm only a few blocks away," she replied.

"See you soon, Ms. Jones." Click.

"Who the hell was that?" James asked, moving toward her.

"Police Chief Sanchez. They are calling professors from past semesters. They are grasping at straws trying to find any kind of lead," she lied as she turned and made her way down the hall to grab her winter jacket.

"You're not walking down there. I heard you say it was only a few blocks. I'll come with you." James followed her down the hall, scrambling to slip his shoes and jacket on in the foyer.

"Do you mind just dropping me off?"

"What the hell is going on Delaney? I've known you for a long time and something is definitely up. The knife, the tears. You never cry. I know I haven't seen you in a long time, but this isn't you." James pulled her arm, turning her body to face his.

"Jesus, James. I'm just worried about my student. I want to help, wouldn't you?"

"Of course."

"Then trust me." Her own words rung in her head. *Trust me.*

"I will Delaney, but you owe me a better explanation," he added, letting go of her arm.

"I don't owe you anything James," she spat back. She stopped herself from the anger that simmered inside. *Stay calm. You can deal with James later.* "Sorry, I'm just…" she stammered, trying to cover her tracks.

"No, you're right. You don't owe me anything. Let's just start with a ride, okay?" he interrupted.

"Sounds good. I'll call Mark on the way. He can give you directions to his house after you drop me off."

21

DAY 4: December 21 – 2:15 p.m.

Theron lied motionless in the bed. Unconscious. It was better this way, V reminded herself. His chest, wrapped tight with white gauze, was blotched with red stains. The IV pumped through his hand. She looked at the clock. 2:15 p.m. It had been almost seven hours. He was stable, but not for long. The shot of etorphine she had jabbed in his neck once they entered into the back of the building would be wearing off. She had dragged him, unconscious, up the flight of stairs with a strap used to haul refrigerators and rolled him onto the cot she had bought used from a friend that worked at Gold Cross Ambulance. She had stopped the blood, sewing him shut the best she could, the needle shaking in her hand as she threaded it in and out of his skin. She had administered the antibiotics hypodermically, but he had lost so much blood. The basic skills class hadn't covered a machete wound.

Sanchez better make this quick, she thought as she looked back at the press conference on her phone screen. The Latino Police Chief wasn't entirely unintelligent. After all, he had searched Theron's cell phone records and would be calling Delaney in for questioning any minute. He would have Delaney's number but wouldn't have the content of the messages. Not yet anyway. As long as Delaney didn't screw it up, it would be fine. She switched over screens to the live feed where she could see an empty, silent house. Delaney and James were gone.

She had seen Holston Parker for a fleeting moment, leaning up against the wall with his hat in his hands. It wouldn't be long before he found her. He had a way of persuading people. She looked up to the brick walls of the attic.

The old loft on the third floor had been vacant for three years, obscured from anyone's focus despite that it was downtown. She had slipped in a quick meeting with the owners three months ago after she had seen Holston Parker in the barn buying the women. Waving a thick wad of cash had kept the eager, older couple quiet, telling no one that she had rented out the space above their apothecary shop. Her late-night visits had increased over the last month as the necessary arrangements to transform the loft had become apparent. A small refrigerator, medical equipment, a week-long stash of food, and working plumbing was all she needed.

Still dressed in her black cargo pants, she stepped over to the window, pulling the tarp an inch to see the Union several blocks away. A car pulled up one block down. The door opened as a woman's heel stepped on the curb. She saw the brown ponytail bobbing up and down, moving toward the entrance, as the car pulled away.

"Take your hair down," V whispered. Delaney paused, pulling at her hair until the waves cascaded down her back. Delaney knew she was more beautiful that way.

"Good girl," V whispered as she closed the tarp. 2:29 p.m. It wouldn't be long.

22

DAY 4: December 21 – 2:29 p.m.

"You can stop here." Delaney looked ahead from the passenger seat to see the building a block away. The sidewalks were scattered with groups of students flowing in and out of the Union. Bundled in winter gear, they huddled together, talking close.

"You sure?" James asked as he pulled the car to the right.

"Yeah, I'll give you a call when I'm done. Thanks for the ride," she turned, giving him a reassuring look before opening the door into the cold wind.

"No problem. Just be safe, Delaney," James called as she shut the door and waved him off. Delaney's heels moved her forward to the old, brick building located in the middle of campus known as the Union - the hub of the university that housed the bookstore and the main dining areas. Small trees poked through the blanket of snow surrounding the building. She remembered walking into the Union for the first time with June, where they had lunch among the students, during the previous spring semester. The Union had been filled with students, white ear buds stuck in their ears and large bags strung on their backs. The college scene was familiar to her, the environment easy to transition to in her first job, but she hadn't quite mastered being on the other side of the classroom. She had taken her job entirely too lightly she now realized.

She stepped up, reaching out to open the glass door to the Union entrance. A man dressed in a police uniform was waiting for her on the other side.

"Good afternoon, Ms. Jones," he said as he stepped to the side, letting her walk through.

"Nice to meet you, Police Chief Sanchez." She met his extended hand and forced a smile. He was shorter and stockier than she'd anticipated, but his presence was nothing short of complete intimidation. Military. He had to be in the service with his stoic body and unrelenting eyes that drilled into her as she walked further into the hallway. *Theron's tags.* He followed her body down to her pink heels before moving back up to study her face. *You have to do this.*

"I'm sorry to meet you under such dire circumstances. Thank you for coming in so quickly. Follow me." She suspected that he often didn't thank people and wondered why he had chosen to use the words with her. He ushered her into the hallway and through the doors on the right to a conference room with one table and two chairs.

"The command center is down through the main area, buzzing with staff taking calls and students pouring in early from break. For such a small community, we have great support. It seems like Mr. Olson had quite a few friends." He paused on the word *friends* before he added, "We'll be able to talk more privately here. Take a seat." He pulled out one of the chairs from the table before moving around to the other side, sitting down in front of an open laptop.

Hesitating, she stood next to the chair and removed her

jacket - glancing down subconsciously to the area she had just scrubbed cleaned of blood - placing it on the back of her chair. She looked down to make sure the blazer was buttoned tight to cover some of her breasts before she slid into the seat. *Be casual, yet concerned. Anything other than suspicious. Start with the truth.*

"Anything to help find Theron and get whoever did this away from campus," she said as she folded her hands on the table, looking across to Sanchez's dark brown eyes set deep in his bronzed face. His skin shone like a worn leather bag oiled several times over underneath his black crew cut. The smell of Old Spice filled her nostrils, reminding her of the first memories of her father. She watched him clasp his weathered hands together on the table, locking his eyes on her. He had done this before.

"Absolutely, time is of the essence and we need as much information as possible. We examined Mr. Olson's phone records and your number is listed as one of the last numbers receiving and sending a text message." He looked down at his laptop. "It looks like just over seventy-two hours before Mr. Olson went missing. When was your last contact with Mr. Olson?"

"Thursday, December 18th. Sometime in the morning, around ten or so. We exchanged text messages." She breathed in through her nose and out through her mouth, trying to calm her body.

"In regards to?" he pressed.

"He asked me to write a letter of recommendation for him." *That sounds so weak.*

"Did you see him on Thursday?"

"No."

"When is the last time you saw Mr. Olson?" His eyes stared

straight, unblinking.

"A day or two after classes ended. Theron came to see me during my office hours to discuss his grade and to ask me if I would provide a recommendation for him." He *did* come to see her during her office hours, but it wasn't for a recommendation. She crossed her legs.

"The exact date?"

"I believe it was December 18th or somewhere around there," she stammered, trying to recall the last day of the semester, as she moved her hands into her lap.

"Can you tell me about your relationship with Mr. Olson?" He was unimpressed, looking for something more.

"Theron was a student in my drawing class this past fall semester. I first met him at the start of class in September." *Leaning back in his chair, watching me the entire class.*

"So you have a strictly platonic student/teacher relationship, is that correct?"

"Yes." She nodded her head, squeezing her hands together beneath the table.

"Tell me a little bit about your impression of Theron. What was he like?" His voice was straight-forward as he continued through the questions, just short of interrogation.

"Well..." She cleared her throat and adjusted her legs in the chair. "He was a good student. He had an eagerness to learn and came to my office hours several times throughout the semester to get additional help. "

"Did he seem to have any friends or enemies in the class?"

"He seemed to get along with everyone fine. No close friends, from what I could tell, that were in the class, but I wouldn't know for sure. I don't think any other football players were in the class. He told me he was on the team," she added before shifting her legs again. *It's hot.*

"What else do you know about Mr. Olson?" He finally broke his posture, leaning back in his chair. Delaney sighed silently, feeling her shoulders lighten with his movement.

"Um, that's about it. Other than he was looking for references to complete his application for a job."

"A job while he's on a full ride, still in school?" His eyebrows burrowed down, puzzled at the thought.

"Um, I don't know," she stumbled, looking down at her hands. Red blotches patched her hands as she rubbed them back and forth. She pulled her eyes upward, catching the shiny name badge on his left side of his chest. *Police Chief Sanchez.*

"Is it customary for faculty to give students their personal cell phone numbers?" He stared straight. The muscles in his face remained static, immovable, as his eyes refused to blink. Delaney cleared her throat and took a deep breath. She envisioned herself standing in front of her bedroom mirror, wrapping her pink mask over her eyes and tying it tight. The reflection smiled back at her. She *would* do this.

"No, Police Chief Sanchez, it is not customary for faculty to give students personal cell phone numbers," she started, placing her hands on the table in front of her and staring her translucent eyes back at him.

"But you did," he interrupted. His face still unflinching.

"Yes, I did. I am in a unique profession at the university that requires its faculty members to foster relationships with their students. The faculty here are dedicated to the students, helping them grow to become successful leaders in our society. I will do what is necessary to help my students achieve what they intend to achieve. Since I was not regularly checking university email, I am not legally contracted to do so during the holiday break, I gave Theron my personal cell phone number so that he was able to contact me to complete the reference within the short deadline," she finished, feeling an inkling of control possess her, a feeling so long forgotten. Her hand reached up to the ring around her neck. *I will do this.*

"For a job," he pressed.

"Yes, for a job. I do not know the details on the position. I was simply asked to provide detailed information on his character and ability to perform in the classroom. That was not information I needed to know in order to complete the reference, and I didn't think it was necessary to ask," she added, shrugging her shoulders. *She was beginning to believe it herself.*

Sanchez broke eye contact and leaned further back into his chair, folding his arms across his chest. He sighed and looked back at his laptop, scrolling through more information. She sensed his leads were going nowhere and for that, she truly felt sorry, but she couldn't risk Theron's life. *Ben, Mark...*

"Is there anything else you want to add, Ms. Jones?" He had already written her off. *I'm in the clear.*

"No, I just wish I was more help. I just can't believe this is happening on our campus," she laid it on, trying to shove any seed of doubt, if there was any, out of his mind.

"Between you and me, Ms. Jones, this is going to be a tough one. We've got an All-American athlete, popular guy on campus, with no known enemies or track record. God damn squeaky clean. But, he's gotten himself into a steaming pile of shit at the moment."

"How do you know it's Theron's blood?"

"The tags. The chain of the tags was severed, the blood indicative of a struggle with a knife or blade that severed the tags and flesh below it. According to a blood spatter specialist in

Milwaukee, we called him up right away. Our guys don't see stuff like this, not here."

She yearned to unfold all the terrifying details of the past two days to Sanchez. He was rough around the edges, but a man determined to do his job. He would dutifully listen. Gunnar. Mr. Rowan. The mysterious man in the fedora. The bloody jacket. The book of matches. The painting in her bedroom. The text. *They have Theron. He's alive!*

Instead, she said, "Do you have any leads?"

"Well, now that you haven't provided any information that may have given us a straw, we're about at the end of our rope." He looked up at her across from him, huddled in the chair. Her face fell. "Sorry, Ms. Jones. I was just hoping that you had something. I thought it was unique that he texted one of his professors," he said as he stood up, pushing the chair back behind him.

"Please let me know if there is anything I can do to help," she said, lifting her body off the chair to wrap her jacket around herself. She had passed his interrogation. *But what's next? The next instruction?*

"Feel free to head to the command center. There are a few staff and plenty of students offering their help. A search party is going out in about thirty minutes." He looked down at his watch. "Back through the doors and into the main hallway will bring you there, which I assume you know."

"Thank you. I will." She held out her hand.

"Ms. Jones." He took her hand in his own, shaking it briefly before casting his eyes down on her red, blotchy hands. "Be safe."

You have no idea. "I will," she said before turning toward the door, looking out the glass to see the tail-end of a man walking by. She craned her neck, shifting her eyes down the hall. Black hair with silver speckles flashed through her eyes.

"Ms. Jones," Sanchez interrupted, pulling Delaney's head back into the room.

"Yeah."

"Do me a favor. Don't wear those high heels in the winter like this." He pointed to the heels with five inch spikes. "You're asking for trouble."

"Oh, sure." She forced a half-smile before turning back to the door, pulling it open and stepping out into the hall leaving Sanchez alone with his laptop. The hall was empty.

Vanished into thin air. It was Sanchez's job to notice the details. She wondered if she had really passed his close inspection; she felt naïve to think she did. Delaney shivered before turning to the right, moving along the hallway filled with colorful posters for campus activities and clubs. The sound of voices ahead echoed through the hallway as she neared the opening to the main commons area. She looked down at her phone. *2:43 p.m.* She had only been with Sanchez for ten minutes. Despite the nagging feeling that she should leave, she was drawn to the noise, wanting to know more about where they were looking. She floated to the entrance and pushed into the main area filled with moving bodies and lights.

Groups of students were clustered together among the tables and chairs throughout the usual open space. Police officers dotted throughout the crowds, some talking with students while others sat behind laptops set up at tables. The panels of windows covering most of the south and east walls streamed in the haze of the late afternoon sun just a couple hours away from dipping below the horizon. The darkness of the winter wouldn't lead the search party far.

Delaney noted two of the counselors on staff weaving in and out of the students, giving reassuring pats and hugs. She stepped to the side and watched the movement of the crowd, her eyes fixed on a man, presumably a student, taking the reins with a stack of flyers in his hand. A warm, wet nudge on her hand startled her. She looked down to see the eyes of a German Shepherd staring back at her before he went back to sniffing her arm and jacket.

"Sorry, ma'am. He's new to the force." A man in a uniform pulled on the dog's leash. His badge read Schaefer. Delaney's eyes followed the badge up to meet his eyes. They were set in a perfectly symmetrical, smooth face. He was gorgeous - the type of beautiful that you usually didn't see in Appleton.

"No problem," she stammered, brushing her jacket off. She looked up to give another forced smile at the man. She had to blend in, seem normal.

"He's got a great nose, but forgets when he's off duty, which is at the moment in here. He got a whiff of the missing student's clothes just a couple of minutes ago," he added before he flashed a bright smile that would have melted any normal woman's heart and walked past her with the dog.

The blood on my jacket. Theron's smell. She brushed her jacket again, pretending to look for something in her pocket. There were no stains. She looked back up, her attention back on the student wearing a backpack, handing out stacks of flyers to other students. He was tall, with a thick frame just like Theron, wearing a LU football knit cap on his head. *A teammate.*

"Yeah, that's his roommate, Mike," a girl's voice said. Delaney turned her head as she overhead the voice of a blonde student. Two girls stood fifteen feet away from her, both wearing outdoor gear.

"It sounds like he was the last one to see him," she added. Delaney perked her head to the right. She couldn't hear the response of the girl with her back turned to her so she sidestepped to get closer to the girls, inching along the wall.

"I don't know. I'm sure he was just out, like usual. Mike saw him Friday and Saturday night. I don't know why Thursday night matters, although it seems like no one saw him Thursday night. At all." The blonde girl emphasized the last words. Delaney shuddered, closing her eyes. *I was with him Thursday night. Make it Friday morning.*

"There are his poor mom and sister," the blonde girl added, pointing to a small woman sitting in a chair across from a police officer. Delaney's eyes followed the girl's hand as she felt her body crave to collapse beneath her.

The woman in her fifties had her arm around a young girl who was sobbing into her hands. Delaney guessed the girl was around ten or eleven. Her thin legs dangled in the chair, striped puff boots like Rainbow Brite swaying in the air. The woman dressed in an old coat and brown rubber boots nodded her head as the police officer leaned in to her. Her hair, frayed a damaged blonde at its ends. The woman wasn't crying, but the devastation was evident. First her husband, now her son. Delaney's head pounded as she watched the mother keep her composure for her daughter.

Delaney hadn't known anything about Theron when she slept with him, but now she knew he had a family and a younger sister Delaney was sure that idolized him. A single mother that worked to the bone to support her two children. Their world had been shattered with his disappearance. *What have I done?*

"Delaney?" She reeled around at the woman's voice behind

her. June and Robert, clad in full winter gear, were walking toward her.

"June. Robert." Her voice squeaked out their names.

"Where have you been? Why haven't you called me? You've got to call with this going on around here," June prompted as she examined Delaney. June's blond hair was tucked underneath a thick wool hat with strings. Nearing her fifties, June dressed like a tree-hugging, hippy artist in hand-made clothing. Usually, it was hemp dresses, but not today. She was in snow pants and a thick winter jacket.

"Agreed, Delaney," Robert added as he put his arm around her. His hat was pulled high on his head exposing his thick black hair, and his gloves stuck out of his jacket pockets. They were ready to join the search parties.

"I just got in and I came down as soon as I could," she lied, Robert's arm still around her.

"Are you coming out on the search party? Robert and I are going to do the first round. I just feel like it's part of my duty since I had him as a student and all. We're leaving in about fifteen minutes," June said as she adjusted her hat over her head.

"Not with those shoes," Robert said, pointing to Delaney's high heels shining ugly in the fluorescent light. His arm dropped from her shoulder.

"I'm sorry, I can't," she said as sweat began to form on her forehead. "I've got a friend in town, and we're meeting Mark. Maybe I can join later?"

"Yeah, sure," June said. "I'm sure there are going to be several rounds unless we find him."

"Let's hope you do," Delaney replied, looking back at Theron's roommate who was still handing out flyers. "I've got to run, though."

"Not in those you won't," Robert joked.

"Be careful!" June yelled as Delaney stepped back toward the entrance of the main area.

"You, too!" Delaney replied over her shoulder, leaving Robert and June standing together amid the crowd of students. She resisted her urge to take one last glance of Theron's mother and younger sister sitting distraught in the chairs behind her. The guilt was too much to bear. She weaved her way through the last of the students, grazing shoulders with them without bothering to apologize. It was too late for common courtesy as she felt the room spin beneath her. She needed to get away. *I need air. Fresh air. And fast.*

The colors in the hallway blurred as the heels of her shoes made contact with the gloss of the linoleum floor. Swirls of voices and conversations circled in her head as her eyes fixated on the glass doors ahead. She saw the reflection of a woman with brown, wavy hair and translucent blue eyes stare back at her. Her face, so unfamiliar to herself, sullen and pale reflected in the glass before she felt the cool metal of the door handle against her hands. She opened the door and stepped out into the crisp, fresh air as she stumbled down the stairs, stopping at the bottom to inhale the coolness into her lungs.

She steadied her breathing, soaking in the briskness of the winter wind. Sanchez. The search party. His roommate. The dog. It was all too much. She knew it was wrong, burning his jacket and not contacting police. Then lying. Obstructing justice. She came from an honest family, a blue-collar family working hard to make a living. She was well-educated with a doctorate and the strong beginning of a career at Leighton.

She closed her eyes as she thought of poor Ann and Michael Jones. What would they say? Her mother, on her death bed, discovering her only daughter was an accessory to murder. *Knee-deep in a pile of shit.* Her father's infamous phrase echoed through her head.

But it's not too late. She turned her heels back toward the Union, facing the concrete stairs and glass doors. *Sanchez has to know. I have to give him the lead. I can't possibly do this by myself. How the hell am I supposed to help Theron by myself?* She whipped her head around to the sound of an engine behind her. Another news van. She placed her hand on the rail about to take her first step back up into the building when a muffled tone from her phone filled her pocket. She slipped her hand in and retrieved the phone. A text from the unknown number.

Do not go back in. Call James. Go to Atlas Pub. Theron's life, your life. V

"Shit." The word escaped under her breath as the female news reporter and camera guy passed her on the stairs. She backed away, paranoid, searching for a phone in one of their hands. The woman only carried a notepad, though, and the man had a camera slung on his shoulder.

"Your day can't be any worse than Mr. Olson's," the woman said as she continued up the stairs. Her lips a vicious red. "Just remember that."

"She's right," the camera man added beneath his black mustache as he shrugged his shoulders, lifting the camera in the air. She watched as they disappeared into the heat of the building before swinging her head around in all directions. Someone had seen her turn to go back in. *He's watching me. Where are you?*

Her eyes scanned the block surrounding her, squinting at the white snow covering the ground and trees. Maloney Hall was just another block down. Reporters filed in and out of the entrance. Empty parked cars filled the street ahead of her. A handful of students scattered the sidewalks, all walking inconspicuously to and from the Union. No phones. A few police uniforms strolled up and down the sidewalk. Her eyes shifted down at the sound of another beep from her phone.

Don't worry, we'll see each other soon. V.

Delaney's hand moved from the rail as she turned and sunk down onto the last step. *I have no choice.* Her fingers slid across the numbers as she dialed James's phone. She breathed deep before lifting the phone to her ear, feeling the immense weight of someone's eyes watching her every move. *Probably listening to my words.* Her skin crawled as she formulated her words.

"Hey, James. Did you make it to Mark's okay?" She rushed, the sense of exposure flooded through her body.

"Yeah, we're just catching up. Are you done?"

"Can you come pick me up? Same spot." Her voice strained as she looked around.

"Are you okay?" James asked with concern.

"Yeah. Let's head to Atlas Pub for some food. I'm starving." The thought of food nauseated her.

"Sounds great. Mark's going to join us."

Mark. "Great." The forced optimism echoed as James fell silent.

"We'll be there in ten minutes," he finally replied.

"See you soon." She clicked end before she heard a response, her hands shaking as she slipped the phone back into her pocket. She had ten minutes. Her eyes fixed back on Maloney. *Fedora, are you there?*

As she neared the brown, two-story academic building, she watched as more reporters gathered outside. A tall man in a long jacket with two men flanking him on either side walked through the doors. *President Givens.* She watched as he turned to the shorter man next to him. She squinted as she walked closer, still too far away to distinguish the man's features. Her body stopped as she watched the shorter man tip his head to place a fedora on it. *His stride. His body. It was him.*

Adrenaline pumped through her veins as she watched him reach out his black leather glove to shake the hand of President Givens before turning to the right. She crept forward, keeping her eyes on the hat moving toward the side of the building, as she skimmed the crowd in front of the entrance. There were too many people. It was too far. Her eyes focused back on the hat as she watched it disappear around the side of the building.

Who are you?

The sidewalk flooded with reporters heading her way. She froze for a moment, feeling guilt rush toward her. She envisioned an onslaught of reporters swarming her, shoving recorders in her face. Accessory to murder, obstructing police. *Did he tell them?*

She flipped her heels to head back to the block she had come from - where James would pick her up any minute. 3:15. She pedaled her feet forward with her head down. Glancing to the right, she watched as two reporters crossed the street, heading off the others. A cameraman pointed at the Union. *Panic resolved.* As she crossed the street, students poured out of the Union and down the steps led by Theron's roommate, now known as Mike, dressed in hiking gear and armed with flyers. The search was on. He marched forward, catching fleeting eye contact with her before hitting the sidewalk. He opened his mouth as if to shout to her, but a voice behind him caught his attention. *Does he know?* Delaney forced her head down, moving only her eyes up to spot Mark's blue truck was parked, just in front of her. She swung the door open and hopped in, glancing back at the roommate leading the search party who was spinning his head around in search of her.

"Atlas Pub?" She shot Mark and James a quick smile before leaning down to readjust her shoes. "Damn heels," she muttered as she kept her head hidden beneath the console as Mark drove forward.

23

V slipped the phone into the front pocket of her leather jacket as she watched Delaney climb into the truck, moving east away from the Union. Moments later, a steel gray sedan turned the corner from Maloney Hall, moving west in the opposite direction. Holston hadn't seen Delaney. He would make a visit to Delaney's house, but she wouldn't be there. V smiled as she envisioned him strolling up to her empty house, waiting for her return. But, Delaney wouldn't return, not tonight. Despite the calm face he had shown on camera earlier, Holston's intricate little empire he had built around himself was crumbling to the ground. Deteriorating piece by piece.

A low, painful groan came from the bed behind her. She turned around to see his eyes moving beneath his shut lids. Her eyes traveled down to his arms and legs in the restraints. She hadn't wanted to use them, but she had to. The tranquilizer would be wearing off sooner than she had expected. She pumped more morphine through the drip as she watched the monitor, reading his vitals. He was safe here. For now. She needed to get him to the hospital soon. It would be close.

She hadn't meant for it to happen like this. Theron was

innocent, but after Gunnar had sliced through Theron, she knew she had a shot at taking down both Gunnar and Holston. Gunnar wouldn't be able to face Holston without finding Theron first, and Gunnar would never find him - or her - here. She would get to Gunnar first. Then Holston. Besides, killing Holston Parker would give her no satisfaction without making him squirm first. He was getting everything he deserved. She needed to save the women he was trafficking and end the bloodshed.

V slipped her feet into the black boots, lacing them up to her knees, and moved the note closer to the edge of the table. Theron would see it, but would he heed the message? *Stay calm. I'll be back with help.* He hadn't known who he was dealing with. He could never know.

She took one last look at herself in the mirror next to the sink and toilet that were floating in the wide open space, waiting to be framed in. Blue eyes stared back at her. "A pixie," Holston had called her when she had walked into the office after cutting it short. She slid the chamber of her .9 millimeter open, double checking the load, and clicked it shut before slipping it into the holster tucked inside her jacket. Always pack light. She gave her leg one final pat, feeling the hard metal graze against her skin on the inside of her boot. She was ready.

"A pixie," she scoffed as she slid open the metal door and slipped out, locking the door behind her.

24

"A round of Miller bottles here." Mark pointed down at James and Delaney already seated on the stools. Mark sat down next to his sister, leaning his back against the wooden slats of the stool. The smell of stale beer and fried cheese filled the air.

"A Sunday afternoon round of beers without a Packer game," Delaney said as she looked around the almost barren bar, an unusual occasion for Atlas Pub. The bar, a staple for the career crowd after work, turned into a low-key lounge for twenty-something's at night. The old pub was one of the first buildings downtown, near the river, making the atmosphere usually nostalgic and cozy. Although those weren't the words to describe the bar to Delaney. Not now. *Where this all started.* It was after 3:30. Theron had little over an hour. *What am I doing here?*

"Looks like everyone stayed home, like they were told, with the potential killer on the loose. Except for us, that is." James nodded at his company, hesitant to smile.

"Like I said on the way over, it seems like they've got it covered and are doing what they can to find him," Delaney forced the words out of her mouth as the bartender came closer to slide the bottles across the bar. His muscles bulged from his fitted shirt, just like they had the night Delaney had flashed her chest at him.

"Glad to see that you got home okay the other night." He winked at her, placing the Miller in front of her. She inhaled, restraining herself from grabbing the collar of his shirt and wrapping her fingers around his neck. His neck, too large for Delaney's thin fingers anyway, protruded from his shirt, his veins popping from his skin like thick snakes. *Just like Gunnar's scar.* Mark raised his eyebrows at his sister, waiting for a response.

"Yeah, I got home just fine. I was here with some co-workers Thursday night for drinks after Mark left," she added, turning to Mark before narrowing her eyes at the bartender. He winked again and headed down the stretch behind the bar.

"All-night drinking benders, pink high-heeled pumps. Who is this Delaney Jones? I've got a lot to catch up on," James teased, spinning Delaney in her chair as she looked him over.

"Wipe that grin off your face, Anderson," she warned.

"And we're back." James raised his bottle in the air in front of her face. Mark reached over, clinking his bottle with James as they both laughed. Sweat poured down Delaney's back. She was sure she would be vomiting in a toilet at this point had there been anything left in her stomach.

"I'm glad I could humor you both," she replied as she peeled the corner of the Miller label off the bottle. As her fingernail caught the edge of label on the chilled bottle, her mind shot to the last vision of her parents; Michael Jones cradling her mother like a child, on the way to the last ditch effort to save her life. Both of their lives, balancing on a teeter totter, waiting to be pushed over. A pang filled her stomach as she felt the ring on her chest. "Do you ever wonder while drinking a Miller if Dad brewed this exact bottle?" she asked.

"Every time," Mark replied spinning the bottle in his hands.

"He's still brewing?" James asked, leaning into the bar.

"Still going strong after twenty-two years." Mark looked up at the flat screen in front of them that had been interrupted by breaking news. A ticker on the bottom of the screen flashed "Student Search Party Begins" while the screen shot to a reporter inside the command center at the Union, now relatively empty of the students. The reporter, the same woman doused with cheap red lipstick on the stairs of the Union, looked into the camera, relating the "heroic" efforts of the students. The same woman that had told her that her day couldn't be that bad. Delaney hadn't been sliced like Theron, but she sat here, like a sitting duck, waiting for instructions from a mysterious killer.

"Poor son of a bitch," Mark muttered under his breath.

"Jesus, Mark," Delaney shot back, her heel tapping relentlessly on the stool.

"Sorry, Delaney, that one slipped, but could you imagine getting sliced open? That's got to be incredibly painful," he added, slowing on his last words when he realized they weren't getting any better by the look on his sister's face.

"I've got to hit the bathroom. Why don't you grab some menus?" she said as she stopped tapping her pink pumps on the metal of the stool, pushing her body up and sliding passed James.

Her leg rubbed against his as he placed his hand on her hip, gently pushing her out. She used to long for that touch from James, but now, it felt dirty – wrong. The heels of her pumps echoed against the walls of the empty space, clicking against the tile as she walked to the back of the bar. Her eyes caught the bartender's head moving with her, staring at her breasts as she made her way passed him. She flashed her middle finger in front of her chest before finding the bathroom.

The door swung shut behind her as she placed her hands on the counter, hanging her head between her arms. *Where the hell is he? And what am I doing here drinking beers?* She slipped her phone out of her pocket. No calls. No messages. *Could he even be alive anymore? How long can you survive without medical attention? How bad was the cut?* Her head swirled as she envisioned Theron, lying motionless in a pool of red.

"What do you want?" she whispered at the reflection in the spanning mirror.

Her eyes drew back to the bathroom stalls behind her, unmoving while half-hidden. She checked the lower halves looking for legs before kicking each of the doors open as a precaution. No one in the bathroom. She turned her attention back to the empty face in the mirror, drained and panicked. Her breasts, now swelling over the corseted top, heaved up and down with each fast breath. She wrapped the blazer tight around her chest, covering what she could. Her mother's ring shone in the light, sparkling back at her as if it were calling her to do something.

Do I tell Mark? James? Someone needs to know. What am I supposed to do? Police Chief Sanchez. She watched as the woman in the reflection began to laugh at the thought of being calm and patient. The voice unfamiliar and so unlike her own. *Only a deranged psychotic killer could be calm in this situation.* She took a deep breath, letting her throat absorb the laughter. *I have to do this.*

Delaney pulled the bathroom door open to find a petite woman, dressed in all black, waiting to go in. Clear, blue, emotionless eyes were set in a small, striking face topped with a brown, pixie-like cut. *Cute. Lethal.*

"Excuse me," Delaney said as she moved to the side to let her in. The black leather jacket slid past her, the cropped hair only coming up to Delaney's chest. She looked down, glancing at the black army boots laced to her knees. *This little sprite is ready to kick some ass.*

As she exited, she noticed canvassed landscapes of new buildings and old structures lining downtown Appleton filled the walls on either side. She hadn't noticed them the first time around – too much anxiety to reach the bathroom. She paused, looking at the black and white large prints, when her eyes caught a photo of the construction site for Parker Tower on campus. Several men in suits stood next to each other, smiling at the camera, President Givens among them. Her eyes scanned to the middle where a man with a shovel in his hand had begun to dig for the groundbreaking. She moved closer to the canvas when his steely eyes penetrated hers. *Fedora.*

"Delaney?" She jumped at the sound of James's voice behind her.

"Jesus, James. I didn't even hear you come up." She turned, his face appearing only a foot away from hers.

"Just coming to check on you."

"I'm good. Let's check out those menus," she replied then looked back at the canvas one more time, skimming the photos for more clues until she relented, following James back to the bar. Delaney gave Mark a quick glance before sliding back onto her bar stool. *Does Mark know him?*

"Did you order already?" she asked as she grabbed the menu from the bar and began to flip through it, despite the fact that she had no intentions of ordering food. She couldn't. *Tick tick tick. Theron, Ben, Mark…*

"Yep, Gorilla will take your order when you're ready." Mark nodded toward the bartender at the other end, out of earshot.

"Gorilla?" she asked, looking down to see the bartender walking toward them. The sound of James's laughing cued Delaney as she forced a small laugh from her mouth as she continued to flip idly through the pages. The words blurred on the page. *Keep it together.*

"Hey, Evie. I didn't even see you walk in." Mark turned to the small woman from the bathroom standing on his right. She leaned casually against the bar as if she had been there all along, but no one had heard her approach. No one had seen her.

"Mark, funny to see you here. I didn't peg you as the Sunday afternoon bar type," she said as her lips turned into a smile. Her clear blue eyes danced, looking at Mark. She had turned from kick-ass bitch who doesn't take shit from anyone to kick-ass bitch with sex appeal. Mark cleared his throat, readjusting himself in his stool. *What the hell?*

"Yeah. All the time. Usually by myself," he joked, lifting up his bottle of beer to his lips. Delaney studied his face, watching as his cheeks flushed a pink when he looked at the woman. Embarrassment was unusual for Mark. *Unless.*

"Pretty quiet in here. That whole missing student thing probably has something to do with that," she said, turning her eyes to Delaney, accusingly. The room stifled with silence.

"Evie, this is my sister, Delaney, and her friend, James. I work with Evie at Parker Enterprises. She's in charge of security for the company and, from what I can tell, a serious security ninja," Mark said, breaking the silence between them.

"Nice to meet you both." She slipped her small, cold hand into Delaney's, squeezing her fingers until Delaney winced with pain. Evie lingered, holding her hand until Delaney pulled hard, trying to escape her grip. She turned to James, giving him a quick shake.

"You look like you are ready to kick some major ass in that gear." James nodded toward Evie's boots.

"She always looks like that. I told you, she's a ninja," Mark added, giving Evie a playful smirk.

"They should outsource you to find this asshole that's roaming around out here," James said, pointing to the screen in front of them that was panning the landscape of campus. The sun, now beginning to make a clear descent, cast a low haze among the buildings. It would be black within the hour. *Chances of finding Theron are dwindling.*

"If they'd give me a shot, I'd take him down," she replied, her eyes watching the screen with serious intent.

"I'm just glad you're on our side at Parker Enterprises," Mark replied, looking at the profile of Evie. "Speaking of which, I assume Holston's been down to campus to smooth over any issues? Considering the scene was essentially at Parker Tower."

"Absolutely. You know the last thing he wants - or needs - is his name splashed across that screen. Or what we need, for that matter," she added, looking back at Mark.

"I'd like to keep my job," Mark added.

"Keep drinking and you will. You know this is his bar, right?" Evie leaned her back on the bar again, waiting for Mark to respond.

"I didn't but good to know I'm supporting my own job." He raised his bottle and took a gulp of beer.

"Speaking of, there he is." Mark pointed his beer at the screen. The screen flashed to a previous shot of President Givens and a man shaking hands. *Holston Parker.* Delaney's raised bottle slipped from her hands, crashing on the wooden bar. Beer foamed from the bottle, spilling down the opposite side of the bar.

"Damn!" She jumped up, tipping the half-broken bottle back up before the bartender moved with towel in hand to the spill, wiping it up with a few sweeps. He shot a look at Evie.

"Too much to drink already, little lady?" the bartender scoffed as he picked up the shards from the bar and remaining bottle.

"Fuck you," Delaney spat back before she could stop herself. *Holston Parker is Fedora?*

"Delaney, relax." Mark placed his hand on his sister's arm.

"Sorry about that," she muttered under her breath as she turned toward Evie, her eyes unmoving from Delaney. *What the hell does Holston Parker want with me? My family. Mark.* Her mind raced as she flashed to the hospital. The church. The mask. Theron's jacket. The pieces lay scattered in her mind with no interlocking pieces and two unsuspecting employees in front of her. She looked back at Mark. *He couldn't know anything about this.* Her eyes floated back to Evie. *She knows something.*

"I've got to get some air. I'll be... back." Delaney stumbled as she moved from her stool.

"I'll come with you," James replied, starting to stand.

"I got it," she said, sliding her shaking feet along the tile, moving toward the back of the pub again.

"I wouldn't do that," Evie added, pushing her body off the bar from her leaned position.

"I got it," Delaney yelled as she moved down the hallway of canvases. She spotted the steely gray eyes, holding the shovel, as she stumbled to the back door. A fedora lying on the ground next to him, near his feet. *Fedora.*

The sound of bass filled her ears as the gorilla turned on music from behind the bar. The back door was only a few feet away. She needed to feel the icy air in her lungs, the coolness on her face. Her hip felt the hard, scratching surface of the mortar as she collided with the brick wall to her left. She stumbled back and pushed the wooden door open with both hands.

25

DAY 4: December 21 – 4:05 p.m.

Evie's eyes trailed Delaney down the hall, watching her stagger along the floor of the bar. Laughter filled her head as she narrowed on the pink heels. Gunnar would be waiting. Watching. Somewhere. If Gunnar couldn't get to Evie, then he would take Delaney because he knew that Evie would follow Delaney. She needed to give Delaney a lead with just enough time for him to take her. Evie knew where he was headed. There was only one place now that the building along the river was out, swarmed with hoards of students and uniforms searching for a trace of Theron. Gunnar wasn't insane enough to go back there. He wouldn't hurt her, but she wondered how much more Delaney could take. Evie would find out just how much Delaney meant to Holston.

"Mark, look at her." The sound of James's voice snapped her back to her current problem, Mark and James.

"I'll get her," Mark said, hopping off his stool before Evie could protest. She threw a hundred dollar bill on the bar before leaning across it.

"Make sure they stay," she whispered to Ethan before turning her attention on James whose eyes were following

Delaney down the hall.

"Stay and drink. I got this. Lady talk. It might be awhile," she yelled over the music as she grabbed Mark's arm, spinning him around. "I've got it covered. We'll be fine."

"Are you sure? You don't know my sister," Mark replied, looking down at her.

"I don't know Delaney, but you know me. Just stay. Trust me," she asserted, pushing him back to the seat. She watched as Ethan turned his back and slipped small white pills into two bottles of Miller. They would stay. Ethan would make sure of it.

Evie's boots made their way down the hall, following the footsteps of the heels minutes before. Delaney was out of sight, already in the alley. She paused as she heard the clanging of a bell and felt a draft of cold air. The door closed, but not before she saw a glimpse of his white hair. Gunnar had been in the bar all along.

26

Delaney pressed against the door and shifted all her weight to burst into the silent alley ahead. The harsh air of the December night pierced her lungs before the heavy door closed behind her, sealing the pounding music of Atlas Pub inside. Her feet slid against the ice, trying to get traction. She knew she would be better off without them, despite the burn she'd feel when the ice stabbed the flesh of her feet. As she leaned down to take them off, a bell clanged behind her. The ringing was followed by the creak of a door closing and a deep voice grunting through the icy air.

"Hey, Delaney."

The voice was deeper and stronger than she remembered. She last heard it two days ago when he had warned her that he had never wanted to see her again. His electric blue eyes flashed through her mind followed by Mr. Rowan's lifeless body in a pool of blood. The rancid smell of singed hair and menthol wafted into her pulsing head. With pumps clutched in her hand, Delaney sprinted toward the end of the alley to the flashes of red taillights ahead. The footsteps pounded heavy behind her, closing in with every step. Her body pulled back as his arms

179

surrounded her. She stabbed the air blindly with the five inch spike of her heel, desperate to connect anywhere on his body.

"Damn!" Gunnar yelled as she finally made contact, connecting with his shoulder.

"LET GO!" she screamed as she wriggled and stabbed, connecting again, this time to his face. His white hair kicked forward as rage filled his eyes.

"BITCH!" He grabbed her wrists, twisting them. The pink heels dropped to the ground as she cried in pain. His hand covered her mouth, stifling the sound. She clenched her teeth, opening her mouth to clamp down on his hand.

"Oh no, you don't." He kicked the back of her legs, dropping her to her knees. She wailed out again as he wrenched her arms behind her back and hard plastic wrapped against her wrists as he bound them together. She stared straight ahead at the taillights before blackness consumed her, feeling a soft black cloth around her head. *God, no.*

"Get up," he whispered in her ear as she felt the fight escape from her body. Her hands were immoveable behind her back, and her knees throbbed with agony. As her mind desperately begged to assess the odds of her getting out of this alive, the soft hum of an engine filled the air. He shoved her to the side of the building, watching as his black car pulled to a stop. He reached out, opening the back door. She felt a slight release from his pull and instinctively lurched forward to run away. Her head yanked back as he grabbed a fistful of loose hair that was still visible beneath the sack.

"Cut the crap. Get in," he hissed heavy in her ear. Her body was pushed forward, sprawling, as she landed on the leather.

"Go." Gunnar's voice rumbled as he climbed in next to her, shutting the door as the car accelerated.

27

Headlights flooded the alley as Evie closed the bar door shut, tucking her head back into the warmth inside. She hadn't expected Delaney to fight as much as she did and was amusingly surprised. The sound of the car passing by prompted her to crack the door again. Evie watched as Gunnar shoved Delaney into the sedan, the black bag over her head disappearing into the seat before he climbed in after her. She squinted, seeing the back of a familiar head behind the wheel, but it couldn't possibly be him. It couldn't be.

Be vigilant. She breathed inward, taking one quick look into the bar before she slipped into the alley, waiting for the red taillights to turn to the right. They were going west, just as she had suspected. She smiled for the first time in months as her boots fell heavily on the surface, propelling her to the car parked three blocks to the south.

Ethan could be trusted to occupy Mark and James. She had known Ethan as long as she could remember. They had found ways to bide the time during those long nights in their childhood. It was Ethan who had taught her to be a fighter.

Evie ran forward onto the second block, passing by garbage

181

cans and a vacant parking lot. The town, stunned by the bloody crime scene, coiled back into their homes while the students went out searching for one of their own.

4:07 p.m. The vision of Theron lying in the bed, his legs and arms strapped to the bed, flashed in her mind. The white gauze wrapped around his chest. But she couldn't bring him to the hospital. Not yet. Not with Delaney in Gunnar's hands. He would never let her live if Theron was dead. The hard metal of her gun, rubbing against her ribs, soothed her as she narrowed in on her gray sedan parked in front of the riverside Victorian homes. She was only ten minutes out.

28

The warmth of her breath inside the black hood comforted Delaney as she lie motionless on the leather of the back seat. The hardness of the barrel against her leg served as a reminder to be still. She winced as the blood trickled into her eye from the blow Gunnar had given her just minutes before as she writhed and kicked in the back seat. A resounding "NO!" had filled the car from the seat ahead of her just before she felt the metal against her skull and the excruciating pain that seared through her head. She screamed in agony before it had swelled, the blood and heat rushing to her head. Immediately after, the sound of hands hitting the steering wheel swirled in her head.

Her body jostled back and forth with the turns of the car while the black fabric clung to her cheeks, wet from the blood and sweat pouring down her face. Her lips were moistened with a salty, metallic taste. *Gunnar.* She had caught a glimpse of his white hair and snake-like scar just before she had connected her heel to his face. It was definitely Gunnar, the man from Joe's shop. He had followed her to Atlas Pub, watching her all along. Her head reeled as her mind played back the vision of Theron's jacket burning in the fireplace beneath the stacked logs. The matches with an embossed V, still in her pocket, singed against her leg. Was *Gunnar V?*

Her bare feet curled up beneath her as she fought to keep them warm. She twitched as she felt a cold finger against her foot.

"Pink toenail polish. Fitting," Gunnar said beside her. She winced, curling her feet deeper into the crack of the seat, her knees now folded so deep they ached.

"Stop whining," Gunnar grunted as the car began slowing. "It doesn't suit you." He tapped the gun against her knee.

"For Christ's sake." Delaney heard the voice whisper in the front seat before two hands pounded against the wheel again.

"Fuck you," Gunnar hissed low next to her. "Just pull the car ahead."

The hum of the wheels against the pavement disappeared as the car bumped her roughly against the seat, stone crunching beneath the tread of the tires. Her body jerked forward not long after as the car pulled to a stop and she settled back into the seat.

"Get out," Gunnar ordered. The wind whipped against her body as the back door opened. She slid her body upright, her jeans sticking to the surface before she clamored out of the car, hands still behind her back. The sharp, rugged cuts of the stones sliced her bare feet, her toes curling up in retaliation.

"WALK," Gunnar boomed. The fluttering of wings echoed through the space followed by short, clunking noises. *Birds. A building.* The birds' wings were hitting the surface of something above her. She felt the barrel point against her back again as he led her forward.

"Couldn't keep her panties up. I tried to help you," Gunnar whispered in her ear, the heat of his breath warmed the side of her head. The familiar smell of stale smoke mixed with a faint hint of diesel filled her nostrils. She closed her eyes, hoping the complete blackness would swallow her, take her away from him. Instead, she could only see Theron's face.

"Keep going," he said. His voice was louder now, but further behind her. She heard feet shuffling alongside of her. *The driver?*

"What do you want from me?" she whispered, turning to the feet next to her. She looked down to see heavy boots half-covered with blue snow pants. A red stripe ran up the leg. Her body froze as she noticed the detail of the red stripe. *Those pants.*

"You know what we want." Gunnar kicked the back of her knees.

"OW!" She flinched at the blow, stumbling along the jagged stones. Warm liquid oozed between her toes as vibrant red streaks appeared among the bright pink polish.

"Lay off, Gunnar." *The driver. His voice. The pants. Joe? Joe's Towing?*

"Don't you start with me. You called me, remember?" Gunnar's voice bellowed behind her. *How am I going to get out of this alive?* She knew Gunnar was a killer. The satisfaction Gunnar had gotten from the knife sinking into Mr. Rowan's chest revolted her. He would do it again to her, without hesitation. The headline splattered in blood printed through Delaney's mind *"Woman, 30, Beaten and Hung."*

"Yeah, I remember. Let's just do this a little more…" The man's voice next to her paused as he lowered his voice.

"Joe?" Her voice escaped from underneath the black hood between her clenched teeth.

"Let's do this a little more diplomatic," Joe ignored her, finishing his sentence.

"Diplomatic?" Gunnar laughed. His voice was low and

raspy, dripping with years of bourbon and cigarettes. The laughter turned to the sound of a low growl. His voice became a discontented, crazed pit bull swarming behind her.

"Diplomacy left me ten years ago when I started working for our boss," he said. "Did you forget that you asked to come with me when I stopped to get my car?" The inflection of his voice hung in the air. *He's crazy. I'm dead. Joe, what the hell are you doing?*

Joe's feet stopped and turned toward her. "This is good." Numb and bloody, she obeyed the order.

"No, in the other building," Gunnar said as she felt the barrel against her back again.

"Come on. You might as well take off the hood. Get started with it before it's too late and somebody else finds that kid," Joe prodded.

"No," Gunnar grunted behind her, pushing the barrel harder into her back. The spot began to throb, radiating out to the rest of her back. *Where the hell are Mark and James? They'll never find me here. I should have gone to the police.* "The other building." Delaney shuddered as Gunnar's words echoed in the air.

"Fine, but we do it my way," Joe interrupted, clearly agitated. The wind flapped in the black hood as they drew closer to the cold. *An opening.* Delaney trudged forward, still stumbling, her feet unable to process her brain's signals. The frozen air stung her hands while a dim haze filtered in through the black hood. *We're outside.* She watched as the black boots left footprints in the snow ahead. Daggers shot through her feet as she pressed into it, leaving small footprints with speckles of red. *How am I feeling this? My feet are numb.* The gun still in her back, she bent forward, trying to jump faster through the snow. The low laughter sounded behind her.

"It's not far," Joe muttered under his breath to Delaney.

"What was that?" Gunnar yelled in the wind as it lashed against her body.

"IT'S COLD. LET'S GO!" Joe yelled. The sound of a spring and creak of a door opening shot Delaney's head up. *The other building. No more snow.* She stepped up onto the filthy concrete as a strong mix of stale manure and animals entered into her nostrils. Pieces of dark brown straw littered the cracks of the concrete. *A barn?* The last time she had been in a barn was with her overly-religious boyfriend back in college; however, she had painted countless barns in the past few weeks. *House_of_Steel?* The door closed behind her, feeling the reprieve from the harsh outdoor elements. The smallest inkling of warmth cuddled her body as she stepped through the hardened manure into the pitch black.

"Up ahead. Turn that thing on," Gunnar's voice sounded behind her. The radiance of a bright light flooded near her feet. *A flashlight.* A rusted, steel pole shot up to her left as she veered her feet in the opposite direction. The sound of feet shuffling along the concrete filled the darkness. A clicking sound perked her ears. She knew the sound as her mind flashed to cutting her own rolls of canvas to paint. *A utility blade.*

"What are you – " Gunnar yelled. Delaney felt her arms being yanked to the side as she tried to propel forward.

"Stay still," Joe's voice cautioned. The blade brushed her skin before the plastic around her wrists released. Her hands ached as she moved her arms forward.

"Thank you," she whispered as she rubbed her hands together. The numbness tingled to the tips of her fingers.

"Don't fuck this up," Gunnar growled toward Joe. "In

here."

A loud scrape followed by the clang of metal banging resonated on her left. He shoved her forward onto the concrete with the point of his gun. Pain jolted her body as she sprawled to her hands and knees. The familiar warmth of her own blood seeped onto her hands.

"A pen? She's not an animal," Joe's voice cut through the air.

"My holding place. It's familiar to me." Gunnar laughed as he followed her in. "Shut it behind you." *Holding place? A pen?*

Joe's boots appeared in front of her. She felt the warmth of the black cloth leave her as he pulled the hood from her head. The beam of the flashlight flashed in her eyes before she squinted and turned away, but the light followed her.

"On the bale." Gunnar waved the gun at the stacks of hay in the corner of the concrete and the steel ten-by-ten pen. She skidded across the floor on her hands and knees, feeling the sting in her palms as she made contact with the surface. Another low spurt of laughter rung in her ears as she crawled onto the first bale, the hay poking at her jeans.

"Alright, I'll take it from here," Joe said as the beam of light moved toward her. The silhouette of Joe appeared before her. His face, partially lit with the haze of his own flashlight, filled the space in front of her. The same gentle eyes she had met two day ago looked back at her from beneath the black ski mask and blue snowsuit.

"Delaney," Joe said. It was the same Joe that had dug her out of the ditch. The Joe who had a run-down warehouse for a body shop an hour away. The Joe who had lost his daughter. The Joe who fixed her car for free. The Joe who was somehow connected to Holston Parker. The vomit came up through her throat before she could stop it, turning just in time to dry heave what little she had in her stomach onto the bale next to her.

"Here." Joe outstretched his hand, holding his gloves.

"I'm okay," she replied, wiping her mouth with the back of her hand. *No hand-outs.* She couldn't trust Joe. Not now. Gunnar leaned against the rusted poles as a low, short chuckle left his throat. The gun was poised on his leg, pointed in her direction.

"Alright. Let's not make this harder than it needs to be." Joe looked over his shoulder, stuffing the gloves into his jacket pocket. "We're looking for him."

"For the kid you fucked. I warned you about him. I didn't want to see you again." Gunnar waved the gun at her interrupting Joe.

"Mr. Rowan," Delaney whispered. "How did you know?"

"That dirty bastard. He's just another initial on my arm." Gunnar smiled, pulling up the sleeve of his jacket to reveal letters tattooed into his forearm. The latest ink near his wrist had puffy, pink skin surrounding it. It was fresh. *R.R. – Richard Rowan.* The letters disappeared into his jacket. There were at least twenty initials searing his arm that Delaney could see. *He's killed all those people. Jesus.*

"But, how – " Delaney started. Her body coiled inward.

"Richard Rowan deserved it. Just like the others. I should have gotten him fourteen years ago, but the police got him before I could. I was waiting for him to be released," he replied. "I'm surprised you didn't know he was out."

"I didn't," she stammered. She had tried to forget everything about him and about that night. The smell of singed hair nauseated her.

"But you liked what you saw, didn't you?" Gunnar accused.

"I…" Delaney looked at the ground, his eye burning her skin.

"You didn't do anything about it. Didn't call the police. You were *satisfied*," he said. Delaney pulled her face up, staring into his condemning eyes. But she hadn't been the one that sunk the knife into his chest. Gunnar killed him, but he was right, she had felt satisfaction. He had gotten what he deserved. Warmth flushed her face as the realization hit her.

"What I did wasn't so wrong after all, was it?" Gunnar began to laugh.

"But how?" she pressed again.

"When we get this little matter straightened out, you can ask Holston Parker about how I knew," he replied. "And why. For now, I need to know where that kid is. Where did she take him?"

"She?" Delaney asked.

"Theron Olson. Where is he?" Joe stepped in, leaning into her.

"I have no idea," she replied, staring into his eyes as he studied her face.

"Come on, Delaney. We want to help you," Joe said.

"I really don't know." She bit her already cracked lip, crusted over with dry blood and salt. "I wish I did."

"Tell us something," Joe cajoled. She watched as he rubbed his goatee with the back of his hand. The scratching noises sent shivers through her already frozen body.

"I can't tell you anything," she lied, looking down at her toes. She shot her eyes back up as the white hair charged toward her.

"Cut the bull," Gunnar spat as he shoved the gun into her forehead. "I know you're working with her."

"OW!" Delaney cried as she scrambled to get away. She felt the crack against her skull when the gun made contact with her head and threw her to the ground. Now on her belly, she felt the familiar warmth trickle down the other side of her head. Hands pulled her arms behind her back. Metal surrounded her wrists followed by a clicking sound. *Handcuffs.*

"Not gonna get these off. Are ya, Joe?" Gunnar scoffed before pain shot to her abdomen from the contact of his boot.

"No, I'm not." Joe stepped back, relinquishing all control to the crazed Gunnar.

"Let's try this again." Gunnar yanked her up by the handcuffs as she struggled to shuffle her feet beneath her. Half-bent, she coughed, trying to catch her breath. He pushed her to the bales, shoving her down as her face scratched against the sharp, yellow ends of the straw. Joe stepped forward as she cried out again, but stopped and moved back to the pole.

"Sit." Gunnar knocked the gun against the bale.

"I'm trying," she whispered.

"Try harder, for that little boyfriend of yours." He laughed as he pointed the gun back at her forehead.

"He's not my boyfriend..." she started before she saw Joe shaking his head behind Gunnar.

"I don't give a shit. Just tell me where he is. Tell me where *she* is," Gunnar said as he leaned down, one knee on the ground in front of her. The jaw of the Neanderthal inched closer to her, his skin pulled tight against his hard face. The scar pulsated in his face, threatening to slither from his cheek.

"I don't know what you're talking about. Who is *she*? I'm not working with anyone and I told you, I don't know where Theron is." Her voice was small, almost a whisper against the wind battering against the wooden planks of the barn. She leaned back as his eyes tore into her. He was losing it, she knew, but she had nothing to tell him.

"Give him something. Give *me* something," Joe interrupted from behind him. The light shone brighter as he moved forward, casting shadows along Gunnar's face. *Gunnar's crazy. He's going to kill me if I don't tell him something. The jacket. The texts. He's not V. If he doesn't have Theron, then who the hell does?*

29

Flicking the headlights off, Evie turned the gray sedan onto the path. What was left of the sunny day had dipped below the horizon exposing the last haze that would soon turn to black. It would be close if she could get to them fast, disposing of Gunnar before Holston found them. It wouldn't be long before he came here, looking for Gunnar. It wasn't his best hire. Gunnar was getting sloppy. Holston had to know that by now. Besides, he wasn't exactly the brightest employee he had on staff. Holston hadn't hired Gunnar for his intellect, however; a machete was far from the correct arsenal for a discreet hit man.

The tread of the tires crunched along the ice packed deep into the crevices of the stones. There was snow surrounding the two buildings that were only set thirty yards apart. The wooden farm and shed, weathered a silvery gray, dirtied the otherwise pristine landscape. The car crawled along the path until she was fifty yards away, stopping the engine. The wind whistled against the car. Gunnar was waiting for her, but they wouldn't hear her coming. She had been strategizing this moment for months. Calculating, planning how the end might come to fruition. Gunnar needed her alive. But she couldn't say the same about

Gunnar – he was dispensable to her. Her bullets would take down her first victim.

She gave her holster one last reassuring check before patting her leg, feeling the hard blade against her skin. Her fist made contact with the glove compartment as it flung open to reveal a flashlight and more knives. She wrapped her hands around the flashlight, turned off the door light, and slipped out of the gray sedan onto the iced stones.

Her lungs burned, letting the disgust invigorate her body. Holston Parker had kept the building after what had happened. It had been twelve years since she had been here last. She had pleaded with him to get rid of the dilapidated buildings – to burn them down. He had promised to take care of them, just as he had taken care of everything else. She had trusted him. Your father was supposed to do anything to protect his daughter.

Her father had done what he thought needed to be done instead. She closed her eyes, smelling the deep aroma of the outdoors and the cheap, spicy cologne that had permeated Henry's body.

Henry had taken her here twelve years ago when she was fifteen. He was nineteen. She had pursued Henry after she had spotted him at one of her father's construction sites during the summer before her junior year of high school. His chest had glistened in the sun, inked with tattoos across his chiseled back and arms. She had slipped her petite body through the framed walls while her father had turned his back to her, occupied with the foreman. Her wavy, brown hair streamed down her back, blowing in the gentle breeze of the summer wind. Standing in her tiny, cut-off shorts and body-hugging tank top, she had introduced herself as he stood with the nail gun poised in the air.

They had been seeing each other for two months before her

father had found out. He had then warned Henry to stay away from her while telling her that he forbid her to see him. Yet, Henry was her first boyfriend, so she had promised him that her father wouldn't find them at the farm. Evie had snuck out her window, running three blocks down to his waiting truck. She hadn't been to the abandoned farm since she had been a small girl.

That night, she had felt the wheat strands graze her hand as she swept along the fields while Henry had parked his pickup. The end of a smoldering summer was coming to an end. The haze of the sun had begun to disappear beneath the wheat fields. They had crept into the farm where they walked across the old beam rafters before falling into the bales of straw. She hadn't questioned that there were bales in an abandoned farm. Not until after.

They had stayed in the straw, kissing each other as Henry began to peel back her clothes. His hands had grabbed at her before she could stop him, groping her neck, squeezing it hard before he had let it go, backing away from her. She had bent down to gather her shirt and cover her breasts when her father had appeared through the shadows of the barn, followed by a man she had never seen before. The man's platinum hair had glinted against his black clothes and shadowed barn.

"I didn't mean to," Henry had started.

"I told you to stay away," her father had responded. She remembered his response, his calm and deliberate voice. voice.

"Nothing happened. I would never," Henry had stumbled through his words.

"But you did before I hired you. I knew. You had such promise to turn it around, but it's too late now." The blonde man stalked forward, his black gloves raised as he revealed a gun that emptied five shots into Henry's stomach. Evie had let out a scream before her father had covered her mouth, turning her away from a still Henry.

"Get rid of him," her father had said over his shoulder. "And the truck, too." Her father had forced her forward, her body paralyzed and unable to fight.

"It had to be done. He would have hurt you, and I will never let that happen."

The words rung in Evie's head as she moved closer to the shed. She had trusted her father, and he had damaged her. He took away Henry. She wouldn't let him continue to control her, no matter how powerful he was. Not after what she saw in that barn in Amberg a few months ago. The poor prostitutes huddled in the barn, being sold to her father. He would pay for the pain he had inflicted upon her, as well as, all the women that she could never seem to find again. So she played his game, every move calculated and strategic, waiting for a chance to avenge herself. As she leaned against the wooden shed, she slipped her hand into her holster and retrieved her gun, stalking.

Silence. She turned the corner and poked her head into the shed. Gunnar's black sedan was parked inside a mere ten feet away. They were here. Somewhere. Bending down, she crept to the car, hiding behind it. Nothing. They couldn't have heard her coming. No, Gunnar wouldn't have hidden. She weaved in and out of the skid-loaders and small excavators. She had never seen this equipment on any of the construction sites. Too small. Too old. Adrenaline pumped through her body. She came to the opening of the shed on the other end, hiding herself on the edge before turning on her flashlight.

The small beam of light shone on the white surface, revealing small, scattered stains of red next to footprints. She followed the path with her light as far as it would reach. The stains fell inside the smaller footprints while larger footprints followed. Another set was five feet off to the right. Delaney, Gunnar, Joe. All three were here. In the barn.

The revenge Evie sought was in the one place she couldn't set foot in. She had envisioned it long gone, smoldering in her mind. He had lied, telling her that he had kept only the shed, and she hadn't gone back. She couldn't. She stood before it, hand on the handle, about to step into the suffocation.

She pulled the door open, sliding into the small opening before silently shutting it behind her. With the flashlight now shoved inside her pocket, she waited for her eyes to adjust to the dimness. The stench of stale manure and animals filled her nostrils. She could almost smell a hint of fiery ashes. With her gun gripped tightly in her hand, she inched through what was once a milk house. The dingy light from the blocks of glass cemented in the wood revealed the old stained sinks still standing in their original place. She closed her eyes as she watched herself as a little girl, standing on an upside down pail, washing her hands under the running water. The heaviness on her chest moved her forward. She had to get out. She had to find them. Knowing Gunnar, they had to be in the pen.

Evie slipped her head into the opening that led to where the stanchions used to be. A haze of light on the other end filled the back corner. The faint outline of metal poles circled the light. She was right; they were in a pen. Her brain scanned through the possible options for attack. She needed to get closer, and she didn't have much time. She couldn't wait too long.

Her feet fell silently against the concrete, moving closer to the target, along the outside wall against the cement blocks on the lower portion of the wall. She crept forty feet forward before pausing as their voices became clearer.

"Tell us something," Joe's voice became audible.

"I can't tell you anything." Evie's lips turned up as she listened to Delaney. Her voice still had fight.

"Cut the bull," Gunnar snarled. It was followed by a scream. Evie watched the bodies scuffle before a small thud registered. A clicking noise followed. Handcuffs.

"Not gonna get these off. Are ya, Joe?" A moan and a cough.

"No, I'm not."

"Let's try this again." Gunnar's voice ordered. "Sit. Try harder, for that little boyfriend of yours."

"He's not my boyfriend – " Delaney started.

"I don't give a shit. Just tell me where he is," Gunnar cut in. Evie heard a whisper, but couldn't make out the words.

"Give him something. Give me something," Joe's voice interrupted. Evie waited. How long would it be before Delaney told them about the jacket? The texts? The person named V? Evie crept closer along the wall now only thirty feet away, still in the shadow of the darkness. The white hair had bent down below the poles, his head bobbing between the poles only six inches apart. She needed a better shot. A kill shot.

Her eyes shifted at the sound of skittering feet just yards ahead of her. A rat. Gunnar sprung up, pointing his gun in her direction. Three shots echoed through the air.

30

Delaney opened her mouth to start from the beginning - the jacket - when she heard the sound of movement in the darkness of the barn. Gunnar shot up, turning to the noise when three popping noises rang against the walls. She caught the last flash of sparks coming from the wall as she sprawled herself flat against the straw. The Neanderthal crumbled before her, his blue eyes staring at her only inches from her face, until he collapsed on the ground.

"Hell," Joe muttered as he yanked a gun from his boot beneath his snow pants.

"DON'T MOVE!" a woman's voice yelled. Joe held his arms in the air, the beam from the flashlight pointed toward the ceiling of the barn. He held the gun loose in the other hand, dangling toward the ground.

"Put them down, Joe," the woman's voice ordered from the darkness. Joe moved slowly, about to place the flashlight on the ground toward the voice.

"The other way, toward her," the woman ordered. Joe obeyed, turning the light toward Delaney.

"The gun," the voice added. She was coming closer to

them.

"V? Is that you?" Joe's question hung in the silence. *Who the hell is V?* A grunt escaped from the ground as Gunnar's hand reached for his gun, sprawled a few feet from him. Delaney pushed off from the bale, forcing her body to move as she kicked her leg forward. She felt the hard metal against her foot as she made contact with the gun, skidding it five feet across the concrete floor. With her hands still tied behind her back, she stood over it, watching the woman creep closer from the shadows.

"BITCH," Gunnar muttered from the floor.

"Evie?" Delaney watched as the small girl from Atlas Pub strode toward them, gun still raised. *Evie is V?* The one who left the jacket in her garage. The painting in her bedroom. The clothes she was wearing. The messages. *This was V?* Delaney's head spun as she wrapped her mind around the small pixie of a woman; the woman behind the elusive V. She was sure it had been Holston Parker. Then Gunnar. But it was Evie.

"V for short." Evie opened the gate, moving into the small pen. She picked up the gun between Delaney's bloody feet. The pink toe nail polish shone bright against her dirty skin.

"Delaney, move back. Get on the other side," Evie ordered as she motioned toward the open gate, .9 millimeter in one hand and a .22 in the other. "Joe, sit down." She waved the gun in her left hand to the bales.

I should run. Evie eyed Delaney as she closed the gate of the pen. "Don't even think about running," Evie added as Delaney made her way to the other side. Delaney didn't have a choice as she looked down toward the end of the barn. *No shoes. Handcuffed. No keys. In the middle of nowhere. I would freeze to death.*

"V, what are you doing?" Joe asked as he slid onto the bale.

"You should have stayed out of this. I had it under control."

"No, you didn't. I was watching." Evie nodded down at Gunnar lying still on the ground. His back lifted slightly with a breath. He was still alive.

"Hey, Gunnar. It's V. Remember me?" Evie's voice strained as she stood staring at his limp body. "The last time I saw you, it was more than twelve years ago. The same place, wasn't it?"

He replied with a groan.

"Well, actually it was this morning, back at the new building. Where you sliced open Theron's chest."

"That wasn't supposed to happen," Gunnar groaned. His body lay crumpled on the ground.

"How did you manage that anyway? You should have let us go. It would have been a lot cleaner that way," Evie retorted, kicking his body. He tried to grab at her leg, but his arm barely moved. "You took Henry from me. Remember that? The kid with the tattoos? You shot him right in front of my face. I watched him take his last breath. I still see those eyes, you fuck. His eyes pleading for help. You're going to rot in hell," Evie added, pointing the gun at his head. A low laughter turned into a small cough as Gunnar gasped for air. Delaney turned her head away.

"That rapist? That kid?" he stammered. "I saved you. That time."

"Henry wasn't a rapist," Evie shot back, spitting on him.

"Ask your father, Mr. Parker," he sputtered. Blood oozed from the corner of his mouth. *Holston Parker is Evie's dad? Evie Parker?*

"Here I thought." He coughed and gasped for air. "I thought. The girl."

"What girl?" Evie shot back at him. There was no response.

"What girl?" she pressed again.

"Joe's girl," his voice choked, barely audible.

"What did you say?" Joe asked as he moved from the bale.

"The girl. The car accident," he sputtered again.

"Elizabeth?" Evie whispered as the guns shook in her outstretched arms, still pointing at the pile on the ground.

"My Elizabeth? What do you mean?" Joe yelled, now standing next to Evie. *Joe's shop. V is the girl in the picture next to Elizabeth. The girl with the hidden face.* Delaney watched as Joe and his daughter's best friend stood screaming over Gunnar.

"Back up, Joe," Evie pointed the gun in her left hand at his chest.

"The girl. It wasn't an accident," he choked out. "It was Henry who murdered her. I made it look like –" He muttered his last words before exhaling for the final time. His body lied motionless against the concrete.

"Like what?" Joe yelled, kicking his body until it flopped around on its back. The shiny blue eyes stared up at the ceiling, completely empty. "Dammit." Joe kicked Gunnar's body again before falling back onto the bale. Delaney's eyes followed Evie as she bent down, a foot away from his body, and emptied one last shot from his own .22 into his skull. The single shot rung in her ears.

"Goddammit, Evie!" Joe kicked the bale underneath him with the back of his boot.

"Do you think..." Evie started, examining Joe's face as she put the guns at her side. He collapsed his head into his hands. Evie cleared her throat, her voice slow and methodical as she processed the information. "Elizabeth never drove that fast," her voice soft as she worked out the possibility in her head.

"I know she didn't," Joe responded into the stifled air. The wind creaked against the walls. "It never made sense to me that she would have been driving fast enough to have hit that tree. It seemed all wrong to me, but she was gone, and I didn't have anyone. I should have asked more questions, but your father." Joe fell onto the bale; his body slumped forward as the details flushed through his head.

"He took care of it," Evie whispered. "But Henry?"

"Who's Henry?" Joe asked.

"A guy I met during the summer Elizabeth was murdered," Evie started.

"Murdered," Joe repeated in disbelief.

"I met him on one of the construction sites. He was a good guy. I thought," she said. "I have to believe he was. I can't believe this murderer on the ground." Evie waved the barrel at Gunnar.

"He killed Henry?" Joe asked, still trying to catch up.

"Yeah, Gunnar shot him right in front of me. My father was there. They both claimed Henry was going to hurt me, but I didn't believe them," Evie replied.

"I knew something wasn't right," Joe said, looking toward Delaney on the other side of the pen.

"What wasn't right?" Evie prodded.

"That your father was hiding something. Not without a doubt, but I suspected something a few months back. Your father started to get real short with me when I started talking about Elizabeth. Almost angry. There was something that I was missing. So I followed him a bit, got close to Gunnar by fixing his car and then your father asked me to help her out," he nodded toward Delaney who was huddled against the poles, trying to conserve any warmth within her body. Her body had gone into survival mode. Her eyes perked up as she felt the other two looking at her. *To help me out. The accident… it wasn't an accident.* The car's lights illuminated so fast in front of her, appearing from nowhere. *It wasn't an accident.*

"And when the blood was found on campus, I knew it had something to do with Holston. I had just picked her up and found a Leighton football roster in her car. I knew there was something with her and the student. So I saw a chance. A chance to play his game to find out the truth, but I never wanted to believe it, Evie. Not Elizabeth. She didn't deserve it." Joe's voice shook beneath his hands. He looked up at Evie, his eyes bloodshot with years of pain and suffering from the loss of his daughter.

"I know she didn't," Evie rushed, her voice louder and stronger. "But Henry? I don't believe it. Gunnar killed Elizabeth."

"I don't know, Evie. I guess they could have made it look like an accident. I wouldn't have been able to live knowing that my Elizabeth was murdered. I would have killed that Henry kid, but it seems like Gunnar took care of that," Joe replied.

"But why Elizabeth?" Evie whispered into the darkness.

"I don't know." Joe shook his head, looking up at the girl his dead daughter had once called her best friend. The little girl he once taught how to ride a bike now stood erect before him, handguns gripped in both hands while standing in a pool of blood. "What is your father doing hiring rapists and murderers? Who is he?"

Evie shook her head as she kicked Gunnar's lifeless body on the cement.

"Before Elizabeth died, I…" Joe started as the wind whistled again, drafting frozen air into the barn.

"You what?" Evie prodded.

"I was looking into your mom. Elizabeth asked me to do it as a favor for her and for you." His eyes met Evie's as his voice trembled.

"My mom," Evie whispered. A heaviness fell on her chest as the memories of the late nights talking with Elizabeth about her mother surfaced. A mother she had never known.

"She said that you didn't know her name. That she was dead. A waitress from some obscure town that he had met and gotten pregnant. She gave the baby, *you*," he nodded toward Evie "to your father to raise and that shortly after giving birth, she died in a car accident." He paused, looking back down at the pool of blood now seeping close to his feet.

"He told me a car accident, too," Evie whispered. Delaney watched on the other side of the pen as the story of the two strangers unfolded, their pasts intertwined. *But why am I here?*

"Elizabeth said that you found a picture at the cabin and that you wanted to know who she was. Just so you knew who you came from. And Elizabeth," he stumbled on her name. "Sweet Elizabeth just wanted to help you. She loved you so much, and I loved her."

Evie shifted her legs before bending down close to the ground, resting the point of the guns on the concrete. Any color she had drained from her face as she listened to Joe's voice.

"I was looking into it, and Holston must have known what I found," Joe added.

"What?" Evie whispered.

"Your mother. She had a family of her own. A husband. Kids."

"A family? Is she alive?" Evie stood back up, guns rested on her hips.

"She might be. I don't know. I stopped looking into it after

Elizabeth died. I just couldn't do it anymore. I didn't have the energy," he stammered. "But I had no idea who your dad was. I still don't know." His shoulders shuddered as he put his head down again.

"Henry couldn't have," Evie whispered. It couldn't be Henry. It had to be Gunnar.

"Holston Parker. Who is he?" Joe asked.

"A killer hiding in plain sight." Evie's words echoed off the walls, resonating in Delaney's ears. Holston Parker was a killer, and he was after her and her family, but she still didn't know why. The pieces floated around her head, unable to connect. She looked at Joe's face, stricken with a revelation that altered his inner core. He was unable to speak, silent as the information penetrated him.

"I know, Joe. It happened for me ten years ago, in this same exact place. Gunnar killed Henry here and my father; he was the one that told him to do it. I've been waiting since then. Waiting to seek my revenge," Evie looked back at Delaney still standing on the other side of the pen. Delaney shifted her body, silent. *What do you want?* "And now Elizabeth. He'll pay for all the wrong he has done." Evie stood straight, slipping one of the guns into the holster.

"Evie, you don't know that it was Gunnar. It could have been Henry," Joe said.

"You're going to believe this thug on the ground?" Evie asked.

"I don't know. I don't know what or who to believe." Joe's voice trailed as he turned again toward Delaney. "But what about *her?* What about that kid? Is he alive?"

"He's alive." Evie bent down, patting down the pockets of the dead body on the concrete. "And for her, I don't know *why* her, but I know that she's important to him." Evie stopped as she caught the glimpse of the beginning of ink near his wrist. She pulled up his sleeve, revealing the initials that ran up his arm.

"Initials," Joe answered Evie's silent question.

"Of who?" Evie asked.

"The last one is the guy that he murdered in front of me," Delaney said, clearing her throat. She shifted her legs and stood up taller, eager to contribute information. She saw no other way out of this barn, out of the murderous mess without showing Evie her value.

"He killed someone in front of you," Evie repeated, turning to Delaney while still crouched on the ground.

"Yeah. The man who raped me when I was fourteen," Delaney added, "R.R. Richard Rowan."

"When?" Evie demanded.

"Two days ago. At your shop." Delaney nodded toward Joe. "After you left, Gunnar showed up with Richard Rowan in his trunk. He sunk a knife into his chest. Killed him within seconds. You could tell, he had done it before. He got pleasure out of it."

"And you didn't tell anyone?" Evie grilled.

"He threatened me," Delaney shot back. "You didn't tell anyone, either, about that Henry kid." Delaney straightened her body, defending her actions.

"I didn't," Evie replied, turning back to Gunnar's arm. She pulled the sleeve all the way up, revealing the remaining initials lining his arm. "There are twenty-two initials."

"Gunnar's killed twenty-two people?" Joe asked in disbelief. "For Holston?"

"I didn't know there were this many," Evie said as she scanned the arm. "H.T. Henry Thomas." She reached into her pocket and retrieved her phone. The white flash illuminated the dark barn as Evie snapped a picture of the tattoos.

"Evie," Joe started as he moved closer to her.

"You better go, Joe." Evie stood up, staring up into his wrinkled eyes.

"Do you have that kid?"

"Joe, you better go," Evie repeated.

"Evie, you're in over your head. What are you going to do with him?" He nodded down at the body.

"Joe, you need to go. My father can't know you were here. Just go. I will take care of him." Evie backed away, holding the keys to the handcuffs tight in her hand.

"I can help," Joe continued, his gentle eyes agonized.

"No, you can't. You have to go. I've got this. I will avenge Elizabeth for you. For the both of us. I promise you that." A tear dropped from Joe's eye as he studied the holster, now hanging in sight. She held the gun tightly in her other hand. The sweet girls he had known were long gone. He turned to open the gate, moving toward Delaney.

"Take care of yourself, Evie," he said as he walked through the gate. "And you, Delaney," he whispered as he moved passed both the women into the darkness of the barn. Evie followed him through the gate, setting her eyes on a shivering Delaney against the bars of the pen. Delaney flinched as Evie grabbed her hands, swinging her around to expose the handcuffs. Evie slid the key in, turning it with a click.

"I'm V," she said, turning to look up at Delaney.

"I've gathered that," Delaney responded, pulling her arms from behind her back. Pain shot through her wrists as she rubbed them with her fingertips. "I guess I should thank you. At least, I think."

"Not yet, but that asshole was the one who took Theron and carved him open. And he kidnapped you to try to get to me. To try to find out where Theron was. I'm guessing he was supposed to scare him, not kill him. He certainly wasn't supposed to slice him with a machete." Evie nodded to the body in the pen. "But he's safe now," she added as she moved back into the pen.

"Where is he?" Delaney prodded.

"He's stable, but he'll need some help soon. You need to trust me, D. I saved your life," Evie spat back as she sifted through the body's pockets again.

"You used me. As a decoy, for whatever this… this mess is," Delaney yelled back. Her heart thudded against her chest.

"I did," Evie replied, unforgiving. "But you slept with a student and you whore yourself out for men on the internet."

"I don't whore myself out," Delaney shot back. "And why does your dad, my brother's boss, care about me? What the hell did I do?" Delaney grabbed onto the poles to steady herself. *I should run. But no keys. The snow.*

"The truth? The truth is that I don't know yet. I know that you fucked that kid, and Gunnar killed the man that raped you. Other than that, I don't know. But, I know that you matter, and I know that you need to trust me if you want to get out of this alive."

Evie began lifting the bales and rolling them alongside the wall. Delaney watched as the slight woman with shocking strength, stacked the bales on top of each other until they reached the wooden planks. Evie looked around, shining the light to their surroundings before slitting the strings of the bale on the top of the stack with a knife she had pulled from her pocket. Evie's petite hands scattered the loose straw around the tower.

"What are you doing?" Delaney asked as Evie slid her hand into another pocket near the knee of her pants. *Who the hell is she?*

"Taking care of this place by doing what I was promised would be done more than ten years ago," Evie added as she retrieved something that fit in the palm of her hand. Several clicks sounded before the red flicker of a flame illuminated from her hand. Evie raised it and held it there, meeting the dry straw near her head until the red spread in front of her. The smoke rose as she waved her hand back and forth, making the flames dance across the yellow strands. It spread quick, swallowing the dry straw with each second as it ignited the top bale resting against the wood planks. *She's burning it down.*

"It should be enough. It's done," Evie whispered as she slid back through the gate to stand next to Delaney. "We have to go. Theron doesn't have much time left."

31

A haze of smoke crawled up toward the peak of the barn as the flames flickered in Delaney's eyes. She felt a compelling urge to trust the woman standing next to her, as crazy as it was. Delaney had no choice except to trust her. Evie had saved her. She had Theron. And she wanted to seek revenge on her father, a homicidal maniac.

"Let's go," Delaney pleaded. Evie stood immobile, eyes transfixed on the billowing haze and orange color that multiplied across the brittle straw. Evie was right. The fire would take. The straw and wood on the barn was weathered and dry. It would ignite and spread fast.

"Over one hundred-years-old. And just like that. Poof. It's gone." Evie smiled before turning the beam of the light to the walkway ahead, falling into a slow jog. Delaney followed her footsteps down the concrete. Her feet like clubs against the hard surface.

"By the way, are you okay?" Evie's voice split through the crackle behind them.

"Yeah, I'm fine," she lied. *Besides the raging headache, numb feet, frozen fingers, and emotional trauma. Yeah, fine.*

"If you want to get out of here, alive, then you're going to have to follow my lead. And you're not going to want to lie." She spun to look at Delaney's face. "That shit doesn't work for me."

"I feel like death then. Not quite warmed over," Delaney replied. "Is that better?"

"I have a jacket in the car. You can put my boots on when we get in, but for now, we have to keep moving." The fire smoked behind them as it spread up to the wall. Several feet of the wooden planks had ignited, illuminating the pen below. Delaney looked back at the body of the man that had beaten her. It was the same man that had closed her wound that had festered for fourteen years and for that, she was grateful, but she had seen his crazed eyes as he'd beaten her. He was a killer. She envisioned Gunnar in flames, his body melting to ash. She turned back to meet Evie's eyes.

"He killed a lot of innocent people. He got what he deserved." Evie turned back, flashing the light to the opening of the old milk house.

"Not all innocent," Delaney muttered under her breath. She didn't want to get into it with Evie. She just needed to get out of the barn and into any place that was warm. Safe. The gray barn blurred in Delaney's mind as she stumbled forward, trying to keep up with the footsteps in front of her when a now familiar sound rung through her ears.

BANG. Pause. BANG. BANG. The gunshots echoed on the other side of the wall, outside.

Evie skidded to a stop and pointed the flashlight on the ground. "Stay here."

"Don't leave me!" Delaney's voice strained to maintain a whisper as she grabbed the air looking for Evie's arm. She was gone. Delaney slid against the wall near the opening of the door to the milk house. Her surroundings were only lit in a slight glow from the fire at the other end of the barn, which revealed the perimeter of the walls. They were made from cement blocks that only reached her chest. As she continued to look around, her eyes caught a glimmer near the floor.

"There are two of them," Evie's voice whispered near the opening of the milk house. *Two of them?* Delaney's eyes fixated on the object's silhouette a few feet from her. *A hatchet.*

"They must have followed Gunnar here," Evie added.

"Who?"

"More of my father's employees."

"You're an employee. My brother's an employee."

"Obviously, not that kind of employee," Evie whispered. She paused before adding, "I thought Gunnar was the only one. I checked over and over. In Wisconsin, Illinois, California. The whole U.S." The anger welled in Evie's voice.

"The shots?"

"Joe. Had to be Joe," Evie said, "I didn't see him. It was too dark, but I did see two men coming from the shed. We can't go out this door. We have to go out the other end." Evie motioned the light, still on the ground, along the concrete toward the fire. Delaney lunged to the side and wrapped her fingers around the hatchet's wooden handle, her aching skin pulling tightly across her hand.

"Follow me," Evie whispered as she sprinted down the walkway. Delaney propelled forward toward the flames, her legs moving as the darkness disappeared behind her. She felt the air warm as they drew closer; her body craved the heat despite its danger. Evie pointed to the right of the pen as they neared the end of the barn then lowered herself to avoid the thick haze of smoke that was developing. Just a foot behind her, Delaney inhaled. The sudden burn spread through her throat sending her into a coughing rage as she bent down lower, searching for oxygen while the smoke scorched her eyes. Delaney blinked wildly before putting the inside of her elbow to her face.

When Evie wrapped a hand around Delaney's arm, pulling her forward, a shot suddenly reverberated through the air. This time, inside the building.

"GO!" Evie yelled, yanking Delaney's arm to the opening on the right side of the pen. Delaney stumbled forward through the thick smoke, still coughing into her elbow. A warm, lightness began to creep over her head as she gasped for air.

Another shot, this one louder, flew passed her head. Delaney's feet stumbled through the opening to cleaner air only laced with a small haze that was rising to the forty foot peaks.

"UP!" Evie yelled in her ear. Evie pointed the flashlight at the wooden beams twenty feet in the air before flicking it off, shoving it and the gun into the waist of her pants.

No. Delaney shook her head, bending down for the cleaner air.

"CLIMB!" Evie ordered. She jumped up, grabbing the decaying wooden slats that started near her head and swung her feet up. Old wire laced together wove between the slats, leading to the beams. Evie flew up, moving her hands and feet in easy synchronization. Delaney stuck the hatchet in the waist of her pants and jumped, her legs kicking the air as she swung them up, trying to get footing. The flat edge of the hatchet slammed into her chest as Delaney gave a final swing. She felt a hardness on her foot as she looked to see it resting on a slat.

"FASTER!" Evie yelled from the nearest beam. She had the .9 millimeter in one hand while Gunnar's .22 rested on the beam.

Delaney grabbed the wire, moving her body up the wall of broken wood and jaded wire, when a sharpness jolted through Delaney's fingers with her next grab. The wire had sliced her hand. She pulled back her hand, grabbing higher as the warm liquid ran down her wrist. Each new foot holding shot tingling pain through her legs as she moved up, now only a few feet from the beam. The metal of the hatchet dug into Delaney's chest, the sharp end flanked outward. The sound of a man coughing became louder.

"Hurry!" Evie whispered, holding out her hand. Delaney grabbed it, feeling the warmth against her own frozen fingers as her hand absorbed Evie's. Delaney's arm yanked up as she felt the heaviness of her body lift upward. Delaney's knees throbbed against the splintered wood as she shuffled them along the thick beam.

A silhouette of a man burst through the smoke as a crouched Evie aimed her gun at him. Her hand steadied, following his movement. *What are you waiting for? SHOOT HIM!* Delaney's head screamed as she watched the man slide back against the wall. Her throat crawled from the smoke like a nest of spiders erupting in her neck. Delaney stifled her cough in her elbow, swallowing to attempt to abide the dryness. Bending her head down closer to the beam, she inched lower from the smoke gathering in the peak.

Delaney slid her hand out from beneath her, trying to adjust her position on the beam and watched the second man rush through the opening. He had his hands on his knees as he coughed into his arm. The hard barrel of the other gun, still resting on the beam, grazed Delaney's knuckles. She stopped, watching the shadowed outline of the gun creep toward the edge, tipping slowly toward the ground. Delaney's outstretched hand grasped nothing as the gun flipped over the edge, plummeting to the concrete with a clank. *We're dead.*

A barrage of shots escaped from five feet away as Evie aimed at the man against the wall. Delaney flattened herself against the beam, landing on the handle of the hatchet still tucked into her pants. Pain shot to her ribs as she gasped for air.

Two shots returned from the wall. Delaney felt a vibration in the wood before she heard the scream. *Evie was hit.* Her eyes shot up to see Evie hanging onto the wooden beam with one arm. She was still emptying shots with the gun in her other hand. Delaney slid forward on her belly, shimmying closer to Evie's hand before the second man stood erect, directly below them, and took aim at the rafters. Delaney covered her head as the gun echoed against the walls, connecting with the beam ahead of her.

The sound of a thud registered in Delaney's ears. *EVIE!* Delaney crept her eyes over the edge of the beam to see two bodies entangled on the concrete. Evie's cries echoed through the barn. Delaney swung her legs down toward the wire and wood planks with her arms still wrapped around the thick beam and then let go, sliding five feet before catching her feet on the planks. The wire scraped against her body and feet as she slid down again, now only a few feet from the bottom. She slid the hatchet out from its place tucked into her pants, gripping it firmly in her right hand.

More screams. Delaney exhaled and released her other hand, plunging to the hard concrete below. Pain jolted her body as her feet hit the surface. She lunged forward until her knees cracked against the concrete and the sound of metal clanged next to her. She continued to hold fast to the handle of the hatchet as she peered forward. She saw the shadow of the first man slumped against the wall. *Dead.*

"Where is she?" the man yelled between Evie's cries as he kicked his leg into her abdomen. *He didn't hear me.*

"Where is she?" he screamed again as he grabbed a fist of hair and yanked her up.

"LET GO!" Evie shrieked as she kicked her legs.

"Not until I know where she is," he yelled again. *Me?* He looked at Evie underneath his hand, his back facing Delaney. Delaney inched her body up to a stand, holding the hatchet close to her body. She stopped, narrowing in on Evie's face twisted with pain. Delaney squinted through the darkness, watching as he shoved his finger into Evie's arm. Evie let out a high-pitched scream.

"He must of hit you, huh? Does that help you remember where she is?" *I have no choice.* She raised the hatchet up, the sharp blade poised in the air ready to land the blow. She wasn't a killer, not like Gunnar, not like Evie, but she had to get out of the barn. She had to save Theron, Mark, Ben... James. Delaney swung her arm down, feeling the hatchet stop when it made contact against his skull. The sound of the thud shuddered through her body. Delaney pulled back, ready to make another attack, but the handle didn't move. It was lodged deep in his head. Delaney let go of the handle, watching his body slump forward as his hand released Evie's hair.

"The guns," Delaney's voice cut through the air. Evie fell to her knees, scattering her hands along the concrete. Delaney followed, searching for the guns along the cracks. A groan came from the slump on the ground. Delaney looked up, contemplating trying to pull the hatchet out again and delivering another blow.

"I got it," Evie said as she jumped to her feet with her left arm hanging limply against her side. Then she leaned down, bent her head over like she had with Gunnar and emptied two shots into his head. The smoke had begun to pour into the opening, stinging Delaney's eyes.

"We've gotta get out of here," Delaney yelled as she grabbed Evie's other arm that still held the gun.

"The other guy."

"He's dead. Let's go."

"Hang on." Evie crept forward to the man slumped against the wall. She raised the gun to his head and, like the previous two, shot bullets into his skull before kicking him over. Evie bent down to examine his face in the darkness. "I didn't know either of them."

"Let's go," Delaney coughed into her sleeve, bending down until her knees almost touched the ground. The warm, light feeling in her head returned.

"The door's this way." Evie emerged from the smoke, stumbling forward away from the opening. Delaney turned around, following Evie straight forward through the vast, empty space to the other end. They reached the cement blocks of the wall as the smoke swirled around them.

"Where is it?" Delaney fumbled along the wall.

"Go left. I'll go right," Evie ordered. Delaney turned her head toward her weakening voice as her hands ran along the clammy cement.

"Where the hell is it?" Delaney cried out as smoke filtered into her lungs.

"I know it's here. Somewhere." Evie's voice was now further away from Delaney as they parted, searching along the wall.

"Any chance it's boarded up? Gone?" Delaney yelled,

frantic as she stubbed her toe along a rise in the concrete.

"I don't know, but we have to find a way out of here, and we can't go back through the smoke," Evie shouted back. "Get down on your knees!" Delaney fell onto her battered knees, crawling along the concrete and running her right hand along the wall, searching for a break in the cement.

"I hit the corner! Should I check this wall or come back your way?" Delaney yelled.

Silence.

"EVIE!" Delaney's scream ended with a cough as the smoke burned her lungs.

"I got it," Evie's voice, barely audible, called from the other side of the barn. "DELANEY! I got it. Come back the way we started." Evie pushed the rusted handle down and pushed her weight forward, but the door didn't budge.

"EVIE!" Delaney called out as she sprinted along the cement wall.

"Follow my voice, Delaney. Here. I pushed the handle down, but the door won't go," Evie grunted as she bent down and shoved her right shoulder into the wooden slab. The door remained unmoved.

"WHAT?" Delaney yelled as she neared Evie.

"The door. It's stuck. It's gotta be the snow," Evie grunted again, ramming the door with her shoulder. The door cracked open an inch. Evie felt the cold draft brush against her face through the small opening. Fresh air. Evie inhaled the oxygen, feeling the coldness cleanse her nostrils.

"Evie?" Delaney reached out her hand, searching for Evie.

"OW!" Evie yelled as Delaney grabbed her arm. Evie pulled back and cradled her arm with her other hand. The blood was still pouring from where the bullet had entered her arm.

"Sorry," Delaney apologized as she felt the cool draft escaping through the crack.

"It moved a bit. Shoulder it on my count. One, two, three, PUSH!" They sprung forward, slamming the door with their shoulders. More cold air rushed in.

"It's open, maybe three inches. Again, on my count. One, two, three, PUSH!" Delaney felt the dull throb against her shoulder as she shoved the wooden slab with her shoulder, and more of the precious oxygen poured in. *Life.* Evie tried to wedge her body through the door.

"There's no way my head will fit," Evie's voice coughed.

"Push some of the snow out of the way," Delaney suggested. She bent down and wrapped her hands around the outside of the door. Delaney shoved her hand down into the heavy layers of snow, partially wet from the afternoon sun and scooped it away.

"It's going to take too long," Evie rasped.

"It's our only chance. Just move over and stay on the ground," Delaney yelled as she nudged Evie over to get a better angle through the door. Her numb hand barely felt the temperature difference as she continued to scoop and toss. Delaney sunk her hand again when she felt something hard against her own. *A hand?*

"MOVE!" A man's voice yelled from the other side of the door as he dug frantically through the snow with his gloved hands. Delaney retreated her hand, pulling it back into the barn before tucking it in her blazer.

"JOE?"

"PUSH!" The voice ordered as he wrapped his hands around the door, yanking it out toward the snow. Delaney lowered her shoulder, shoving the slab again and causing it to crack open several more inches. The clean air hit Delaney's lungs, immediately invigorating her senses. She gulped the oxygen, feeling the life pump through her veins.

"EVIE, let's go!" Delaney began to wedge herself through the door, but there was no response. "Evie?" Delaney bent down, feeling around for Evie in the dark against the wall. She felt Evie's body, slumped against the wall. Delaney grabbed her arm and pulled her closer to the opening of the door. The gloved hands reached for the door again, opening it even further.

"COME ON!" the man's voice exploded. Delaney wedged through the door. Her bare feet sunk into wetness as she met the man's eyes set in a chiseled face that wasn't Joe's. *The bartender.*

"Where's V?" he yelled in her blank face.

"She's passed out. Help me pull her through." Delaney bent down, shoved her hand through the opening, and grabbed Evie's arm. Delaney managed to yank her several inches closer to the door, but Evie's body was jammed against the wall.

"MOVE!" Ethan moved forward, pushing Delaney off to the side and into the snow. Delaney lied there, feeling the moisture sink into her clothes and letting the air penetrate her entire being. His hand disappeared into the opening and retrieved more of Evie's body.

"She's stuck," Ethan grunted as he pulled Evie's body harder before turning to Delaney, motioning his hands. "You gotta go back in and turn her body so it can be pulled through the door."

"The smoke…" Delaney started as she watched the smoke streaming through the crack. *She had to go in, though. Evie had saved her life.*

"GO NOW!" He stormed toward Delaney. "Cover your face with this." He peeled off his glove and handed it to her. Delaney scrambled to her feet, glove over her mouth, and slipped back through the opening over Evie's body into the smoke while Ethan continued to shovel with his hands. Delaney squinted, desperate to shut out the slow burn that agonized her eyes. She dropped down and fumbled to find Evie's legs. Evie's body was contorted and folded against itself. Delaney straightened Evie's legs and angled her head toward the opening of the door as Ethan's hands wrapped around the door, pulling it open further.

"Try again!" Delaney sputtered as the smoke scorched her lungs before she could get the wet glove back up to her mouth. Pushing Evie's body forward with one hand, it moved toward the door slowly. Delaney pushed harder until the body suddenly vanished from beneath her hand.

"I got her! COME ON!" he shouted through the door. Delany crept forward as her lungs blackened and her head spun. It became lighter and lighter with each movement. *It's so close. The door. I need air. Fresh air.* Delaney clawed forward, feeling the cold flow over her head before she felt her body empty into total blackness.

32

DAY 4: December 21 – 5:45 p.m.

"I've got 'em." The words rang in the back of her head as she fought to open her eyes. Her head screamed from the repetitive pounding. The rapid beating of what felt like a hammer against her skull echoed through her head. His voice was close. Warmth blew on her face and feet while tiny needles stabbed at her feet as the heat penetrated her skin.

"Yeah, both of them." His voice was louder, clearer. She felt her body shift to the side, brushing up against hard plastic. They were moving. The man talking cleared his throat.

"She was hit in the arm, but I've stopped the bleeding, for now. She's going to need help." Eyes still closed, Delaney concentrated on her arm but didn't feel pain there. Just everywhere else. *Evie.* Delaney's eyes peeled open. She felt the sting of the salt and smoke coat her lids as she blinked, adjusting to the glowing lights in front of her. *A car.*

"Only a few minutes. In the back." Delaney turned to see the chiseled profile of the man in the driver's seat, phone to his ear. *The bartender. The fire.* Her mind shot to the small opening of the door and outstretched hand she was crawling to before it all went black. *It was his hand.* He clicked off the phone, turning to

223

her in the passenger seat. *Where was Theron?*

"You're awake," he said. She opened her mouth, but her throat felt scorched with ash and refused to form the words.

"Here." His hand extended a half-empty bottle of water to her. She took it in her hands, desperate to stop the burn lodged in her throat. The bottle reached her lips before she stopped, looking back at him while he studied her. He couldn't be trusted. No one could be trusted anymore. She pulled the bottle back down to her lap before handing it back to him.

"There's nothing in it," he said. She thrust the bottle back in his lap while her throat crawled.

"See?" He took a small drink and offered it back to her, his eyes half on the road ahead of him. "Just take it. Your throat has to be burning. You inhaled a lot of smoke." She felt the plastic crunch in her hands as she brought it to her lips and felt the cool liquid slide down her throat, soothing it for a second. She paused, letting the bottle rest in her hand, as she looked back at his profile staring at the road ahead. Tipping the bottle back, she gulped it down, her throat and mouth desperate to relieve the sting.

"Better?" he asked.

"A little."

"I'm Ethan by the way. Are you okay?"

"I don't know." She twisted her head to the left as she recognized Evie's black boots in the corner of her eye. Turning further, the pain in her neck amplified before she made out the rest of Evie's body. A white bandage was wrapped around her arm and her body lied still except for the gentle rocking caused by the car. Her arms rested behind her back. *She's alive.* About to turn around, Delaney spotted white around her black boots. *And tied up.*

"It's for her own good." His voice pulled her back to the front.

"What does that mean?" The headlights slowed as they turned onto the main street of downtown Appleton. A section of the Leighton campus lined the left side of the street. Delaney's eyes fell to the large oak trees running alongside the sidewalks where large, blue ribbons were tied tight around the thick trunks of the trees. As she scanned the trees, her eyes fell onto a small group of students huddled near the next tree. A woman reached inside the backpack of a man next to her. The blue fabric fluttered in the wind before she gathered it in and wrapped it around the bare tree. Another man armed with flyers pointed to the other side of the street where more bare trees were located. They were students looking for Theron.

"She knows where Theron is," Delaney started. "He needs help and you have her tied up in the back seat."

"It's for her own good," he repeated. "She's safe this way."

"Safe? Is Theron safe?"

Delaney's head jerked forward as Ethan hit the brake, letting the engine idle to a stop. *Red light.* She pulled her head up to look at the familiar buildings edging the street. *I need to get out.* She reached her hand up slowly, placing it on the handle of the door before a clicking sound registered in her head. As she glanced back toward Ethan, she could see his hand resting on the door controls.

"Don't even think about it." He turned to her while he slid his other hand into his jacket. He pulled out a gun, placing it on his lap.

"What the hell is going on?" Delaney spat back as she sunk back into the seat. "Who the hell are you? Who was that back at the barn? Why is this happening?" Her head fell into her bloodied hands. *The jacket. Evie. The fire. Holston Parker.* It didn't make any sense. *Why me?*

"We'll be there soon, and if you can't control yourself, I'll tie you up, too." He smiled as he looked back at her. "I figured you wouldn't fight. I guess I was wrong about you."

"Evie, is she okay?" she asked. *He was wrong about me?* She had only seen Ethan three times in her life, twice at Atlas Pub and now. She had barely uttered any words to him.

"She was hit in the arm. The bullet's still in there. And she inhaled a lot of smoke."

"What about my brother? James?" Her voice hesitated, wary of the answer. The sound of shots resonated through her head. *What did I get them into?*

"Those two?" He laughed as he hit his foot against the gas in response to the green light ahead. Delaney's body stiffened with dread. "They're fine. Passed out in the back of the pub. Thanks to me." He jerked the car to the right, turning down a side street before taking another right into an alley. She exhaled. Relief flooded her body as she watched the alley narrow. The car stopped.

"We're here."

"Here?" Delaney asked, looking at the backs of a row of buildings.

"Yeah. And like I said, if you run or fight..." He slid the gun in his hand and tapped it against his leg.

"What do you even want from me?" She looked back at Evie bound in the seat behind her. *Where did she put Theron?*

"First of all, let's get something straight. It's not me. It's him." He tapped the gun against his window at the brick building adorned with a worn, metal sign with vintage letters. *The Apothecary Shop.*

"The Apothecary Shop?" she asked.

"Mr. Parker is waiting for you. For her." He nodded to the back seat. "He wants to have a quick chat with you both."

"Holston Parker?"

"Yeah. Your brother's new employer. My boss. Her dad." His voice became impatient as he turned to open his door.

"Wait. Why?" she pleaded.

"Listen, all I know is that you better do what he tells you. He's powerful, D." He lingered on his last word, smirking at her. The chat room. *This is a sick game.*

"Yeah, he knows about your little secret." He paused, contemplating his next words. "He told me to request a show. To see what you were doing," he added, his eyes dominated her as he looked at her chest. She wrapped the blazer tight around herself.

"Asshole," she spat.

"Don't worry, it was only once. You denied me after that," he replied. "Although, I could have handled another show." Delaney's body crawled as his eyes fixated on her. She had only stripped a few times in that first week and apparently Ethan had been one of them. She had never seen their faces, so they hadn't been real people to her. She reached up to slap his face.

"Whoa!" Ethan warned, catching her hand mid-air before it landed. She wound up and spit into his face, just under his eye.

"Really?" He let her arm go and wiped away the spit with the back of his hand. "Are you done?"

"I don't know," she retorted, falling back into the seat.

"You better be." He waved the gun in her face before he opened his door and swung his leg into the alley. Delaney eyed the keys dangling from the ignition. "I better take these," he added, sliding back into the car to grab the keys. She opened the door, feeling the cold wrap around her body, and slid her feet onto the icy layer that covered the concrete. Her toes curled as the temperature of the ice burned the bottoms of her feet. She scanned the alley, looking for anyone that might see her. There had to be someone out there. Somewhere she could run to. Someone who would hear her. She opened her mouth.

"Don't even think about it," Ethan's voice snapped behind her in a whisper. Delaney turned at the sound of another door shutting behind her to see the small body sprinting down the alley. *Evie.*

"V," Ethan yelled, sprinting after her. Delaney turned to the alley ahead of her, moving her legs forward into a run in the opposite direction. The nearest side street was only about thirty feet ahead of her. Her feet skid across the ice, trying to grip the surface, as she felt her leg give out from underneath her. Her toes flew in front of her face before the pain shot through her tailbone. The thud of her head against the ice registered before the pain radiated to her skull. Blackness.

***

"Don't say I didn't warn you, D," Ethan said as he hovered over Delaney's unconscious body, hoisting her up and over his shoulder. He had become adept at carrying bodies except, this time, the body was much lighter than what he was used to. He had been Holston's "removal man" for the past six months, disposing of bodies at his discretion. As long as he didn't have to kill them, he was fine with it. Gunnar took care of the "dirty" work. It was the least he could do for the man that had saved his life as a child, regardless that he feared and despised him at the same time. He disappeared into the metal door underneath *The*

Apothecary Shop sign and into the dim hallway. His eyes adjusted as he paused, looking for the stairwell.

"Where is she?" Holston's voice sounded down the hall.

"She... uh... she," he stuttered. "I've got Delaney here."

"I see that, but where is Evie, Ethan?" His voice neared as his audible footsteps made their way down the hall.

"She's gone," he stumbled on the words, looking down.

"Gone?"

"Yeah, she's gone."

"How could she possibly be gone?" Holston pressed, now only a foot away from Ethan. His steel eyes hardened, flashing even in the barely lit space.

"She somehow got out of the restraints. She must have had something, a knife or something, on her," he started, rushing his words. "I checked her, though. I patted her down, looked everywhere."

"Ethan," Holston spoke as if he was scolding a small child.

"Mr. Parker, I tied her up. She was passed out. She must have slit the ties when I was dealing with this one," Ethan replied as he hit Delaney's leg, her body still slung over his shoulder.

"And where do you suppose she went, Ethan?" His voice was calm and steady.

"I don't know, but she ran south, and I chased her for a bit before I saw this one run the other way."

"And?"

Ethan fidgeted, feeling the intense pressure of Holston's eyes penetrate into him. He had known Holston long enough to tell that he was losing his patience. His composed demeanor at the moment meant nothing to Ethan, he knew better. "Well, I figured you would find Evie, that she would come back, but this one, I didn't know." He spoke slowly, carefully choosing the words that articulated his lie. Ethan didn't think Evie would come back. He *knew* she wouldn't come back. Sweat poured down his forehead as he waited for his response.

"You're right. She will come around." Holston stepped back, taking the fedora off his head and resting it on his chest. "And the wound?"

"She'll need medical attention. The bullet's still lodged in her arm. She'll need someone to take it out," Ethan spoke truthfully.

"And anything else?"

"It looked like she was knocked around a bit, and it looks like this one was, too. She has blood on her head and possibly frostbite on her feet." He raised her feet up near his face.

"George and Frank?" Holston stood waiting for the report.

"I didn't find them, but three cars were there. I'm guessing that's where the bullet came from in Evie's arm. I'm sure they were in the barn."

"One from Evie." Holston waited, his eyes bearing into him again. "One from George and Frank, and the last car?"

"A black Buick. There was a body in the shed." Ethan paused. "It was Joe's."

"Joe?" His eyebrows and voice rose as he stepped back, closer to Ethan.

"Yes, Joe." Ethan's voice cracked. He had intentionally left the details of the barn out of their phone conversation on the way over, but he knew he would eventually have to tell him about Joe and the barn. Despite his size, Ethan knew that Holston Parker could and would end his life. "His body is in the trunk."

"The trunk," Holston repeated. He lowered his voice as his

hands gripped his hat.

"Yes." Ethan exhaled as he watched Holston rub the brim of his hat, running his hands across the fabric. Holston nodded his head while his steel eyes remained fixated on Ethan, the messenger.

"And the smoke?" His face sullen and unflinching. "I smelled it the moment you walked in the door." Ethan's eyes cast down to his feet. "Ethan, this has been a painful conversation so far and I have been nothing other than generous to you. I have much to do as you know. Did she burn it?" he hissed in the darkness.

"Yes."

"To the ground?" His voice was deep as his face and neck tensed, making Ethan cringe. He had never seen him like this despite the fact that Holston Parker had witnessed many murders. Burning a barn to the ground seemed much less offensive than killing.

"Yes, it's gone. Or it will be by the time anyone gets there. They were in the barn and the smoke was so thick. There's smoke inhalation, for the both of them…" Ethan felt the intense need to unfold the details for the unrelenting man.

"That's why you didn't find George and Frank. They were in the burning barn," Holston interrupted, his hand moving fast now against the brim. "Ethan." His voice boomed before he lowered it again. "Why didn't you tell me?"

"There was nothing to do. There was no time, so I just left and brought them here," he responded, shifting his feet. The weight of her body tugged on his own, the sweat now dripping down his back.

"Bring her upstairs. I'll be up in a minute." He turned his back to Ethan, slipping his phone from his pocket and bringing it to his ear. Ethan trudged forward onto the steps as Holston's voice carried into the stairwell.

"I just got word that my property at 2516 Larsen Road is on fire. I'm sure you've seen the dispatch. There will be two bodies in the barn. Convicted felons, released from prison. I do not know any of these men. They brought two cars to the scene, none of which are registered to me. One car is. It is my daughter's car. She's gone missing. I will take care of it. Your discretion is appreciated and will be awarded appropriately." He paused before answering, "Yes, I realize he'll be on it. I know he's close. Do your job." His voice disappeared into the hallway as Ethan neared the top of the stairs. Holston hadn't asked about Gunnar, and Ethan wasn't about to tell him. What would Holston do without his trusted hit man? He pulled the metal door open, the wheels squeaking against the track, and walked into the vast loft.

Ethan's eyes fell to the empty white cot across the room, blotted with red stains. Evie must have brought Theron here, but now he was gone. Ethan wondered how this had happened – how Evie had gotten to this point. He thought he would have known.

"On the other side. Put her down over there," Holston ordered as he appeared next to him, pointing across the room at the cot.

"Thank you for bringing *her* to me. Your services are no longer needed here. Go back to the pub. Make sure her friends don't wake up and take care of Joe." Holston paused as he spoke Joe's name before taking a glass vial out of his jacket. Inside was a single white cotton swab. "If she comes to you, bring her to me. You can go."

Ethan bent down, rolling Delaney's body onto the cot, when

he spotted a small, black bag strapped directly underneath it. He slid his hand beneath it, pulling it loose, as he pretended to check the lock mechanism of the wheels. Ethan shot his eyes up to see Holston's back, turned to him as he set his fedora on the table. Ethan slid the bag into his jacket before he walked across the loft and disappeared through the metal doors without saying a word.

***

Delaney's eyes fluttered open to the light above her, squinting as her eyes adjusted to the silhouette standing before her. His face demanded her attention before he stepped back, placing the cap on the small black tube filled with smelling salts.

"Welcome back." His voice was low and steady. "It's a pleasure to finally meet you." He held out his hand, firm, as if he was shaking the hand of a business associate. His gray eyes were set deep in his face among his high, tight cheekbones, just like the photo back at Atlas Pub. His black hair was speckled with gray, just as she remembered it from the hospital. It was him. *Holston Parker.* She lay still, unable to move her hand forward to meet his. The distinguished, mysterious killer stood before her.

"Breathtaking," he said as he studied her eyes first and then moved to her hair, reaching out to run the strands between his fingers. The sweet smell of cigars filled her nostrils before she flinched away, her body rigid, as she turned her head. Her eyes fell on the fedora, resting on the table next to her.

"Well, you'll warm up to me. You have no choice," he said as he leaned in. *You have no choice.* The words stuck in her throat as she watched him study her. Those were her mother's words. *Was it purposeful?* The anger welled in her body, consuming her

233

as she scanned the room.

Her eyes narrowed on a line running across the room. Hung from it were canvases with various shades of black and gray, but all forming one distinct and common feature - a barn. *Holston Parker is House_of_Steel.* She felt her stomach crawl up through her throat as she heaved, but her body was empty. Her head fell back onto the pillow beneath her.

"They are beautiful. Your work," he said, nodding up to her canvases strung across the room. Delaney let out a small moan of disgust, averting her eyes.

"After I saw the first one, I couldn't stop," he mused, walking over to the other side of the room to take a closer look. "Your passion. Your talent. It's astounding," he added as he looked up at the canvases. *I never should have done it.* "You never should have started your little masquerade, though. I needed you to stop your little shows with strangers, so I gave you a reason to. I hadn't intended to continue, but it became …" he paused to turn to her, lifting his hands in the air in a grand gesture as if he was about to say something earth-shattering, before he finished, "Curious. Addictive."

Holston strode back to her, his black jacket moving effortlessly with him across the room. She eyed his pristine gray pants and black shoes that exhibited a sheen only achieved by regular buffing. In his late fifties, she guessed, his face was taut and almost handsome-looking. Yet, she couldn't wrap her mind around his appeal, not with the frightening details that had unfolded in front of her. He was a monster, capable of things she couldn't even imagine. A beautiful creature capable of destroying her world. His mere presence made her body coil inward. *What does he want with me?*

"And you, of all people, know the true meaning of

curiosity, which is a cordial term for your addiction to your self-destruction. First, the indiscretion online, and second, the unfathomable. I can barely speak the words. The affair with your student," he said before adding, "but I'm getting ahead of myself. Let's go back."

"What do you want from me?" she uttered, her voice raspy.

"You knocked your head. On the ice," he said, not answering her question. *Evie. Did she get away?*

"She's gone, but she'll come back," he assured her, as if he knew what she was about to ask.

I'm alone. Delaney turned back to the vast, open space with exposed brick walls. Her eyes moved along the wall to the corner where a toilet and sink, recently installed, stood with no walls. She looked down at the white sheets underneath her, blotches of red soaking through the white near her right hand. She pulled her hand from the sheet, moving it to rest on her stomach. *Theron.*

"Evie had him here strapped down to the bed. His wound was covered and taken care of. She had even placed an IV in him," he continued, looking at the ground where an IV pump on a wheeled pole lay next to the bed. Delaney's eyes moved up to the table where empty plastic bags and medical supplies littered the surface next to his fedora. "She must have drugged him. The needle was on the table."

"Theron?" her voice rasped.

"He's taken care of," he replied, his hardened eyes unmoving from her as he slid down to sit on the cot next to her. Delaney cringed, pulling her legs toward her to inch away from his body. The weight of her feet felt like concrete blocks. She felt a sudden pang in her stomach.

"Taken care of? How exactly?" The words flooded from

her. "Like Henry?"

"So she told you about Henry?" He turned to her feet, placing another blanket around them. She looked down to see that her feet were wrapped tight with cloth. "Did she tell you she's had a hard life? A troubled past?"

"A troubled past because of you," she shot back.

"Delaney, love. Theron's alive, at the hospital by now," he replied. "I'm sure she didn't tell you everything about Henry. He was a barbaric young man with no hope. A rapist. A slaughterer. Despite my best attempts, he wasn't worthy of saving. I gave him a shot to work for me, but his darkness prevailed, leaving me with little to decide. After Gunnar found Elizabeth's strangled body in the field, it was just a matter of time before we found him. Evie had no idea." His eyes wandered out into the loft. *Theron's at the hospital, thank God.* Relief swarmed her body.

"They said it was an accident," Delaney prodded. Despite her urge to scream at the insanity of the Parker family, she found herself drawn to defend Evie. She had saved her, in a twisted sort of way, and now that Theron was alive, she felt a renewed sense of energy.

"Gunnar made it look like an accident. Joe wouldn't have been able to live knowing that his Elizabeth was murdered," Holston replied as he turned back to her. "And besides, we had destroyed the evidence. Henry that is."

"Leaving your own daughter shattered," Delaney muttered.

"My daughter," he paused, slow to let the word twist from his lips. "It wasn't time for Evie to know. Look what she's done," he replied, lifting his arms up toward the room.

"She's dying right now from a bullet lodged in her arm. It was one of your guys that shot her. You can live knowing that you killed your daughter?" Delaney asked.

"She'll come back." His eyes shifted to her. "You need to trust me."

"And if I don't?"

"There's no other choice. You need to trust me." Her mother's words stung her again.

"My mother," Delaney said. Her voice trailed through the air.

"Your mother is in good hands," he said as he peeled off his jacket. "Dr. Jackson is the best surgeon in the U.S. He'll take care of Ann, there's no doubt. He needed a little convincing, of course, to take her on such short notice." He reached out to touch Delaney's hand that lay on the cot. She pulled it away as if she had touched a hot fire. My mother, Ann Jones. The maniacal man before her was watching over her mother, over her. *Mark's boss*. A deep smile spread across his face.

"But why do you care?" she pressed.

"Your mother is an old friend of mine."

"She's never mentioned you," she replied. There was no way this man was a friend of her mother's.

"It was a long time ago, and Ann holds a special place with me." His words drifted.

"How so?" Delaney asked as she studied his face, trying to regain any control that she might possibly have. Although, she doubted there was anything she had control of at this point.

"That's all you need to know. If you do what I tell you, your mother will stay safe. If you don't, well, you know the devastating result. Your family would be crushed with her slow and painful end," Holston warned as his voice darkened. "And don't forget your devoted Mark and precious James, passed out just down the street."

The words hallowed her as she closed her eyes, trying to escape the cot. The room. Holston Parker. She had put everyone close to her in danger. The pain in her head radiated through her body ripping through her gut, leaving all of her exposed.

"But why me? What do you need from me?" Delaney asked as she slowly opened her eyes to see him standing next to the cot.

"I need your discretion, Delaney. You've made some huge errors in judgment. These things," he said as he moved his hand into his pocket of his pants, retrieving the pink satin fabric of her mask, "I thought you would clearly have sorted out by now." He held the mask from his forefinger and thumb, allowing it to dangle in front of her eyes.

"By now?" she accused. *How long has he known me?* "You almost killed me, running me off the road."

"I didn't almost kill you. Slowed you down, that's all. I've been around for a while, being silent, yet vigilant. But I couldn't be silent any longer. I needed to step in to stop the destruction. Do you think that Leighton would have hired you, a recent graduate, without a little encouragement? A little negotiating with the President?" He crumpled the fabric into his hand, squeezing it into a small ball before putting it back into his pocket. Delaney's face flushed. It had been a leap being hired at Leighton, but she thought she had earned the position with her graduate work and exhibits. Shame scolded her body.

"You're talented, no doubt about it. I've seen your work," he added, leaning toward her again, watching the color drain from her face. "No, not that work. Your paintings. I admire your painting, as you can see." He nodded toward the barns streaked across the room.

"What do you want?" Her eyes focused on the metal sliding

doors on the other end of the room. Her head screamed to her body to sprint out of the room, to rid Holston Parker from her life, but her body lie battered and bruised on the cot.

"Are you happy here?" he asked.

"I thought I was."

"Until?"

"Until this." She pointed to the streak of blood dried on the side of her face. "Until that." She pointed to her canvases hung in the air to mock her.

"I brought you here because I needed to keep an eye on you. Make sure Ann's daughter was staying in line. I needed to help you and your brother. I brought him here because I thought he would help you and *me.*" He paused before walking along the wall near the windows, covered with black tarps. "But this," he spread his arms out toward the room, "this was too much. This was too far. My Evie threatened that boy's life. She killed two of my employees. Two of her coworkers, and Joe is gone now, too. She created a mess that needs to be cleaned up."

Two? He couldn't possibly know I killed one. Delaney felt the handle of the hatchet in her hands, still stuck in the man's skull as she tried to pull it back. The sound of the metal hitting his skull crawled into her stomach as she pulled her knees into her chest to cradle them. Her stomach lurched again.

"That mess that she created. Tell me more Delaney. After all, this can be the first of many ways you can help me. See how this works? I help you. You help me. An understanding," Holston said as he walked back to the cot. "I've found that this is how all relationships work."

"But I don't want a relationship with you."

"It's too late. We already have one. You see, this could have all been avoided had you not made your errors in judgment.

Need I remind you? First, the mask. Second, the student. I was trying to help you," he added. His face was calm and steady, although she could feel his patience waning. "Gunnar was supposed to warn that boy. Keep him away from you, but my daughter took things into her own hands. That boy would have been fine had it not been for her. How Gunnar managed to split him open is beyond my understanding and once I find him, he will pay for his error of threatening that boy's life. Putting *me* in peril."

"Too late for that," she muttered under her breath. *He didn't know about Gunnar. Make it three employees.*

"I didn't quite hear what you said," he said, leaning in to her.

"It's too late for that. That bastard is gone."

"Gunnar?" he said, his eyes searching her for confirmation.

"Yes, Gunnar. The man who killed Richard Rowan in front of me two days ago. The man who kidnapped me to question me about Theron. The man who - "

"Killed Richard Rowan in front of you," Holston interrupted. "Where?"

"He stuck a knife in his chest and killed him in seconds. Why?"

"Where?"

"Joe's shop. I assumed it was you that called Joe to get me out of the ditch," Delaney accused. She felt the vulnerability seep into her bones as she added, "And you knew about Richard Rowan."

"I did. I know quite a few things about you, Delaney," he replied as he studied her face. Delaney shuddered, turning her eyes away from him. *How can I be tied to this man?* "And how did you feel watching him?"

240

"Disgusted," she replied, looking down at her dirty hands.

"Yet relieved," he suggested.

"Yes," she breathed, still unable to look at his eyes.

"It was warranted. Richard Rowan didn't have the right to walk this earth like you and me," he said.

"And Gunnar did? He did this to me," Delaney said, turning to face him. The dried blood ran down the side of her face from the large welts on her head.

"Gunnar has spent the last twenty years in redemption. He has saved himself from the sins he committed when he was young with the work he has done for me, but the time was nearing. He was straying from his work, resorting back to his old ways. It was becoming *addictive*," he replied. "And you know what that's like."

"Whatever sick game this is, I don't want to be a part of it. Your friend, Joe, is dead. Gunnar is dead and your daughter is dying as we sit here."

He smiled before his eyes became emotionless again. "Joe was a good man. Elizabeth was a special friend to my Evie. Special friends are important, aren't they?" he asked.

James. The hospital. She lied still, cradled on the cot. "Did you make the call to James's office?"

"Things were spiraling, as you know. It seemed necessary. Unsuspecting, caring person that James Anderson is. I have always been fond of him. He would be a good influence on you. He doesn't know, if you were wondering. He's oblivious to this all."

"Stay out of my life," she whispered.

"The barn?" His eyes darkened.

The barn was important to him. "Gone. She burned it to the ground with all three bodies in it." The words dripped from her mouth with pleasure.

"Quite a mess to be cleaned up," he responded as if a child had spilled a glass of milk on the table.

"What do you want from me?" Delaney pleaded.

"Your discretion."

"My discretion? If I help you, you'll leave my family alone?" Delaney shifted her body weight, leaning on her elbows. *I need to negotiate if I ever want to get out of this monster's wrath.*

"I will promise to leave the rest of your family alone, except for Ann, of course. I will continue to help her as I always have," he replied evenly. *Help?* Holston Parker had done nothing to help her, except to tear her life apart. There was no bargaining chip. There was little she could say.

"Mark and James? You will let them go?" she asked. Her heart slammed against her chest as she thought of Mark and James passed out in the bar, vulnerable.

"Yes. Mark will continue to work for me, and you, my dear, will continue to work at the university," he said, leaning in again. "And this. Everything that has happened, you will keep it to yourself. Sounds like a reasonable arrangement, doesn't it? You will find I am a reasonable man. Powerful, too. I have many arrangements with various constituents. The police being one."

Delaney studied his face, his words carefully formulated. He was warning Delaney, promising that she would suffer consequences if she went to the police. *I have no choice.* The words branded in her mind as a tear rolled down her cheek.

"How am I supposed to help you?" she asked, her voice small.

"You already have, my Delaney. You already have," Holston answered as his hand tightened around the glass vial inside his pocket.

33

Evie slumped lower, sinking into the sticky filth of trash bags and grease before silently swinging the cover toward her. Complete blackness. The nauseating stench of the industrial garbage permeated into her nostrils as she attempted to steady her breathing. She winced as she shifted her weight off her arm. The crinkle of the garbage bags filled the inside of the box. Evie froze as she listened to the footsteps coming closer. They paused.

She stopped breathing, feeling the excruciating pain radiate down her arm. The sound of footsteps registered again. This time, they were going back to the right. Ethan was going back the way they both had come from. He was going back for her. Ethan knew he needed Delaney, not her.

Evie waited, motionless, among the leftover French fries and half-eaten, stale buns from Atlas Pub. The smell of moldy, decomposed garbage made her eyes water as she bit down on her lip. A metallic taste soaked into her mouth before she realized she was bleeding. Her lungs burned with each breath of the cool, bacteria-filled air. She moved her right hand slowly up to the front of her left arm. The searing pain consumed her as her fingers felt the white gauze that covered the exposed, torn flesh.

A tourniquet had stopped the bleeding. She knew Ethan must have done it, but the bullet hadn't gone through, and she needed help. Someone needed to get the bullet out. She gasped as the fumes filtered through her airway; she needed air.

"One, two, three, four, five," Evie whispered before she rolled to her right side, against the metal wall. She pushed up, cracking the lid an inch. Her eye poked out to a dark and empty alley. Evie exhaled again before pushing the lid higher. With her knife clenched in her teeth, she hoisted herself with her right arm over the edge of the wall. Her black boots staggered onto the concrete among the patches of ice. She slid her hand into the empty pockets of her pants, checking to see if any of her other belongings remained. Ethan hadn't discovered her knife in her knee pocket, but her phone was gone, along with the picture of Gunnar's tattoos and her gun. They had pulled right in front of her loft, so Theron had to be safe; Holston couldn't make him disappear. He was too high-profile at this point.

"Be resourceful, Evie," she whispered as she looked at the back of Atlas Pub. Mark and James. Ethan had left them, most likely passed out, if not worse. Exactly what she needed. She slipped through the door. The clang of the bell dinged as she moved along the wall, leaning her back against the "Employees Only" sign. She reached her arm behind her and twisted the knob, cracking the door open to slip in.

Evie's hand fumbled against the wall, feeling for the light switch she knew was on her left. She had been in the stock room plenty of times before, but this night was different. Ethan wasn't here to protect her. To talk to her. To help her. She was running from him. She flicked the lights on.

"Turn it off," the voice groaned from the middle of the room. Mark and James's bodies were slumped together on the floor. Silver racks lined with bottles and cases that surrounded them on all sides. Evie caught movement from Mark, his body shifting against James.

"Move over," Mark slurred with his eyes still shut. Evie waited, watching Mark before his arms stopped moving. Their bodies were heavy, motionless; Ethan had drugged them at her request. She crept over to Mark and patted down his jacket. Nothing. She slid her hands into the left pocket of his jeans. Nothing. Evie winced as she crouched down and reached her hand underneath his body. She felt the hard plastic against his jeans, wedged between the floor and his body. He was lying on his phone. She knelt down, pushing his body over with her right arm. Just a few more inches.

"Get off!" Mark yelled as she latched onto his phone and slid it out from underneath him. She waited, still on her knees next to him. His eyes moved beneath his lids.

"Mark, it's V. Everything's fine," she whispered in his ear. He groaned in response before his head slumped to the ground again. She staggered up to her feet and put the phone into her pocket. As she was about to turn toward the door, she caught the shimmer of the racks. Alcohol.

Her boots stumbled to the racks where she stood, eyeing the crates and bottles of varying shades lined up in perfect rows. She scanned the bottles until her eyes fell on the black and white label: Everclear. The 190 proof grain alcohol - illegal to sell in Wisconsin - stared back at her, calling her. She pulled the bottle off the shelf, holding it between her legs as she twisted off the top. Her hand shook as she raised the bottle to her lips, letting a shot of liquid slide down her throat. It ravaged her mouth, scalding her before she felt it settle into her stomach.

Evie looked behind her at Mark and James still slumped

together on the ground. It wouldn't be long before Ethan would be back to check on them and to find her. Her eyes turned back to one of the small wooden crates filled with bottles. The handle of the crate was broken, dangling by a few splinters. She cracked the handle off, placing the wood between her teeth as she clenched down. She peeled back the white gauze, saturated with red, to reveal her wound. Her outer skin was shredded, drowning in blood. With the bottle still open, she trickled the alcohol onto her left arm. The stinging stabbed her arm like short knife jabs. She bit down, letting out a low moan before she poured more, letting the excess liquid drip down her arm and onto the floor. A pink pool gathered on the linoleum in front of her boot before she wrapped the stained gauze back on her arm.

Exhaling, she brought the bottle back up to her lips, swigging another shot of fire down her throat. She slumped forward as her stomach attempted to reject the liquid, but her throat stopped it, pushing it back down into her stomach where it settled. A groan rumbled behind her from the ground as she slid the bottle back onto the shelf. Evie crept around them, giving them one last glance, before turning off the light to leave them in blackness. Mark and James would be fine. Her father needed them alive. He couldn't make them disappear, either.

She pulled the door open, eyeing the hall to her left, toward the empty bar. She slid out into the hall where the pictures of her father decorated the wall ahead of her. His steel eyes stared back at her, watching her as she moved closer to his face. She reached up, her claws ready to shred his existence in the picture, before she lowered her hand. Her eye had caught movement down the hall. She registered the blurry outline of a man walking toward her before she turned and moved back to the door.

"Hey!" the voice called behind her as she sprinted the last

five feet to the door and shouldered it open, sending the bell into a clanging frenzy. Her boots hit the pavement as the cold air reenergized her body, propelling it forward into the alley. She took a left between two smaller buildings, weaving her way into the backyards of the old Victorian houses lining the residential streets. Delaney's house was only a few blocks away, and she wouldn't be there – at least not anytime soon.

Evie cut through the backyards in the dark night, coming to Drew Street where Delaney's bungalow stood silent. She retrieved the key from beneath the tree stump and slid it into the back door, popping it open to the warmth of the house. Her boots squeaked against the wood floor as she crept into the darkness. White, chalky coals smoldered in the fireplace and the small hiss of smoke filtered into the chimney. The jacket was gone. So was Holston's barn. Her lips turned up into a smile before she stumbled down to the bedroom.

She reached her hand up, turning on the lamp on the desk before opening the closet to retrieve a large bag. She slung the bag onto the bed, throwing clothes in it as she scanned the rest of the room. Her eyes fell back to the desk where Delaney's laptop should have been. Delaney hadn't unpacked before James had shown up at her door. Bad timing. She smirked as she scavenged the medicine cabinet to gather supplies. Bandages and rubbing alcohol; it wouldn't be enough. She needed help.

Evie slid down the cabinet onto the hard tiles. She had no one. Elizabeth was long gone. Now Joe was gone. Joe's body was left to her father who would dispose of him discreetly. The bodies seemed to just disappear. Then there was Mark. Mark could have been an ally. She had seen something in him, something that had drawn her to him. When he had made a pass at her after work one day, she had almost relented and given in to her desires, however, she hadn't known if she could trust him. Now he was passed out on the floor of her father's pub.

Ethan. She closed her eyes, envisioning Ethan tying her up. She had trusted him for the last twenty years, and he had betrayed her. They had grown close for a short period in their childhood. Her father had taken Ethan in until a foster family could care for him after Ethan's father had abandoned him. He made her who she was. A fighter. But why go through the trouble if he was going to betray her anyway? There was no one left.

She moved to her knees, the alcohol seeping into her bloodstream as the room spun around her. Her throat gagged and emptied onto the floor in front of her just as she crumpled to the floor, letting her cheek rest against the cold surface. Her head clouded over, filling with a dizzying haze while the wall in front of her blurred. She succumbed to the warmth creeping over her body as she lied still on the floor, her body craving the darkness.

***

Evie felt the weight of her body leave her as she was lifted into the air. It was as though she was floating, traveling through the air in complete stillness. She heard Ethan's voice whisper in her ear as she hovered over the ground, her legs dangling into nothingness. A quiet bang stirred her as her body turned. Another bang, this one louder. She felt her body lower and come back up. Another bang. Her eyes shot open to see the kitchen cabinet door shutting. It was followed by a soft glow of light and cool air that brushed against her face. She was staring at the contents of an open refrigerator.

"What the hell?" her voice rasped as she suddenly felt the

hard arms wrapped around her body.

"V," Ethan whispered, looking down into her eyes.

"Let go of me!" Her body fought to drive an elbow into his chest as she wriggled in his grip.

"Stop, V," his voice ordered. He tightened his grip.

"Leave me alone!" Her legs kicked in the air, trying to loosen his arms.

"GODDAMMIT! STOP, V!" he shouted in her ear. She felt her body squeeze tight against his, her bones aching as he pulled her in. She relented, letting her legs dangle like a rag doll.

"Thank you," he said, shutting the refrigerator door with a kick. Evie took in her surroundings. They were in Delaney's kitchen. The neon lights of the microwave read 7:15.

"Ethan, let me down," she ordered.

"I can't."

"Let me down!" She elbowed again, feeling her elbow bounce off his chest as she panted. Her head began to swim again. She took a deep breath and let her body relax in his arms.

"V, I'm here to help you." His voice softened as he looked into her face.

"Just like you helped me at the barn by tying me up?"

"I saved your life."

"Not exactly, we were about to get out," she rebuked. The smell of the smoke burned in her throat as she flashed to Delaney scooping out the snow in front of the door.

"You wouldn't have gotten out if it wasn't for Delaney and me." He paused. "After she was out, she went back in to get you." His deep brown eyes glistened in the dim light.

"I can't trust you. You tied me up to deliver me like a package," she spat back. Her body tensed, rigid in his arms. The leather of his jacket rubbed against her body. "Theron?"

"He's alive, at the hospital. I know I made a mistake," he said, shaking his head.

"And Delaney? Where is she?"

"She's with him. At the shop."

"Why?" she whispered.

"He won't hurt her. I don't know what it is about her – "

"Why?" she demanded.

"Your dad can be - "

"Persuasive?"

"Yes."

"And now?" Her eyes rose, penetrating his.

"Evie, I'm here to help you. I've known you forever and know that you won't get help, you'll run instead. I couldn't let him get you or have you disappear without me not knowing what happened to you." Ethan's voice cracked as he placed her in the chair at the kitchen table.

"I went to your apartment, but it was being watched. A car parked one street over. I found this address in that asshole's pocket - her friend or whatever he is - after he passed out." He held a small piece of paper with Delaney's address scribbled on it. "If I hadn't come, V, no one would have found you. You would have died," he started before he added, "He won't know that I came back for you. Not until tomorrow. We need to get you to a hospital, and we can't go here. We have to drive a bit. Otherwise, he'll find us; like he finds everyone else."

"I can't trust you," she started as she watched him pull the bag from the floor she had started packing on Delaney's bed. He tossed it on the table, filling it with a half-eaten box of crackers and two bottles of water before he began to zip it shut.

"Wait, her laptop." She shuffled her feet underneath her and steadied her arm against the table.

"Don't get up. Tell me where it is. We need to go." He rushed to her, coaxing her body back into the chair.

"It's got to be in a bag somewhere. Check her room again," she said. Ethan fled the room, disappearing down the hall toward the dim haze of light. "Behind the door, check behind the door," she yelled, her voice echoing in her own ears. She placed her head down on the table as her body began to shake.

"Got it." Ethan flooded into the kitchen, holding the laptop above his head, to see Evie's body shaking in the chair. "Evie?" He skidded forward, kneeling before her in the chair. Her body collapsed into his arms, becoming limp. He threw the laptop into the bag before he zipped it shut and slung it over his shoulder. He lifted Evie into his arms and out into the winter night to the gray sedan parked in the driveway, waiting.

34

The sunlight streaked through the half-closed curtains, the bright light reflecting into her eyes. Delaney groaned, rolling onto the other side of her body away from the sun. She lifted her hand to her head, feeling the bandage covering the tender spot. A moan escaped from her lips before she shot up, her mind drawing his bright blue eyes and laughing face. *Gunnar.* He was the one who had hit her. Almost killed her.

She shivered as she pulled the blanket closer to her body, looking down to see stains of pink and red near her hands. The watercolor from the painted portrait of the mask. Her fingers released the softness, letting the blanket fall back to the bed. She scanned the familiar room. The walls a stark white. The desk in complete order. Everything in its place. The lamp. The pictures. The pencil holder. No laptop. In its place sat a small, mahogany box. Her mother's ring. Her hand fluttered to her chest, feeling the metal against her fingers. She was in her own bed. In her own room. In her own house. Except she was not wearing her own clothes. She glanced down to see the letters LU covering her chest and leg. The t-shirt and sweatpants were new.

Delaney fell back onto the pillow, her neck feeling strained with the movement. Her whole body ached. It craved the warmth and comfort of the bed at the same time that her lungs and throat burned with dryness. Her head throbbed, the pain searing from front to back. Her feet felt heavy as if they were wrapped in thick cloth. *How did I get here?* Her mind jogged through the night. The jacket. The pub. The barn. The fire. The shop. *After the shop, where did he bring me?*

She exhaled, turning to her bedside table where a small plastic container with a prescription label and glass of water sat, waiting for her. Her arm slid from the warmth to secure the bottle. *Oxycodone. Painkillers.* She popped open the top to reveal five white pills settled on the bottom. She flipped it over, dumping all five pills into her hand, when a woman's voice rang in her head. *"Only one at a time. To take the edge off, honey."* Her voice had been smooth and clear as she had leaned closer to her, her breath smelling of pink bubble gum. A flash of her blond hair surrounding her round face above her green shirt jogged her memory. She had been lying in a hospital bed while the woman dressed all in green walked around her bed. It was a nurse, but she didn't remember coming back to her house. *How did I get here? Was Theron at that hospital?* Her eyes strained, moving back down to look at her outstretched hand holding the pills, before she poured three pills back into the container. *Is Holston still here?*

A soft knock rapped on the door, causing her to jump. Her heart raced as she scanned the room, looking for something, anything, to fight with. There was nothing. Besides, she could barely move. She relented, letting her body sink deeper into the bed. The door cracked open a few inches to expose a small mop of sandy brown hair.

James. Unsuspecting James. It opened further as he struggled to poke his head through the door. His brown eyes, bloodshot, locked on hers. Her body relaxed, comforted by his presence.

"Delaney?" he whispered into the bedroom.

"I'm up," her voice rasped before she cleared it. She reached over, taking a gulp of the water to soothe the dryness in her throat. She felt the pills slide down her throat in two small lumps.

"Delaney." He moved into the bedroom, his steps attempting to be light, but he staggered toward the bed anyway. "What the hell happened last night? Your head?"

She reached up to feel the bandage again as if she had forgotten about it. He slid onto the edge of the bed, near her covered feet. She tried to slide them back, but they barely moved, wound so tight with layers of cloth. "I must have hit it pretty hard," she said as she looked back at the container of pills. She would have done anything to avoid his eyes while she lied. "Who wears high heels in the dead of winter with ice on the ground? I must have slipped in the alley. I think Evie found me, but it's just… all a blur," she finished, wishing her words were true.

"Tell me about it. One second we're chugging down beers after you leave and the next, nothing. I've got nothing on the night. I woke up here, on your couch. I have no idea how I got here, but my rental car is here. I can't imagine I drove," he said, shaking his head.

"Is Mark here?" she asked, even though she wasn't sure she wanted to know.

"Not that I saw."

"You don't remember anything, James?" She looked up into his bloodshot eyes. He looked like hell. *Like he was drugged by one of Holston Parker's henchman.*

"No. I can't tell you the last time that's happened. Maybe, back in college," his words trailed off as he looked down at the floor. The blonde sorority girl clad in her underwear popped into Delaney's head. It seemed so irrelevant now.

"When's the last time you saw Mark?"

"We were at the bar, drinking. Gorilla kept feeding us drinks. We both were knocking them down. We were having a good time. Then nothing," he said.

"Well, you look like hell."

"I feel like hell. Like I got run over by a truck, but somehow, unfortunately, survived," he groaned as his head fell into his hands. "And there is nothing in your kitchen. No food, no leftovers. Nothing. Do you even live here?" he joked, knocking her foot with his hand.

"OW." She flinched, pulling her feet away.

"Sorry."

"That's okay," she said, smiling back at James.

"What's wrong with your feet?" he asked as he looked back at her feet underneath the covers.

"Those shoes killed them. Being a woman is a hazard, James," she lied, looking back at the pills.

"You're eyeing up those pills pretty hard core. Do you need some more?" He crawled across the bed, reaching for the pills.

"I'm good, thanks."

"They're pretty much gone, anyway." The few pills rattled as he shook the container. "Some prescription. Did you go to the hospital?"

"Yeah, Evie must have brought me, but I told you, I don't remember much. Just bits and pieces," she lied again, this time with her eyes closed. She opened them to see James's face only a few feet from hers. He was sitting on the bed in the same spot Theron had laid. *And now Theron is, lying in a hospital bed somewhere. Safe.*

"Well, I'm here now." His eyes studied her head before he reached up slowly, brushing the hair from her face.

"Good." She exhaled. She needed this. She needed the comfort of someone familiar. Someone she knew from her previous life. A life before Holston Parker had come storming in. A life that seemed so much simpler, uncomplicated, and safe.

"You just tell me what you need, Delaney."

"Well, for starters, I need my phone so I can call Mark and make sure he's okay," she started, staring back into his face as she felt the pit of her stomach growl. "Then some food. Before all that, though, can you hold me? Weird, I know," she said. Despite the fact that she wanted to tell James to leave, to get away from her, she was desperate to feel the warmth of someone she could trust.

"I thought you would never ask." James snuck under the covers and cradled her body into his, wrapping his arms around her. Her body sunk into his warmth. She had forgotten what he felt like. What it felt like to be safe again.

"Have you heard from your dad? Did they make it to Chicago okay?" His voice tickled her ear as the soothing sound absorbed in her head.

"I haven't heard yet, but that's the second phone call I'll make." A feeling of guilt washed over her as she thought of her small mother, cradled in her father's arms. She had been so consumed with her own night with Evie. *Evie. What happened to Evie?* The loose ends piled in her head. She remembered Evie sprinting down the alley into the dark night with a trailing Ethan. She had run the opposite way, but she hadn't gotten far before she slipped on the ice. She reached up to touch the bandages on her head.

"She's one tough woman. If there was anyone to make it through something like this, it would be her. You know that, right?" he asked before adding, "Not unlike someone else I know."

"Yeah, she is," Delaney said. Her voice cracked as her mother's smiling face filled her mind, her brown waves blowing in the wind. It was the day they both left Amberg, leaving her father behind. *What was Ann running from? Was she running from him?* Her mind sought answers as her body melted further into his arms.

"I never wanted you to leave, you know that right?" he whispered in her ear.

"I had no choice, James." The words carved a hole in her stomach as she thought of Holston Parker. His steely eyes pierced hers as he talked about her mother. *How could he have known my mother?*

"I know I made a mistake with the blonde, you don't need to remind me, but Delaney, you were the one who said we would never work. You told *me* to move on. Then you showed up at my door, without calling," he said, his voice rising at the end.

"It had been one week, James. One week gave you enough time for the blonde and how many more?" She turned toward him, the pent up frustration with James talking about their past had finally bubbled over. It seemed so far from her in this moment. All she needed was someone on her side, to feel safe.

"That's not fair, Delaney, and you know it," he shot back.

"We never talked about this. I never got a chance to tell you how that felt. How it felt standing on that doorstep. To see you with someone else." Her voice was strained as her cheeks flushed a deep pink.

"You never gave me a chance. Never returned my calls. My emails. I tried, Delaney. How long was I supposed to try for?" he asked.

"I don't know," she said, her voice creeping back inside her.

"How did it feel, Delaney? To be crushed?" His voice welled, full of resentment. "I loved you since the day I met you, yet, you pushed me away. Time and time again. You dated other guys and I had to listen to that. I just couldn't do it anymore." She shifted her body away from him, leaving his hands empty.

"Delaney, don't go," he pleaded, backpedaling. "It doesn't matter anymore. It was so long ago. All that matters is now. How we feel now." He scrambled underneath the sheets, flipping them over to uncover the red and pink stains. He stopped, looking down at the blotches on the sheets between his fingers.

"What is this? Is this blood? Delaney, are you okay?" He rushed toward her, examining her head.

"It's just paint," she said, pushing his body away.

"Delaney, don't do this again. Don't push me away." He jumped back and hopped off the bed.

"James, don't," she started as she began to pull her body out of the covers, but stopped as she felt the heaviness on her feet. *How do I explain this?*

"Don't what, Delaney? I'm not going to be a part of your game again. I came here to say I'm sorry, but I'm not going to be your punching bag." He moved toward the door. She exhaled, letting her head fall back down into her pillow.

She wanted to tell James everything. About Theron. Evie. Holston. The hatchet. Her body shuddered as the sound of the blade suctioning to his head echoed through her mind, but she couldn't. Holston Parker had made sure of that. *I need to find Mark and Mom. Did she make it to Chicago? Did he have her now?*

"I know you're going through a lot, Delaney," he started.

"You have no idea," she said, staring at the white ceiling cracked in several places. *I never should have bought this place. Never should have come here.*

"I want to be here for you. I really do, but you have some stuff - you stuff - to figure out before that happens," he said before adding, "I need to stop in Milwaukee before heading back to San Diego. My flight leaves tonight. I should get going."

"Yeah," she said. The one person she trusted was leaving her when she needed him, but she couldn't let him stay. Not with Holston breathing down her neck.

"Do what you do best, Delancy. Push me away," he said before walking through the door. "But just remember, I won't always be here." *DON'T LEAVE ME,* her head screamed as she thrust her fist into the bed. She heard him slide something down the hallway before the front door slammed shut. The sound of an engine revving muffled through the house before complete silence enveloped her room again.

Delaney sat up and swung her legs from underneath the covers to reveal her wrapped feet, covered in thick socks. She carefully peeled the layers back, moving her toes with less restriction. She glanced back at the prescription on the counter. The pain was tolerable, thanks to the painkillers. As she peeled off the last layer, she closed one eye, afraid to see what was underneath.

"OW." The sound filled the empty room as she touched the skin on her toes, blackened at the tips. Cuts ran all along the bottoms of her feet. *The stones. The ice.* She rubbed her finger against her toenail where the pink polish had been removed. *No more pink mask.* She could deal with that. But she didn't know if she could deal with everything else. Exhaling, she wrapped her feet back up, slipping the wool socks back over the layers. *Theron is safe, but I need to find Mark.*

Delaney carefully set her wrapped feet onto the floor, easing her weight onto her feet. The heaviness rushed down, followed by sharp blades that stabbed her toes. She fell back down onto the bed. *I need a phone.* She studied the room, looking at the desk again to see the mahogany box. If her mother had the strength to endure after all these years, after all the hospital visits, after all the chemo treatments, she had to get up. The sound of the skidding object down the hallway jogged her head. *Her phone.*

She placed her feet back onto the floor, supporting her weight along the bed with her hands until she neared the edge. She let go, hobbling until she grabbed the door to see her phone in the middle of the hallway. *Thank you, James.* As she hung onto the door, she crept down to her hands and knees to release the weight off her feet. Pain shot to her knees and a stinging sensation burned her hands.

"This isn't much better," she said as she crawled down the hall to her phone. The steel eyes glared at her from the screen, his face solemn underneath his fedora. The image burned in her mind before she let the phone fall through her fingers and crash to the floor. *A reminder.* She closed her eyes, letting out a groan before she picked up the phone again and found Mark's number.

"Pick up. Pick up the phone, Mark," she repeated as the other end continued to ring.

"Delaney," a man's voice answered. It wasn't Mark. She paused, not answering back. "We thought you might be calling.

How's your head?" His voice became clearer in her mind as she placed it. *Ethan. We?*

"Mark better be alive," she yelled into the phone, her hand shaking as she fought to hold it up to her ear.

"I'm sure he is. Holston needs him alive," he answered back.

"This is a sick game," her voice cracked into the phone.

"I know it is, Delaney. That's why I'm out. I left," he responded quietly.

"What are you talking about?"

"Delaney, I left. I was waiting for your call before I destroy Mark's phone," he responded. "She thought I already did, but I knew you would call. I knew you would want to know if she was okay."

"She? What the hell is going on?" Delaney whispered into the phone.

"After I brought you to Holston, I went looking for Evie. I found her a couple hours later, passed out in your bathroom. She had Mark's phone. She must have gone back to the pub and got it." His voice lowered even more, "We left Appleton. Holston. For good."

"Evie. Is she okay?"

"Yeah, she should be now anyway. I found a hospital out of town, but we're leaving soon. We can't stay long, otherwise he'll find us."

"And Mark?"

"The last time I saw him, he was passed out at the pub. He should be fine. He's probably back at his apartment. Check there," he rushed.

"Where are you going? What am I supposed to do?"

"Do what he tells you to do for now, but be careful,

Delaney. He's powerful. And..." his voice strained before he finished, "toxic."

Silence.

"Ethan?" she whispered into the phone before pulling it back from her ear. The call had ended.

35

"Are you ready?" Ethan asked. Evie's head turned on the pillow toward his voice before she felt his hand grip hers. The tape on her hand held the tube in its place. She felt the long metal of the needle inserted into her hand move as he rubbed her hand. It was a tube just like she had inserted into Theron's hand. She looked at the sunlight pouring through the glass of the hospital window hoping that Ethan's words were true about Theron, wondering if he had made it out alive.

"Ready as I'll ever be. Are you?" she responded, looking up at Ethan's restless eyes staring back at her. "Did you sleep at all last night?"

"What do you think?" he asked, sitting on the side of her hospital bed.

"Are you going to be able to drive? I might be able to. One handed." She tried lifting her arm off of the sheets, moving it only a few inches before she laid it back down with a low moan.

"I'm driving. Don't even think about it. I'll be able to stay awake long enough until we get there." He raised a large plastic cup in the air.

"Do I want to know what's in there?" she asked, shaking

her head.

"Probably not."

"Theron?"

"He's fine."

"The nurse?"

"She's at the end of the hall with another patient. We'll have to go now. There's a set of stairs on the other end. Good thing we stopped at this hospital. Limited staff." He smiled as he gulped down the last of his drink and threw the empty cup in the garbage.

Evie tore the tape off her hand and slid the needle out, watching the drops of blood collect on her hand before they rolled onto the bed. She placed the tape back on her hand, stopping the flow of the blood.

"The monitors. On your chest," Ethan whispered, pointing to her hospital gown. She reached inside her gown, tearing off the patches adhered to her chest. A loud beep filled the room as the monitor flat lined for a moment before it stopped. Evie looked up to see Ethan by the outlet, the cord of the monitor in his hand. He dropped the cord and scooped her up into his arms, hiding her tiny body inside the bulge of his arms. Evie tucked her head into his chest and closed her eyes, feeling the ripples of his body rub gently against her face. The pain in her ribcage screamed as he made his way down the hall and into the stairwell. Her body jerked with the jolt of the steps, but they needed to go. Holston would be here soon, and she couldn't confront him now. Not when she wasn't ready.

Ethan hit the door open, rushing them into the bright sun and cold winter wind of a brisk Wisconsin day. Evie felt the sting on her cheeks, letting the burn sink deep into her skin. She knew she wouldn't feel the Wisconsin wind much longer. They would go far away where he wouldn't find them.

"The car is just twenty feet away. Are you okay?" he whispered as he darted in between cars, her feet dangling from underneath the hospital gown.

"It's freezing, and we probably look suspicious as hell," she muttered into his chest, the heat of her breath grazing against her face.

"Yeah," he grunted as he bent down to open the passenger door of her gray sedan. He had removed the GPS tracker according to Evie's instructions, leaving it twenty minutes just outside of Appleton. He placed her in the car, slamming the door shut before hopping in and revving the engine. He tore out of the parking lot and onto the pavement of the road. They sat in silence waiting at a red light before Ethan pressed his foot heavy on the gas and turned right onto the highway. Evie exhaled.

"You said the drive was only one hour or so from here?" Ethan asked as he looked at Evie. Her body barely filled the passenger seat.

"Yeah. It's not far after the Michigan border." She squinted in the wicked glare of the sun. They would be there before dark but could only stay long enough to get what she needed.

"He'll know we've been here. Once he figures out that I've helped you, he'll check my accounts and see that I withdrew all my money," Ethan said.

"Ethan, you shouldn't have - "

"I had to. We'll need as much as we can to get as far away as possible. Out of his reach."

"I can't let you do this, Ethan." Evie sat up, wincing at the pain that radiated through her body.

"It's not your choice, Evie. I make my own decisions, and I made this one a long time ago. We both knew that he was destructive, but we both had to play along. Be puppets in his show. You're a fighter, Evie, and I'll fight alongside you as long as you'll let me." Ethan reached over, placing his hand on her leg buried in the loose cotton.

"Ethan, it's not your fight."

"He made it this way. He started it with Henry. I never wanted to see you hurt like that."

"When you convinced me to be a fighter."

"You were always a fighter, Evie. I just had to convince you to bring it out."

"Well, it looks like it didn't turn out well for either of us," she sighed, pulling his hand away from her leg.

"Don't give up yet," he said reaching his hand into the backseat, pulling a plastic bag onto her lap. "Your clothes are in here."

"Thanks."

"Your knife's in the black bag in the back," he said, gripping the steering wheel once again. The hum of the engine filled the silence between them. "And your wallet and the money."

"You found it? How?" she asked. She had stashed her wallet with her counterfeit IDs, passport, and stack of cash in the bag underneath the cot. She had planned on coming back to the room to get Theron and her bag.

"Dumb luck," he replied with a smile.

"And the barn? How did you know we were there?" she asked, studying the profile of his face.

"When you tore out of the pub, I knew something was going on. I slipped Mark and Joe a little something and took off after you. The barn was my first stop. It usually was -" He stopped before looking back at Evie.

"What?"

"The usual spot for Gunnar."

"For what?" she asked, knowing the answer to her question, but she wanted someone else to say it. To make it real.

"Do you really want to do this, Evie?" he asked as she nodded her head. "Where I picked up the bodies."

"Why?" she whispered, feeling her body sink into the seat.

"I don't know, Evie. He's Holston. I felt like I owed him after he had taken me in. I was abused, broken from my father, and Holston, he convinced me. It wasn't hard. It was actually pretty easy; I've only done it a couple times. Ever since Gunnar wanted to stop running the bodies," he said before he added, "I wanted to tell you. I really did."

"And Joe?"

"I left him for Holston to clean up."

"I can't believe Joe is gone. I didn't know," she started, letting the conversation fall. She couldn't think about Joe's body lying somewhere, waiting to be dumped.

"I don't know what to say," he muttered.

"Did you get rid of your phone and Mark's?" she asked as she sifted through the bag to find her pants. She pulled out the black cargo pants and put them up to her face. The smell of smoke permeated her nostrils as she inhaled. At least the barn was gone.

"Yeah. Both phones crushed and in the garbage at the hospital," he replied without looking at her. Evie watched him, staring at his defined jawline, his eyes fixed on the road. He had, after all, come back for her. He had saved her from the barn and from Delaney's house. She owed him something.

"And my phone?"

"In the bag," Ethan replied. Evie dug deeper into the bag

and pulled out the phone. She flipped to her photos, finding the picture of Gunnar's arm.

"There's so many," Evie breathed. "So many more than I thought."

"What is that?" Ethan asked, leaning over to look at the phone.

"The initials of the people Gunnar killed. That my father killed," Evie replied, studying the arm. "Henry's here. H.T."

"How many?"

"Twenty-two."

"I haven't taken care of twenty-two bodies, I can tell you that. Only two," Ethan said, looking at Evie. "One on Friday and one a few months ago. I had no idea."

"Richard Rowan was on Friday," she said as she took one last look at the initials before she slid the screen away. "What happened to Theron?"

"Some students found him in an alley on the other end of downtown. Away from Atlas Pub and your space at the shop. The news is reporting that he is stable at Appleton Medical Center." Ethan's voice drifted off. "How did that happen anyway?"

"Gunnar, that Neanderthal. He was slicing at me with a machete, and he missed. Slit right into that kid's chest," she sighed. "It's a long story." She slid the gown off and pulled her shirt over her head. She looked over at Ethan, smiling back at her.

"You know I had to steal a peek." He held his hands up as he laughed.

"Really?"

"Yeah, really. I was curious. I always have been." He turned to study her face, waiting for her reaction. She sat in silence before a small smile crept onto her face.

***

The gray sedan pulled into the long driveway, winding along the dense evergreens. "The driveway is plowed," Ethan said, his voice stirring her awake. She blinked several times, letting the landscape of the cabin soak in as she shifted her body up to look out the windshield.

"Hector takes care of the cabin and yard even though my father..." she paused, the word father felt dirty in her mouth. "He doesn't come here in the winter. Hector's the groundskeeper." The compacted snow crunched beneath the sedan as they rolled up to the entrance. "The last time I was here was with Elizabeth, more than ten years ago," she added as she surveyed the expansive cabin stuck in time against the same trees and same lake that she remembered from her teenage years.

The cabin itself seemed more ominous against the beauty and solitude of the nature surrounding it, darker now as if someone had suffocated the light much like her father had snuffed out Elizabeth's light. Henry's light. Now, he was meddling with Delaney Jones, a woman she had thought she hated up until yesterday.

"Pull off to the side, near the back," she said, looking closer at the cabin and adjacent out building to the left before she finished, "In case someone decides to show up." He pulled around the side of the house, moving the car out of sight from the main entrance.

"Do you think he'll come here?" Ethan turned the key, stopping the engine. The silence hung in the air as he looked back at Evie examining the cabin.

"No, and I'll be quick."

"Do you want me to come in?"

"No, stay out here. It will only be a couple minutes," Evie said as she pat her leg, feeling the metal of the knife against her leg. "You have a gun, right?"

"Yeah," he said, sliding his hand into his jacket.

"Keep it, for safe measure." She smiled at him before she pulled the handle of the car door and felt the ice break beneath the tread of her black boot. She shut the door, feeling the stillness of the winter surrounding her. The silence of the familiar woods from her childhood had once soothed her, but now, the trees stood watching her, waiting for her to make her move. She had never been to the cabin in the winter. Her father had only brought her here in the warm summer months. The barren trees stood stark, void of the life and vibrancy she had remembered.

Evie's legs and body ached with each movement as she crept up to the cabin along a path that had been cleared. "Thank you Hector," she whispered into the silence as she made her way up the steps to the porch on the back side of the house.

As she reached the top, she turned her body to the shores of Lake Michigan where the waves crashed against the white beach. Large chunks of snow and ice thrashed in the water, the waves bringing them closer to the piles of snow accumulated on the beach on which Evie had once buried her feet into the warm sand ten years ago; it was now deep beneath the inches of snow and ice. The sweet warmth of the summer wind and sun had been replaced with the churning, freezing water threatening to seize the remaining shore. It was all an eerie reminder that everything had changed.

Sliding her hand into her pocket, she retrieved a tension

wrench and a long, thin pick, and then bent down, inserting the wrench first into the lock. She knew she would destroy the lock, but it didn't matter. They would be long gone before Hector ever figured out she had been here. She placed her hand on the knob, turning it once until she felt the plug inside the lock release. She pushed the door open, a high-pitched beeping resonating in her ears as she slipped through the door.

"No," Evie whispered as she scanned the dark room. She hadn't anticipated an alarm system. Last she had checked, he hadn't installed any alarm systems in the cabin. She would know, or should have known, considering she was the director of security. He had entrusted her with all his properties, or so she'd thought. She ran to the hallway near the garage, finding the control panel for the system and punched in 1197 - the same code to his house in Appleton. The beeping stopped.

"It's not secure if you use the same code." She smiled as she turned back to the main area of the house and navigated her way to the living room. A wall of windows facing Lake Michigan streamed the light gray sky into the room. The brown leather furniture. The cobblestone fireplace reaching twenty feet in the air. The bookshelves flanking the fireplace filled with books. It remained undisturbed, just as it had been since her last visit. Her eyes scanned the bookshelf on the left, looking to the third shelf almost ten feet up. She narrowed in on the navy blue book with gold trim and lettering. It was still there. She pushed an overstuffed chair against the bookshelf, climbing onto the chair to reach the first row of books.

"Too short," she whispered as she looked at the shelf. She slid the tip of her boot onto the first shelf, launching herself another couple of feet into the air as she grabbed the wood with her right hand. Her wounded arm dangled at her side as she gripped onto the shelf, pausing before she reached it up slowly. The pain shot through her arm as she raised it higher. Just as her fingers reached the navy cover, and she secured it in her grasp, she lost her grip on the shelf. Evie's legs crashed into the chair below her, causing her knees to buckle before she fell to the floor where her bandaged arm slammed against the hardwood planks, sending jolts of agony through her body. The book sprang loose from her hand, landing on the spine as the pages fanned out into the air.

Evie rolled over, looking at the blank pages standing straight in the air. It was the same book she had found when she was a teenager. A blank book, no type on the pages. She flipped the pages to the front of the book, exposing the inside of the back cover. The eyes of the woman in the picture, still neatly taped inside the back cover, stared back at her. She traced the outline of the woman with her fingertip as the woman smiled back at her. Her mother.

She had last seen the picture over ten years ago, the last time she had been at the cabin with Elizabeth. They had begun to settle in for the night while Holston and Joe were outside, drinking beside the lake. Curled up against the brown leather couch, Elizabeth's long blonde curls had bounced on her shoulders as the breeze filtered in from the windows off of the lake. Evie had pushed the chair against the bookshelf, climbing along the shelves as they searched the books for something to read. Elizabeth had pointed to the navy blue one with intricate gold lettering.

"Looks fancy," she had said as Evie reached higher, pulling the book from its spot.

"It's empty," Evie had said as she flipped through the book before handing it to Elizabeth on the couch below.

"Let me see," she had responded before flipping to the back cover where a picture of a woman was neatly taped. "Except for her." They had leaned over the book, sitting side by side on the couch, staring at the woman before her father had walked into the kitchen.

"Staying out of trouble, I hope," Holston said as he strolled into the kitchen, reaching into the refrigerator for two more beers.

"Of course, we are, Dad" Evie had answered as Elizabeth shut the book and tucked it into the side of the couch cushion.

"Good." His voice had deepened as his eyes settled on them before he turned to walk outside. Evie had reached over Elizabeth's lap, pulling out the book from the cushion before Elizabeth's hand had stopped her.

"You better not," she had whispered in Evie's ear. "I don't want to get into trouble."

"We're fine," Evie had said, reaching back for the book.

"For my dad's sake. He works for your dad now and he's finally making some money with his shop. I don't want to cause trouble," Elizabeth had whispered, gripping the book tighter in her hands. "I'll put it back."

That had been the only time Evie had seen the picture. The picture that they both agreed had to be Evie's mother. She had never seen pictures of her mother during childhood because her father had always told her that her mother wasn't worthy of posing before the camera. When she asked again as a teenager after the night they saw the picture, he had warned her about her mother's drug addiction that caused the car accident. He had cautioned Evie to be mindful of the "addictive personality" she may have inherited, but Evie had never believed that she was gone. She could feel that she was still alive. Her mother had to have answers to her own past. Answers to her father's true identity.

The woman in the picture was dressed in a waitress uniform, her dark hair pulled away from her face in a low bun at the back of her head. The uniform was tight against her body, buttoned to the top to cover her full breasts. She squinted at the nametag placed above her right breast and could just barely make out the name of the restaurant - House of Steel. Her lips were a bright red, the color of a cardinal against the white snow. Evie peeled back the tape, loosening the picture from its spot before she turned it over. In blue ink, a date on the right corner filled the otherwise blank space. 1986.

"You know she's dead," Holston Parker's voice cut through the silence. The hairs on Evie's neck spiked as she turned to see her father sitting on the couch behind her. He was lounged deep into the seat, his legs folded as if he had been there all along. His fedora sat lightly on his head. His black leather jacket and shoes were still on. She scanned the back door, looking for any signs of Ethan.

"Did I surprise you?" he asked, "My head of security doesn't even know anyone is in the house that she breaks into. Isn't that something?"

"I see we're past the formalities of asking how I'm doing after I've been shot by one of your employees," she spat back, still on the ground.

"I see you're doing fine, so there's no need to ask." The low, steady calmness of his voice she had once admired enraged her as she watched the stillness of his body.

"Did you kill her?" she said, positioning her body into a crouched position, like a cat ready to pounce. She raised the picture in the air. She wondered how long he had been in the house.

"I would have never killed your mother."

"What about Henry? Or Elizabeth?"

"Elizabeth. Poor Elizabeth was a casualty of the situation. It was Henry who raped and strangled her then left her lifeless body in the field. Gunnar found her, and I knew Joe couldn't live with it. Elizabeth needed to be avenged so I had Gunnar make it look like an accident. I took care of the funeral arrangements and Henry, of course, he needed to be disposed of," Holston replied.

"I don't believe you," Evie accused.

"That's why I didn't tell you at the time. You wouldn't have believed me, but Henry was vile," he retorted.

"Then why did you hire him?" She tore into Holston.

"He had the ability to be rehabilitated. He had a chance at redemption, or so I thought. Henry proved me wrong. Whether you believe me or not, that's up to you," he replied evenly. His gray eyes penetrated her skin, making it crawl beneath her clothes. "This is what you came for. The picture." He nodded toward the picture still gripped in her hand.

Silence.

"I wish she wasn't dead. I truly do." The words slid out of his mouth, a rehearsed phrase that meant nothing to him.

"I wish she wasn't, either," she replied, staring straight into his lying eyes. The man sitting before her was a complete stranger to her. Her father had long left her, if he had ever really been there at all. "She could have helped me."

"I don't believe she could have. It seems as though no one can help you now. I tried, Evie. I tried to help you, but you wouldn't let me. You didn't follow my lead. There was so much promise for you," he said, leaning forward to rest his arms on his legs.

"Promise? To run the family business of buying and selling broken women?" she accused.

"Selling broken women," he repeated the words as if he had never heard them before, his face still unflinching.

"I saw you. Buying those women back at that barn, you sick bastard," she spat as the rage exploded inside her.

"The women in the barn," he paused to formulate his next words, "were unharmed only *after* I bought them."

"You bought them."

"Yes."

"To do what with them?" she demanded.

"Evie, I'm not about to divulge my personal affairs to you. You wouldn't believe me anyway. Not after you have caused such a mess. That poor boy along with murder and arson. Although," he contemplated, "last night showed me that you could have potential, but I don't like cleaning up messes. I had to call in quite a few favors." His eyes pierced into her beaten body.

"I will never be like you," she breathed back.

"It's a shame that it had to turn out this way. If you would only go along with what I say, just like your sister, our situation would be much better," he said.

"Sister?" Evie choked out the word.

"Delaney is coming along quite nicely now," he replied as he looked out of the vast windows. "The lake is beautiful this time of year, isn't it? Ethan would find it so peaceful out there. Where is he by the way?"

Sister. Evie couldn't digest the word. She slid her hand into her pocket and retrieved the knife, hiding it along her leg as his eyes moved back to her.

"Did you think I came alone?" He let out a small, low chuckle. Her stomach sank as she envisioned Ethan still sitting in the car alone, unsuspecting and exhausted.

"No. More of your thugs, the convicted felons on your secret payroll," she retorted as she stuffed the picture into her pocket. "Did you clean up the mess yet? Gunnar and your beloved barn?"

"See. You're not so unlike me after all," he said as he moved to stand up. Evie sprung from her position on the ground and thrashed her arm through the air, making a single long stroke against his knuckles. The flesh seared open as the blood gushed from his hands. He shot up, reaching inside his jacket before she jabbed another shot into his leg. She felt the metal pierce his skin as she pulled the knife back out and sprinted to the kitchen.

His voice growled behind her as she clamored through the kitchen, knocking the chair over on her way to the door. A popping noise rang in her ear as she ducked down, avoiding the bullet as it ricocheted against the corner of the wall. Plaster shattered to the floor beneath her, crunching underneath her boots.

"EVIE!" he yelled as another shot fired against the wall behind her. She looked forward; the glass door was just a few steps ahead. Ethan's face appeared in the glass, his eyes flashing panic before the glass shattered in front of her, the shot ringing in her ear from behind her. She covered her head as the shards sprinkled down onto her arms and legs as the door swung open. Her eyes shot up, searching for Ethan's face, but it was gone.

Evie slid through the door, maneuvering around Ethan's body on the ground. She fell to her knees next to him. Blood spewed from his chest. Her hands rushed to his body, covering the wound with her hands as she tried to stop the flow of the blood. Her eyes scanned down to his legs where more blood poured from his upper thigh.

"It's too late, Evie." The words sputtered as red liquid seeped from his mouth.

"No, Ethan. No." She could feel her hands being covered with warmth. "Don't leave me."

"You have to go. I got the other two. I'll stop him... one shot left." He shook the gun in his hand.

"You can't."

"Evie, just go!" he yelled.

"I promise, Ethan," she whispered.

"GO!" he tried to yell, but the words stuck in his mouth as more blood poured out. Evie turned to run along the side of the house, her boots covering the ground with leaps as the adrenaline pumped through her veins. She couldn't let it end this way. Holston would kill her now, she was sure of it. Her boots pushed straight ahead, avoiding the stairs and path where two bodies laid in pools of red. As she neared the edge of the porch, she heard a shot fire before she slid down the pile of snow leading to the car. Ethan's gun. Another shot fired. Ethan was gone. She inhaled the sharp air, feeling the pain of his death sink into her. He was gone because of her.

Evie whipped around the car and pulled the driver side door open, hitting the gas before she turned her head to see her father standing on the porch. His gray eyes pierced her as he rested his gun at his side. The blood dripped from his hands, landing in droplets in the thin, white layer of snow beneath his feet. The car's tires spun in reverse as she propelled back, his face disappearing behind the corner of the house as she swung around to the front. She shifted to drive, thrusting her foot into the pedal as she tore down the driveway. His black eyes, filled with disgust, burned in her mind as she watched the evergreens vanish behind her.

36

Three Months Later ~ March 13

Delaney stepped onto the porch, feeling the rays of the afternoon's spring sun soak into her skin. The sound of trickling water flowed from the eave troughs to saturate the dingy grass already soaked in mud. The blades of bright green scattered throughout her yard showed signs of an early spring.

"Are you sure it's okay?" she asked, turning to lock the door behind Mark while resting the last box on her hip.

"Let me take that." Mark reached out, grabbing the box to free her hands. "And yes, I already told you it's okay. What am I going to do in the house alone anyway?" he asked as he walked down the wet steps, damp from the last remnants of melting snow.

"I don't know, you tell me," she provoked, not wanting to actually know the answer.

"Are you sure you're ready to sell?"

"The sign's up. This wasn't the right house for me," she said, pointing at the for sale sign flapping in the gentle breeze. "Small kitchen. Detached garage. Should I go on?" *How about the microscopic camera hidden in the bookshelf?* Delaney had found the planted camera on her books while she was boxing up her belongings. She had crushed it with the hammer her father had given her.

"What prompted you to buy it anyway?" Mark asked. "You didn't even ask one of us to come and see it before you signed the papers."

"To be honest, it reminded me of home," she said, following him down the steps. "But I'm ready for a new beginning. To start fresh."

"I've known that feeling," he said as he turned to her. "But it was a long time ago, when Dad picked up me and Ben in the hardware store."

"You remember how it felt?" she asked.

"I do. I remember the day pretty clearly," he said. "I wasn't afraid. I wasn't hesitant. Dad was sure of taking us home. I felt free."

"From what?" Delaney asked, longing to feel free, to start over and erase the past winter.

"From my past. From my parents. From everything that was tying me down, holding me back from becoming something better. It was as if Dad knew, the moment he saw me, that I needed him to lead me out." His voice softened as they neared the truck packed with boxes of her belongings. Although Delaney had heard the story from her dad when she was young, Mark and she had never talked about that day - not until this moment.

"Did you feel ... suffocated?" She stopped near him, placing her hand on his arm.

"Yeah, I guess I did."

"But now you can breathe?"

"Yeah, I guess," he said, staring back at her.

"Well, I want to breathe, too," she said.

"And getting rid of the house is going to do that?" He slid into the driver's seat, setting the last box on the passenger seat next to him.

"Not yet, but I think it's the first step," she said as she stared forward at the door of the empty garage. She blinked, trying to remove the memory of Theron's bloody jacket clumped in the middle of the concrete. The logs that started the crackle of the fire inside the living room. Her fingers reached absently to graze the metal hanging from the chain on her neck. She traced the outline of the engraving on the ring, soothing her as she turned to look at Mark.

"And all the other steps?" he asked, leaning in to hug her. She exhaled, feeling the comfort of his closeness. *Another advantage of moving in with Mark. I won't be alone.*

Prior to December, moving in with Mark wasn't even a consideration, but Holston Parker had changed that. He had changed her whole world. Delaney was under his watchful eye, playing to his whims without even knowing why he cared. She would stay at Leighton like he had demanded, and Mark would stay employed with him, although Mark had no idea what had happened. His employer, for all he knew, was a wealthy philanthropist giving back to the community while still building his empire. She, on the other hand, had vowed to find out why he cared so much about her and her family. She craved to break the tie between them, whatever that was.

"I don't know yet," she started, feeling the memory of Holston's steel eyes creep along her skin. "I guess I'll have to figure that out."

"Looks like you've got a visitor." Mark nodded his head toward the rearview mirror. Delaney turned to see a man walking up the driveway, his hair tucked in a baseball cap with

LU splashed across the chest of his hooded sweatshirt. His stride, a casual and familiar one that had once sent excitement through her body, now coursed dread and guilt through her veins. *Theron.*

"I'll catch you in a bit back at your house, if you don't mind. Just leave my stuff in the truck so I can help you unload it when I get back," she said as she walked away to leave Mark sitting with the door gaping open, her gaze concentrated on Theron. She heard the door shut behind her and the roar of his engine as she crossed behind it. Mark waved to the back of Delaney's head. She had never turned around; instead she'd kept her eyes focused on Theron as his steps drew him closer.

"Theron." His name caught in her throat.

"Ms. Jones," he replied. His eyes, set deep beneath the shadow of his hat, met hers. Her eyes led down to his chest, where he had been slashed.

"It's all healed. Although I have one bad ass scar," he mused.

"Theron. I'm sorry -" she started as her legs fidgeted beneath her.

"You don't have to apologize, Ms. Jones."

"Delaney," she corrected, feeling the uneasiness of the power dichotomy between them.

"Delaney. You don't have to apologize for not returning my calls. I didn't return your text that day after I realized that sleeping with my professor wasn't probably the best idea I've had. I saw the For Sale sign, and I wanted to stop in," he said, pointing to the sign. "I saw it just a few days ago."

"Theron, I'm sorry for what happened to you. The whole ordeal must have been terrifying. I just can't imagine," she said as she stumbled through the apology. "I just didn't have the …

courage to answer... I guess." *For fear of the man that ultimately did this to you.* "But I'm glad you stopped by."

"I get it, a lot was going on."

"How's spring training going?" she jumped in, trying to rescue them both from the awkwardness of the conversation. She couldn't stand to rehash the events that led up to that night, but as the words left her mouth, she realized the topic couldn't possibly alleviate the clumsiness between them. *Nothing can be normal between us.* The feeling of being watched wasn't settling well with her, either; although she hadn't seen or heard from Holston in the last three months.

"Good. The scar has healed for the most part, so I'm just getting back into things," he replied. "It really hasn't been that bad."

"That's good, Theron," she encouraged, studying his face. His strength and forwardness had dulled. This version of Theron was much different than the first day of class. "Your tags, did you get your father's tags back?"

"They're in evidence right now, but I'll get them back when the trial is over." He paused before continuing, "I wanted to come by in case you were leaving. I wanted to tell you something before you left."

"Oh, I'm not leaving Leighton, Theron. Just selling the house and moving in with my brother," she replied. *I wish I could leave Appleton. Leighton. Leave this all behind.*

"Oh, okay. Well, I still wanted to tell you something that's been sticking with me since I was... kidnapped," he said, looking up into her eyes as he let out a half-laugh. "It still sounds weird, kidnapped. How does an adult male get kidnapped?"

"I don't know," she said, letting out a nervous laugh. "It's pretty strange."

"Yeah, it is. Anyway. I don't remember much from that whole ordeal between having a bag over my head and being drugged, according to the doctors." Delaney's stomach dropped, remembering the feeling of the cloth rubbing against her own skin. The feeling of the warmth of her breath permeating to the rest of her face stung. "But the one thing that I remembered, I think anyway, is a woman helping me. She came in to 'save' me - or at least I thought - from the man who had taken me and cut me," he said as his eyes began to glass over. "Anyway, I don't remember much of her. Just that she was a small woman who I trusted right away, but she took care of me somewhere else before leaving me in the alley, without telling anyone. Why would anyone do that? I just can't seem to fit the pieces together. No one ever found her; she never came forward," he said, his words running from his mouth. Evie sprinting down the alley, flashed through Delaney's mind, but Delaney knew that she hadn't left him there. It had been one of Holston's men. Maybe Ethan. She hadn't quite figured out the details.

"But there was something that made me trust her. It was her voice and her eyes that made me trust her. They were familiar to me. I spent weeks trying to figure out who she was and even though I don't know who she is or anything else about her, I finally realized what it was that made her so familiar to me." He paused looking closer at Delaney. She felt her cheeks warm, waiting for him to finish. *How do you know Evie? What is it?*

"I can still see her eyes, like flashes burned in my mind," he said, adjusting the cap on his head. The tufts of his brown hair stuck out over his ears.

"And?" Delaney breathed.

"The blue eyes. They were so clear. Unlike any other eyes that I've seen before, except for one other person," he added, stepping closer to her. "And that person's you." Delaney swallowed hard, feeling tightness in her chest. The thought had never occurred to her as she began to draw Evie's face in her mind. She had brown hair and blue eyes, just like a million other woman she had seen before.

"A lot of women have blue eyes, Theron." Her voice dropped as his words began to sink in, but the night she had seen Evie had been a blur. She had only seen her in the dark. The pub. The barn. She was passed out in the back of Ethan's car. *Were her eyes like mine?*

"I know it sounds crazy and weird." His face flushed. "But I felt like I just had to tell you. I was so drugged out of my mind. I guess I could have just imagined that it was you," he backtracked, trying to make sense of something so undeniably painful. Delaney stood quiet, unable to overcome the guilt that plagued her.

"But they arrested the guy they think was responsible," he said, filling the silence.

"They think?" she asked.

"Yeah, I'm not entirely convinced, but I guess all the evidence adds up. Along with the fact that he admitted to it," he said. "I'm not supposed to talk about it, though, until the trial is over. Jesus, here I am, in your driveway, just spilling everything out. It's kind of embarrassing."

"Don't be embarrassed. Apparently, I have trusting eyes, remember?" she joked, trying to relieve Theron of his worries.

Her mind tried to connect the pieces of the puzzle, attempting to figure out how Holston Parker had pinned the kidnapping on someone else and how he had gotten rid of Joe's body. The local news had reported it as a barn fire started by a drug deal gone wrong, the three men convicted felons. Holston had played it perfectly, a shocked businessman with an old, abandoned property full of antiquated machinery.

He was more than cooperative with police officials, donating close to half a million dollars to enhance the drug unit on the force and to placate the frenzied citizens of the blue ribbon town. Although there wouldn't be any remnants of Delaney's DNA in the barn that had burned to the ground, she was sure she had left a bloody trail from the shed. There was never any mention of unidentified blood, no body found in the shed, and no mention of Evie's car, either. Evie, who had allegedly taken a sabbatical across seas. Holston had made it all disappear.

"Yeah," he laughed, shifting his legs.

"But what do you mean when you say that you're not convinced?" she asked before she realized that she didn't want to know. The man ultimately responsible was Holston Parker, but Theron could never know that. No one could ever know that. Gunnar was the one that took Theron. *What had Holston concocted?*

"Well, from what I can remember, I thought I heard a thick accent from the guy that put the hood over my head. He seemed like he was from Holland or some Norwegian country. I sound crazy, right?" he laughed.

"I don't know, Theron. Did you talk to anyone about this?"

"I did. The investigators, but they don't believe me," he said. Holston's words rang through her mind about his influence. His connections. *Who does he have ties with in the police department? Sanchez?* His reach was far beyond what she could imagine. "They told me it was all part of the drugging process -

286

that I don't remember much because of the drugs used, and maybe I don't. All I know is that it just doesn't seem to add up."

The sound of an engine pulled her eyes up – taillights of a gray sedan. *I will never feel normal again.*

"Well," he said. "I just wanted to tell you that. For whatever it's worth."

"Thanks, Theron. It was good to see you," she said as she put her hands on her hips, glancing at her Civic parked and fully packed behind her. "I should get going."

"Of course," he said. Delaney felt a surge of pain rush over her as she longed to tell Theron everything that happened. That Gunnar had taken him and that Evie had saved him in her twisted sort of way, but she knew she never could. She knew she could never take back that night with Theron. With all her heart, she wanted nothing more than Theron to move on and never look back. She had a feeling he would.

"Take care, Theron," she said before adding, "And be careful."

"You too, Ms. Jones." He smiled as he turned to walk back down the driveway, his hat disappearing down the sidewalk. She blinked, trying to keep the tears welling in her eyes from falling, as she thought of his head bobbing down the sidewalk the morning that she had kicked him out of her house.

37

Delaney watched as Ann Jones stood in front of the kitchen sink wearing the apron she hadn't worn for more than a year. Her hands moved with fierce efficiency in the scalding water while Delaney sat at the counter on the same wooden stool that had been part of the kitchen since she was seven-years-old, in awe of the woman turning another year older. Ann was just as strong as the years before she had been diagnosed, still denying anyone's help with dishes. She had gained weight, looking like a healthy and vibrant sixty-three-year-old. Her wig, still intact and quite beautiful, covered the sprouts of new hair growth.

"Where's Mark?" Ben asked from the table, Meghan next to him. The newlyweds of three months were undeniably attached at the hip, a feeling Delaney never imagined for herself.

"Right here," he said, striding into the kitchen.

"What is with people walking into this house without us knowing? Michael, we're going to need a bell on that door." Delaney's eyes shifted down as the clang of Atlas Pub's door rang through her head. She closed her eyes as her mind begged her to cover her ears to escape from the clanging. She watched as her family moved around, speaking to each other and hugging in slow motion. Their mouths moved, but the words were silent as Delaney blinked, trying to focus her attention back on them.

"Delaney," Mark said again, louder, as he moved toward her. She felt his hand grip her arm before she finally turned to him to respond.

"Yeah?" Her voice came out louder than she anticipated. All five faces of her family stared at her.

"Someone is here to see you," Mark said as he nodded toward the opening of the dining room. Delaney turned her body, still seated on the stool, to see a man standing with his hands stuffed inside his pockets. His lips curled up in a half-smile before he lifted his hand from his pocket to give the familiar wave. *James.*

"James!" Michael welcomed, putting his hand out to shake James's hand.

"So good to see you," Ann said as she walked past Delaney, giving her a side smile before she embraced James like a long lost friend. Delaney turned toward Mark who shrugged his shoulders and shot her a smile before retreating to dig in the refrigerator. Her eyes shifted back to James.

"Why don't we give these two a moment to catch up? Then, James, you can join us for cake," Ann directed, not giving anyone a choice. She knew no one would argue. No one argues with a recovering cancer patient.

"How about outside?" Delaney stood up, nodding to the deck overlooking the backyard.

"Sure," James replied as his body relaxed, following her. Delaney slid into the wooden chair facing the fenced in backyard, curling her feet underneath her body, as she watched James fall into the chair next to her. She wrapped her arms around herself, feeling the cool traces of the Wisconsin winter still present in the air.

"Delaney, I didn't know we were coming here... well, until we got here," he started. His eyes studied her as her eyelids closed and her hand reached up to graze her forehead.

"Classic Mark," she interrupted, opening her eyes to settle in on James.

"This is awkward," he said, shifting his legs before adding, "Should I just go?"

"Of course not," she rushed, looking back into his warm, brown eyes. His tanned olive skin had lightened and his dark brown hair had grown back to the curly mop that she had remembered from ten years ago. His facial hair was unrelenting, a scraggly, yet handsome beard was settling onto his face, maturing him. She exhaled, feeling his comfort from five feet away.

"You sure?"

"Don't tempt me," she warned.

"Your mom looks amazing," he said, glancing back at the door. Mark and Ann's heads disappeared from the window and then Ben's face appeared, smiling as he waved.

"Subtle, aren't they?" She laughed as she waved them off. "She does look amazing, doesn't she? It's unbelievable that she made it through surgery."

"And the cancer?"

"Gone," she said as her eyes wandered to the grass in front of them.

She reached down and plucked a strand of grass, noticing it wasn't green. She twirled the single, brown strand between her fingers, watching the color change in the light. The dull hues of yellow and brown from the dormant months littered the strands of grass. It was yet another reminder of the past winter that left her desolate and chilled to the bone. The large oak trees with fresh leaf growth rustled next to them in the wind. *But there's always a chance for a fresh start. To be reborn.* She looked back at James staring at her. He was waiting.

"She's in the clear, for now," she added.

"It's amazing and, don't get me wrong, but if there was anyone to beat it, Ann Jones is the one," he said as he leaned back into the chair.

"You told me that. The last time we were together... at my house," she hesitated. She hadn't wanted to drudge up the last time they had seen each other so soon. Delaney attempted to change the conversation by adding, "She is certainly stubborn, that mother of mine."

"A trait that I hate *and* love about your family," he said. His lips turned into the playful smile that she had missed for so long. She craved to reach out to feel the softness of his lips against hers. To feel the warmth and comfort of his solid body against hers. *I can't. I can't get involved. Not with Holston Parker breathing down my neck.*

"I know. I'm working on that stubborn thing."

"Good."

"Are you back in Milwaukee now?"

"For the past month. I'm downtown right now, but I'm scoping out some houses about ten minutes west of here. Crazy, right? Back in the stomping grounds." He laughed, putting his hands behind his head. "Never thought I would be back here."

"Me, neither. Remember that afternoon when we were studying outside? When you told me you were leaving? That you were never coming back?"

"Vaguely," he said, nodding his head with a smile.

"Always a flair for the dramatic, James Anderson," she said, raising her eyebrows.

"It was a day like today, studying for Mr. Johnson's chemistry final. Do you remember that guy? I wonder if he's still alive. I bet he'd be almost a hundred by now. I feel bad for poor Mrs. Johnson if he isn't dead yet." He laughed, again, leaning forward.

"It's amazing what a knock-off Silly Putty invention can bring you. Millions of dollars and a gorgeous, yet spiteful Latino wife," she joked as her eyes watered, envisioning the rumor that had circulated during high school. Mr. Johnson had apparently suffered two heart-attacks during lectures, a year apart. Both times clutching his chemistry beakers as he stumbled to catch his breath, mumbling, "Put on your safety glasses, don't forget," as if in that particular moment, he was about to mix his final and most memorable masterpiece. However, he hadn't died on either occasion. James had lamented this fact, along with Johnson's thirty-five-year-old Latino wife, who stood to inherit the millions he had managed to hoard in the bank. "God, you hated him," she laughed.

"I did. He gave me my only F."

"Funny," she said, wiping the tear away from her eye.

"Yeah, it is."

"I miss that," she said softly, looking back out into the yard again. *Don't do this, Delaney.*

"I do, too."

"That was a long time ago. We can't exactly go back to that. Do you see these wrinkles?" she said, pointing out the crow's feet her mom had always dutifully noted for her. In the last three months, she could have sworn they had multiplied by ten.

"That's nothing. You're gorgeous as ever." He leaned in, putting his hand on her leg. She inhaled sharply, feeling his warmth against her jeans.

"Damn you, James Anderson," she whispered, her voice barely audible.

"Come on, Delaney. You know this feels right."

"It does," she relented.

"I'm ready to be a part of your life. If you'll let me."

"I don't know if I can..." she started, feeling a nagging feeling in her chest. Holston Parker's gray eyes burned in her mind again. She couldn't bring James into that.

"I promise I won't go after a blonde sorority chic," he said playfully as he tapped her knee.

"It's not that," she said, falling back into her chair.

"Then what is it? Are you seeing someone?" The realization that she might be with someone else spread across his face.

"No," she denied, feeling the redness flush to her cheeks. *Holston Parker is seeing me.* She hadn't worked out the details in her mind of what it would be like to actually have a life. For the past three months, she had immersed herself in work and teaching, coming home to the empty house on Drew Street to walk past the fireplace day after day. She had denied dinners with June and Robert. Cancelled meetings with co-workers. Deflected Mark's request for occasional visits. Too worried about *his* perception and influence to even say hello to any students outside of class. Up until, of course, when Theron visited two days ago

"I didn't want to pressure you three months ago - what with your mom and that student - it all seemed like pretty horribly timing. I was just moving back to Milwaukee, but the dust has settled, Delaney. If not now, then when?" he pressed, leaning back into his own chair.

"I don't know. It's just..." She realized that she had no way

293

to finish the sentence. How could she possibly explain to James what had happened that night? How could she explain Holston Parker? Or her inability to even brush her teeth without feeling like someone was breathing down her neck? She darted her eyes around the yard. *They're probably here now.* She felt as if she had a noose around her neck, the itchy rope tightening with every movement she made. She felt trapped. *Suffocated.*

"Delaney?"

"I'm here," she said. Her voice rang in her ears as she cleared her throat and sat up in the chair.

"Whatever it is that's going on, Delaney, I want to help you. I want to be here for you. I love you. I have always loved you. I know you're not ready for us, but you at least need to let me into your life. As a friend," he pressed again. "I can't see you like this."

"I know."

"Can you promise me something?"

"What?"

"A coffee. Can we try that coffee thing one more time?" Her stomach balled up as she thought of herself tearing out of the Alterra parking lot just after she had heard the news about Theron. "Except this time, you don't leave me hanging by myself for an hour," he teased as he let go of her hands.

"I can do that," she replied reluctantly. *And if I see James, what is Holston Parker going to do?*

"Tomorrow? Ten a.m.? Alterra?" His eyes pressed into hers.

"Tomorrow, ten a.m.," she repeated, feeling the rope around her neck loosen with his gaze. *A good influence on her.* "Let's try the Starbucks downtown this time. Change the venue to give me a no-excuses second chance."

"I like where your head's at, Jones," he said as the playful grin that drove her wild spread across his face. She stood up, feeling the heat of the sun's rays escape from beneath a cloud. *New beginnings.*

***

"Hurry, help me, before the wax drips on the cake," Ann laughed, waving her hands to the family surrounding her on all sides. Mark and Ben jumped forward, blowing the rest of the candles out amid laughs. "Whose idea was it anyway?" she accused, pointing her eyebrows around the table.

"Don't look at me," Delaney said as Ann paused at her, narrowing her eyes with a smile, before she added with a whisper, "I think it's your lovely husband over there." She held up her hand and pointed to a grin plastered on her father's face.

"Guilty," he confessed, holding up his hands. "I thought it would be quite the sight to see. Celebrating sixty-three years."

"Can't get rid of me quite yet," she teased, moving over to embrace her husband. Delaney's chest welled up as she watched the embrace of a couple passionately in love after so many years. *Maybe it's not so bad after all.*

Laughter and joking filled the air around the table as the plates exchanged hands as if it were a well-rehearsed, orchestrated event. The Jones family, including James, had done this before. She moved the fork in and out of her mouth, chewing and swallowing without tasting the sweetness of the cake. The constant buzz of chatter and joking filled her ears as she looked around, studying the faces of her family. Sweet Ben and Meghan huddled next to each other, teasing and touching as a young couple in love would. Mark stood by her father, both the protectors of the family. Then there was Ann who sat strong in her chair, the pale gray coloring had vanished and been replaced with vibrant, rosy colored skin that exuberated life.

I would do anything to protect them. To keep them safe. I need to know who Holston Parker really is. Delaney nodded and smiled, following the orchestrated cues as everyone finished their cake and began to filter into the living room. She cleared the plates, carrying them into the adjoining kitchen to stack them next to the sink.

"Do you want to wash?" Her mother appeared behind her.

"Are you kidding? You, Ann Jones, are relinquishing your right to wash dishes in scalding water?" Delaney asked as she examined the woman behind her, "Are you feeling okay?"

"Yeah, yeah," she said, hitting her on the arm.

"It will be the first time in twenty-eight years. You realize that?"

"Don't make me go back on my words," Ann warned as she stepped toward the sink.

"Go sit down," Delaney ordered as she hit the faucet, letting the warm water rush into the sink. "I feel so powerful," she joked, turning to Ann who had slipped onto the stool across the counter. Delaney glanced back into the empty dining room, hearing the chatter of her family in the other room.

"Funny. How was your talk with James?"

"Oh, I see why you wanted to get me alone," Delaney accused.

"You know, he's not always going to be around. James is…" she stopped, looking down at her bare fingers. "Nothing short of amazing. He's everything any smart, beautiful woman would look for and, to be honest, I'm surprised he's not off the market. He has a good job. A house. He's handsome. I've always liked him, but you know all that."

Delaney felt the burn of her mother's ring on her chest as her mother talked about James. She was talking about commitment. True love. "I'm sorry, Mom. I never asked you if you wanted your ring back. Please take it." Delaney's hand shot up to her neck, pulling out Ann's ring beneath her light sweater.

"No. It was a gift. I stopped wearing it after I got sick." She cleared her throat. "I think it's better for you to keep it. I never thought you would get married, but after seeing you with James today, I think that could change and don't deflect the conversation. Let's go back to James."

"What about him?" Delaney plunged her hands back into the water.

"Don't let this moment pass you by. I think you'll regret it later in life," Ann directed.

"Do you have regrets?" Delaney asked.

"Of course, we all have regrets, don't we? Some are simply bigger than others. It's avoiding those big ones that are important, like James."

"He's a great friend, Mom. He always has been, even with our seven year hiatus. He comforts me. Makes me feel…" she paused as her mind searched for the right word, "normal."

"That's good. Your dad does the same for me. We love each other. Feel comfortable with each other," she replied.

"But doesn't comfortable get boring? I mean, I love you together, and I can't imagine it any other way, but did you ever find yourself looking for something else? Something that would make you feel alive? In all those years?" Delaney pressed, hoping that she would bite on the bait she had thrown out to her.

"When I was young, sure." Ann leaned in, placing her elbows on the counter.

"What do you mean?"

"There were other men that I thought were *interesting*, but nothing ever compared to your father. He is my rock. He is the only one to ever bring pure joy to my life. He gave me you along with Mark and Ben. What man do you know would stop into a hardware store, see two boys that needed help and bring them in? That's what I love about him. One of many things," she said, glancing back into the living room as a burst of laughter exploded from the other room. "I would have missed that sound."

"I'm glad you don't have to miss it," Delaney responded.

"Me, too. Dr. Jackson saved me. I feel so lucky. So... blessed. Like divine intervention," she said, focusing on the last words.

"Does this mean you'll be frequenting church with Dad?" Delaney joked as she dried her hands and slid onto the stool next to Ann.

"Probably not," she laughed. "But someone was looking out for me for once." *Yeah, a murderer with gray eyes. His name is Holston Parker. Do you know him by chance?*

"Well, I'm happy you got connected with Dr. Jackson, however that happened," Delaney said while grabbing the *Journal Sentinel* on the counter. Despite receiving the daily newspaper for as long as Delaney could remember, she had never once seen her mother read the paper. Delaney began to flip through it, idly turning the thin pages as her eyes scanned the pictures and headlines.

"You know I never really read the paper," Ann confessed with a small laugh, "Even when I worked there. Your Uncle Walt would be so disappointed."

"Your secret's safe with me."

"Look, someone donated $30,000 to the youth art program you used to be in. An anonymous donor, how generous," Ann said, pointing to a picture of smiling children holding their creations. Delaney smiled knowingly; her mother hadn't needed the money Delaney had collected after all, so she'd found somewhere else that did. Her only condition had been that the program screen and hire more qualified instructors.

Delaney turned the page, feeling her heart stop as she paused on the third page of the business section. His defined face and steel eyes stared back at her, as if he was mocking her. *He's still watching. He will always be here.* He stood next to President Givens in front of Parker Tower which was set to open in the upcoming weeks at Leighton. She cringed before she turned the page over, not wanting to look at his face. She couldn't read about how Holston Parker, philanthropist, was saving the community, one building at a time.

"Wait, go back," Ann said as she grabbed the corner of the newspaper to flip the page back to the black and white picture of the two men. Delaney glanced at her mother, staring at the picture of Holston Parker and President Givens. Her eyes squinted, scrutinizing the picture before they became watery.

"What is it?" Delaney breathed, watching her face.

"Nothing," she sighed, sliding back into her chair.

"What?" Delaney pressed, hesitant to know why her mother had paused at the picture to look directly at Holston Parker.

"The picture just looks like someone I knew a long time ago," she said, waving her hand in the air, dismissing the notion.

"Which one?"

"The shorter one. The man with the distinguished face and serious eyes. He looks like someone I used to know," she said, sitting back up to reread the caption. "But it says his name is Holston Parker. I don't know Holston Parker of Parker Enterprises. That's the company Mark works for. Is that Mark's boss?"

"Yeah," Delaney replied, feeling her heart thrust against her ribs.

"The similarities are just astonishing. That's how I would envision him to look." Her words softened as her eyebrows scrunched down, "But it's been almost thirty years. Is that the building Mark has been working on?" She pointed to the building in the background. "I haven't exactly been involved in your lives lately."

"Yeah, that's the one. It's a striking building." *Funded and built by a manipulative, threatening killer that you seem to know.* "Who did you think it was? What was his name?" She waited while she studied her mother's body shifting in the seat. Ann's cheeks flushed as she waved her hand to dismiss the thoughts. *You remember. This is my chance. Who is Holston Parker?* Delaney leaned toward her, closing the gap between them.

"Mom?"

"The man that I was thinking of. The man that looks like Holston Parker. His name was George Boyd. I met him at this little diner I used to work at. It was a funny name for a restaurant if you ask me. It was called the House of Steel."

38

The Same Day ~ March 15

Evie stepped onto the street, feeling the unevenness of the damp cobblestones beneath her boots. The slow trickle of the snow melting filtered through the cracks as she moved toward the line of boats in front of her, leaving the snow-capped mountains behind her. The chimneys of the small houses puffed white smoke into the air, adding to the already foggy mist that plagued the mountainous region. Their small, lit windows illuminated the otherwise dark, night sky providing a soft glow as she examined where the waves crashed up onto the shores, rocking the queue of boats that sat perched in the bay. Most of them were back from their daily runs. Only a few men remained in their boats, finishing the last clean-up and preparation for the next day.

She had waited all day, sitting in the coffee shop just a few blocks down, watching the tour boats filter in and out of the bay carrying sightseers on scenic fishing excursions. She had learned, through the broken English of a waitress and an American man that visitors flocked to Norway's Lofoten to fish during the annual cod spawning. The chain of islands' mild temperature and gorgeous scenery added to the allure. But Evie hadn't come there to vacation. She was there to find someone she hadn't seen for a decade - a fisherman on the Norwegian Sea.

He had made a good decision to move to Norway. The serene and natural atmosphere suited him. He could blend in without anyone finding him. She contemplated the notion for a moment, wondering what it would feel like to disappear to a foreign country. To immerse herself in the land and culture. Europe was the birth land of beautiful churches and rich history.

She stopped to sit on a bench next to a path that overlooked the sea as she thought of the prospect of running and never looking back. Holston Parker would never find her here. It was a corner of the world where he couldn't touch her. She adjusted her wig, letting the blonde hair fall down her back. It was long, just like her sister's. It was months later, and she still couldn't reconcile the fact that Delaney Jones was her sister.

She breathed in, feeling the brisk air of the night. She smelled the fragrances of the sea mixed in with the scent of new grass. New growth and life surrounded her. Spring was on its way in Norway, just like it was in Wisconsin. She sighed before setting her eyes back on the boat rocking in the waves. She couldn't make out the letters anymore, but she had found it earlier that morning, noting its place among the line of boats. The name "Betty" had been splashed in red across the white hull. She watched as the outline of a man finished moving on the boat and climbed down. He was heading straight to her, moving slowly along the path.

Her body relaxed as she felt the familiar feel of metal knocking against her knee. She knew she wouldn't need the knife, but she had bought one anyway before she had even checked into the hotel. It brought too much comfort to her, too much control.

His body moved closer, his boots knocking against the path. The gear she had envisioned him wearing was gone. He had left the rubber boots and jacket on his boat. Instead, he wore jeans and a canvas-like jacket that hung open, swaying with his movement. His orange hat sat high on his head, letting the cool air breathe onto his dark hair. She couldn't make out his face in the dark, but she was sure it was him. "Betty" had been the final piece that had assured her.

"Ryan." Her voice cut through the sound of the water knocking against the boats. The man stopped and turned toward her.

"Pardon?" His voice was laced with a Norwegian accent. He hadn't been speaking English.

"Ryan Gordon."

He took two large steps toward her as she shifted her hand near her leg, feeling the metal beneath her pants.

"I'm sorry, you must have the wrong person," his voice answered. He was now standing only a few feet from her. She studied his face as it tensed from the threat. The same gentle eyes as Elizabeth's looked back at her. He still had his thick eyebrows; it was him, Elizabeth's brother.

"It's me. Evie Parker," she whispered, watching his shoulders and arms fall back down.

"Evie?"

"Yeah. It's me, Ryan."

"What are you doing here?" he asked as she stood up to stand in front of him, inhaling the aromas of the sea from his body.

"I'm here to see you." Her voice was even and steady.

"How did you find me?" he pressed, looking close at her hair. "What's with the hair?" Evie pulled off the blonde wig, letting the wind air out her cropped hair. "That's better," he said as his eyes settled on her dark brown hair. Evie smiled as she ran her fingers through the strands.

"So how did you find me?"

"I just did," she said. "But it took me three months, so don't worry," she finished, trying to reassure him. It was clear that she was an unwanted visitor. She couldn't blame him.

"I didn't think anyone ever would. Or at least I hoped," he replied, looking out into the sea before turning back to her.

"You made it hard, but I was determined to find you because I thought you might have some answers," she started.

"Evie, I can't do this," he interrupted.

"Ryan, I need you. You knew what happened to Elizabeth, didn't you?" She stared into his eyes as they softened and welled.

"What do you mean?"

"I've been on the run for three months. From my father," she hesitated on the words, still hating the sound of it from her lips. "I found out about Elizabeth. That it wasn't an accident. That she was murdered."

"How did you find out?" Ryan asked as he fell down on the bench, taking the hat from his head.

"I had a little conversation with the man who covered up her murder," she said as she slid onto the bench next to him. "Before I killed him."

His head shot up as he turned to her. "Evie, you need to go."

"Please. Just give me a few minutes," Evie pleaded. She had known this would be hard. She swallowed before she asked a question she wasn't sure she wanted answered. "How did you find out about Elizabeth?"

"I can't," he replied, shifting his feet to stand up. Evie put her hand on his knee, drawing his eyes to hers.

"Please, I need to hear this," she whispered.

"I've never told anyone. It was the reason I left," he started.

"I know," she encouraged.

"I was working in the field that day Elizabeth was killed. I saw her that morning. She said she was going to spend the day with you and your boyfriend." Ethan glared at Evie before continuing, "I was cutting hay for the Schmidt brothers when I lost a spring for the chopper. I had gone back late that afternoon and was looking around the field when I saw your father and a man with white hair. The guy you killed, did he have white hair?"

"Yes. Gunnar," she replied.

"They didn't know I was there. At first, I almost called out to them, but then I saw them carrying what looked like a big burlap sack. Out of the end of the sack, I saw strands of curly blonde hair. I flattened myself down in the field, unable to move," Ryan said as he rubbed his hands back and forth together. "I should have done something. I should have confronted them, but I just couldn't."

"It wasn't your fault. She was gone already," Evie whispered.

"I know that now. I didn't know it was Elizabeth then. I couldn't allow myself to think that," he replied. "But when the officer called that night about an accident. That she had hit a tree from going too fast -"

"She never drove that fast. It wasn't like Elizabeth."

"I knew it wasn't right. I knew something bad had happened, but I didn't know what it was, and your father came in to take care of everything when my dad - he was just out of his mind," Ryan rushed as his chest welled.

"I know. We all were," Evie said as she put her hand on his knee.

"I didn't know who to turn to. I wanted to call the police, and I almost did, had it not been for your father. He knew that I had seen something or felt that something was wrong. He pulled me aside the next day. He told me that something unimaginable had happened to Elizabeth and that he had found her, but that he knew my dad couldn't live with it. He said he made it look like an accident to give my dad some peace of mind. That he had taken care of the man who had murdered Elizabeth. Whoever that was," Ryan finished. His shoulders fell forward as if a huge weight had been lifted from his body.

"Henry," Evie whispered.

"I didn't know if I could trust your father, but I didn't see any other option. He didn't give me an alternative. I had nothing to go on except that I maybe saw something suspicious that day. I knew your father would ruin me and my dad if he had to," he said before adding, "Who was Henry?"

"Henry was the boy I was seeing. He was one of my father's employees," Evie replied.

"He worked for your father?"

"Yeah, I met him on one of the construction sites. He was nineteen. Gunnar - the man with the white hair - killed him in front of me the day after Elizabeth died. They hunted him down and shot him. My father never told me what he had done to Elizabeth. He just said that Henry was going to hurt me," Evie said. "Whatever that meant."

"Your father. Who is he?"

"I don't know."

"And Gunnar told you about Elizabeth before you killed

306

him?"

"Yes, he told me that Henry murdered Elizabeth and raped her."

"And you believe this Gunnar guy?"

"Yes. It has to be true. There is no other explanation."

"And then you killed him? Does my dad know any of this?" Ryan asked.

"Your dad knows," she added, hesitating at the mention of his dad. She had played this moment out on the airplane a hundred times over. How she would be able to tell him that his father was gone?

"I haven't heard from him in a few months."

"You kept in contact with him?" she asked, her voice hesitant. She had known this. This is how she had tracked him down, finding the incoming calls to Joe's shop. It had taken her months and treks across three countries to find him.

"Just a call, two or three times a year, when I travel out of Norway, but you said 'kept,'" he replied, questioning her.

"I'm sorry?"

"You said you 'kept' in contact with him. Not keep in contact with him." He watched her, waiting for her to respond.

"He's gone. I'm so sorry," she whispered.

"Was it your father? Was it Holston?"

"No," she started, "Well, yes. It wasn't him directly, but it was one of his employees."

"God, no," he said, shooting his body off the bench. "You have to go." He pointed toward the town of houses. "You can't be here. You're poison. Your whole family is poison. If it wasn't for you hanging around that murderer, Elizabeth and my dad would be alive. I wouldn't be here."

"I know," she said, unable to argue. He was right.

307

"I came here to get away from Holston. From your family. I left my dad because I knew he would never leave. He would never believe that Elizabeth had been murdered and for whatever reason, Holston Parker was covering up the murder. No one would have believed me. Damn," he yelled as he paced along the bench. "I thought if I left, my dad could live the rest of his life in peace. That we both could, but I left him to die."

"No, you didn't," Evie rushed. "It's not your fault. Your dad was catching on and that's what got him into trouble. He was there when Gunnar told us what happened with Elizabeth, so at least he knew what happened. He could stop questioning himself," she said, trying to reassure not only him, but herself, of what had happened to Joe. She hadn't meant for Joe to get mixed up in her plan for revenge.

"Don't, Evie," Ryan warned. Evie exhaled, moving to stand next to him again. She knew it wouldn't be easy, but she couldn't run for the rest of her life. She needed to stand up and fight, just like Ethan had taught her.

"I came to you for help. For revenge." The words rolled sweetly from her tongue before her lips curled up into a smile as he locked his eyes on hers, the waves of the Norwegian Sea crashing in behind them.

39

He knelt down, letting the wetness of the muddy grass seep into his gray pants. He scanned the area, letting his eyes fall on the green-brown strands littering the ground. Spring would be coming soon and a renewed surge of repentance was needed. It was a sign of new life and fresh beginnings. However, the lines of headstones and dark graves interrupted the fresh growth. The cemetery at St. Luke's Parish was at capacity.

The engine of his gray sedan idled twenty feet behind him. He wouldn't be here long. He bowed his head and grasped the fold of the fedora into his hand to expose his silver speckled hair. Bringing his hat to his chest, he closed his eyes. He opened his mouth as the quiet, daily ritual left his lips, "Romans Chapter 10, verses 9-10. That if thou shalt confess with thy mouth the Lord Jesus, and shalt believe in thine heart that God hath raised him from the dead, thou shalt be saved. For with the heart man believeth unto righteousness; and with the mouth confession is made unto salvation. Lord Jesus, I am a sinner. Please forgive me. Wash me clean of all sin and give me strength to endure with your power. I ask this, in your name, Jesus. Amen."

As he opened his eyes, he brought the white roses to his

nostrils to inhale the sweet fragrance one last time. He laid them down in front of the black granite monument before he stood. He pulled out the book of matches, flipping them over repeatedly until he finally stopped at the embossed letter – V. His finger traced over the raised letter before he tucked it back into his jacket and brought the fedora to his head. He was a week early. He had visited March 22 every year for the last fourteen years since the headstone with a large cross affixed to the top had been erected to his orders, but he couldn't come next week. There were too many preparations that needed his attention. It was his deepest and only regret in life. Holston Parker would spend the rest of his life repenting his sin and begging God for forgiveness. No date or name adorned the headstone. Instead, one large word sprawled across the four foot wide stone. The word met his eyes, burning into his irises. *LIVE.*

ACKNOWLEDGEMENTS

I have many people to thank on my arduous journey of fulfilling my life-long dream of completing my first novel.

A special thank you to my husband, Brandon, for being incredibly supportive and for pushing me to pursue my dreams. I couldn't have done this – or much else – without you.

Another thank you goes to my two sons, Cole and Holden, who have made me laugh, cry, and above all, made me realize that life is short, and we all grow up way too fast. Without your laughter and simple take on life, I don't think I could have brushed myself off and finished the challenge.

To my siblings (Jenny, Matt, Stephanie, Eric, Heidi, and Chalyce), thank you for reading drafts and offering suggestions. I know you were tired of it all – I was too. And Kyle, I can't leave you out; thank you for being you.

Thank you to my parents, Ralph and Sue, and mother-in-law, Lydia, for watching the boys while I worked. Your relentless worth ethic has given me something to shoot for; although, I highly doubt I will ever achieve your status.

Thank you to my editors, Alizon and Kris of C&D Editing, for providing sound advice and to Mike Olson for providing information on firearms. Any mistakes are my own.

Last, thank you to all the beta readers. Your advice and keen eyes were extraordinarily helpful with this process. Reba, your cheerleading skills pushed me forward, and Lydia, I removed *most* of the Drews.

UNRAVELED #2: HOUSE OF FIRE

Prologue

"And do not fear those who kill the body but cannot kill the soul. Rather fear him who can destroy both soul and body in hell." Matthew 10:28.

The thumping in his trunk persisted.

He tapped the volume control on his wheel until the rich soul of Frank Sinatra's croons drowned out the sound. The thumping ceased for Holston Parker.

He stared ahead at the oncoming lights, the flash glaring in his eyes before blackness eluded him again. He adjusted his headlights, allowing the high beams to illuminate the pavement. The residual light made the familiar passing fields and trees glow a comforting scene. He had driven the road many times before but never with a man in his trunk. *Alive.*

The Mercedes glided along the road at a smooth forty-five miles per hour, exactly on the small tick line on his odometer. His tires had rolled tirelessly at this pace along the country roads for almost two hours. The sleek gray sedan shone in the full moon, the epitome of luxury and success. Power. The humming of the road soothed him, coaxed him to finish what he had started. God had given him the strength, the will to continue *His* plan. Taking Kurt Dodd's life was the beginning of the end.

Holston breathed the polished leather of his seats as he turned off his headlights. His gleaming Oxfords eased the gas. The steering wheel shifted to the right in his hand, sliding against his palm as the gravel crunched beneath the wheels. He begrudgingly silenced Frank Sinatra, the echo of his serenade replaced with the thumping and muffled yells. He entered the driveway as silent as he could. He didn't want her to stir, not yet anyway. She was a restless sleeper, a result of a fateful night more than fifty years ago. It hadn't stopped her husband, though, from sleeping like the dead. His snores would reverberate off of the bed and into the rest of small, run-down home – if it could be classified as such.

He pulled along the dilapidated out building behind the house, crumbling from the decades old mortar that barely held the bricks together. It would serve as Kurt Dodd's resting place, just like the scathing devils before him. But unlike Kurt Dodd, the countless other men were already dead before they had gotten here. Gunnar had already taken care of them. But Gunnar was gone, and compromises needed to be made. Holston reached in the glove compartment, pulling the eight inch blade wrapped in a white cloth. He rolled it in his hand, letting his finger graze the tip. It was only fitting that he used Gunnar's weapon of choice. The gravel crushed beneath the sole of his shoe as he stepped out of the car, silently shutting the door behind him. The black surrounded him as he perched his ear to the sound of crickets and the rustle of leaves, a light breeze gracing the warm summer night. The trunk opened with a light push of his finger, the muffled screams moaning through the air.

Kurt Dodd thrashed in the trunk, desperate to reach the edge of the opening. But his body was bound in plastic wrap from shoulder to knee, preventing his body from moving fluid to his own commands. He jerked instead, like a fish out of water, flapping before its final breath. The duct tape secured over his mouth puffed back and forth with his breath. Blood spilled down his face from a wound that had rendered him unconscious after he had given Holston his boss's name. He had thought it was his pass to freedom, to life. But Kurt was wrong. Kurt Dodd now knew he was going to die.

Holston stood over him, gripping the handle of the blade as he emulated Gunnar's stance he had watched so many times before. Killing had looked effortless, almost peaceful to Gunnar. But for Holston, it was a necessary means to an end. The peace would come later in the stillness of the body – in the realization that he was one step closer to his final kill. One kill closer to *her*. He slipped his hand into his jacket to retrieve a small pink ball of fabric. The mask dangled beneath his fingertips before he tucked it inside the plastic wrap near Kurt Dodd's chest. It was time for the mask to go, for Delaney's sins to be buried deep with Kurt Dodd. Holston slipped his hand in his jacket again, this time pulling out a small vial with a blood stained cotton swab. He hesitated for a moment before tucking it back into his jacket. He couldn't part with it quite yet; he may need it. Holston Parker raised the blade above his head. Kurt Dodd deserved it. He wasn't worthy of walking the same ground he walked on, drinking the same water he drank.

"Lord Jesus, I am a sinner. Please forgive me. Wash me clean of all sin and give me strength to endure with your power. I ask this in your name Jesus. Amen."

But he wasn't Gunnar. Holston had never killed before, not with his own hands. He slipped his hand inside his jacket and emptied a single shot from his .9mm into Kurt Dodd's waiting forehead.

House of Steel is Raen Smith's debut novel. When she isn't writing novels, she spends her time wrangling two small sons and teaching at a technical college. She lives in Sherwood, Wisconsin with her husband and two boys.

Visit raensmith.com or follow Raen on Twitter.

20033133R00174

Made in the USA
Charleston, SC
24 June 2013